Ursilla and the Baron's Revenge

The Fentons, Book 5

Alicia Cameron

To Lyndsey, who supplies me with cocktails, from your Wicked Stepmother

Copyright © 2024 by Alicia Cameron

All rights reserved.

No portion of this book may be reproduced in any form without written permission from the publisher or author, except as permitted by U.S. copyright law.

This is a work of imagination, not AI.

Contents

1. Not all Heroes Return — 1
2. Lady Grant's Decision — 19
3. Avoidance at All Costs — 37
4. Cole's Discovery — 49
5. Settling In — 57
6. A Life of Luxury — 73
7. Out of Darkness — 81
8. Gentlemen Conspire — 93
9. Female Wisdom — 109
10. The Stalker Stalked — 126
11. Accustomed to Her Face — 147
12. Sadie Intercedes — 159
13. A Knowledge of Evil — 173

14.	Ursilla's Stand	181
15.	Retribution	196
16.	The Submission	199
17.	Dinner with Friends	217
18.	Epilogue	225
19.	First Chapter of Honoria and the Family Obligation, The Fentons #1	231
20.	First Chapter of Georgette and the Unrequited Love, Sisters of Castle Fortune #1	240
About the Author		249
Also By		251

Chapter 1
Not all Heroes Return

'My sister!' Duvall's voice was hardly more than a groan. Grant looked grim. It had taken him two hours to find his friend after the battle. There was a ball still in his own shoulder, but the gory sabre wounds on John Duvall made it clear his friend would not survive this day. A light was already fading in his eye.

Grant and Duvall had ridden out together towards the enemy, feeling less bold than they looked in their splendidly frogged uniforms, shako hats, and shining boots — and they had exchanged a glance that knew it. They had been old hands in battle now, too experienced to shirk betraying their fear, at least to each other. In the first three minutes of the noisy confusion of the battlefield, Grant had been knocked from his mount by the force of a ball and the last he had seen of Duvall was the rear end of his horse as it rode ahead. John had made it as far as close combat, evidently, and as Grant looked down at his friend's terribly slashed and wounded body, Grant understood that the cursed ball in his own shoulder had saved him.

'Sister?' said Grant. They had spoken little about life before the cavalry, when they had only known each other slightly. But Grant now remembered the letters that arrived for his friend, and that Duvall collected seeds here and there for a sister who loved the garden.

'Direction ... in my effects. She lives with ... people who do not like her.' As these words were dragged out, Grant held the hand of his friend, the noble Viscount Duvall, reflecting that death is blind to rank. John continued, with an effort, 'Lawyer will give her what I can. But my cousin inherits. Look after her.'

What was this ... a deathbed bride arrangement? The dying man's eyes had a moment of sharpness, for he said with a twisted grin, 'Not that. Just look in, oversee...!'

This Grant could do. 'Yes.'

John's eyes gleamed a little as his life seemed to congeal there for a moment, and then he was gone.

It was months before Grant got back to England. The ball had been removed from his body, and he had mended quickly, apart from a certain stiffness at times. However there had been the affairs of a woman he had met in Spain to take care of. Grant had an arrangement with the woman: they had both known from the first that the end of their affair would be with his return — but before he left he had things to do for her. She had been a woman of the night, of course — a camp follower, but still ... he had cared for her, and she for him. She had been his for two years and they had been happy enough in the little time he could be with her. So before he left, he had tried at the last to improve her life from the one that she had lived before him. An introduction to a music academy that might nurture her undoubted talent. Dormitory life with other female musicians. Joining the academy required almost the life of a nun, but she thanked him. She did not wish another lover, another heartbreak, she said. *Not*, she added with a smile, *quite yet*. He remembered her beauty and her warmth and thought that she would meet someone again. He hoped it would be someone she could share her life with.

Now it was time to go to London and find himself a wife. He was obliged to for the sake of his family. On the boat home, remembering his promise to his friend John, Viscount Duvall, Grant had a brief fantasy of meeting the sister and solving both his obligations at once. He had a pack of her letters, her present direction, and that of her lawyer's, as well as some other of Duvall's effects in his trunk. He had not read her letters to her brother, but there were a deal of them. Opening one at random, to see what it was, he had seen a sketch of a tree included in the text. It was ill-achieved, he thought; the lady was no artist. The handwriting, too, was almost indecipherable. Had she received no gentle education at all? But how could this be? Her loving brother had been at home three years ago.

Grant's conscience, not a faculty that often bothered him, had chided him somewhat about the delay in keeping his promise to his friend. He had contacted her lawyer, explaining that he had been entrusted by his friend the viscount to look into the matters pertaining to his sister. The man wrote back, expressing his relief. He said that he would delay the process of the bequeathed sums until Grant returned, for he had reservations that he needed to discuss. What Duvall's sister's inheritance had to do with himself, Grant did not know, but he agreed by letter, to meet the lawyer.

This was a month ago, and something of the urgency in the request had led him to visit the lawyer at Beltane Buildings the day after his arrival. A tall, ice cool blonde of rare beauty dressed in a velvet pelisse of stylish cut, passed him in the corridor. That he did not recognise such a beauty showed him how long he had been from Town. She had a peculiarly upright bearing, causing Grant to stand back more paces than usual, and bow more deeply than he was used to do. She did not look at him and passed by.

'Is that she?' His eye following her form as she left, Grant asked the lawyer, the rather dusty and elderly Mr Rigby-Blythe, after he had introduced himself.

The lawyer seemed to be in great hilarity at this. 'No indeed, baron. Apart from age, the two young ladies could not be more different!'

'Indeed?'

'Well, I should not say so. That young lady's situation, is at last secure, and she is happily married, also. That cannot be said of Miss Duvall. And in appearance, too...!'

'Is Miss Duvall left penniless, then? I understood that John had left her at least with something.'

'After the death of his father, I think the viscount regretted that his earlier rackety ways — quite normal I should say for a young buck — had prevented him save money. Still in battle, there was little he could do to improve his private funds and I think the possibility of death, and the realisation of how completely his father's property was entailed worried him greatly. While alive he could provide amply, and he lived somewhat sensibly, so as to save his income for her in the event of his death. He left her with £1000 in his will, which, if safely invested might well be adequate to live a quiet life if she failed to marry. She might chose to buy a house, or employ a companion, for example. If she did marry, it was to provide her dowry,

'It is not a princely sum for life. One hopes that you invest it wisely, Mr Rigby-Blythe.' The old man grinned, but Grant saw that he still looked concerned. 'But it will surely afford her some security to settle herself independently now.'

'It ought to, Lord Grant. This is delicate, my lord, and really, too, it is perhaps beyond my lawyerly duties to discuss it with you. But I once saw another young lady in a dreadful situation, and I could do nothing. I do not wish to do the same with Miss Duvall.'

Grant was bored with the lawyer's sense of the dramatic, and said, as though to a reporting lieutenant, 'Get on with it, man!'

'The Viscount provided a quarterly sum to the Cole family to keep his sister while he was at battle. He also provided a sum for Miss Ursilla Duvall's use alone, in addition, but I do not believe the girl ever saw a penny of the sum.'

'Miss Duvall is named Ursilla?' For some reason this rang a distant bell in Grant's head. 'Why would John leave her with such people?'

'It was his father that left her to them, when he was still alive. The viscount was at war and was unable to look for alternate provision, since the cousin who was his heir, and might have been expected to help, loathed him. The Duvall siblings were not happy in their provision of family. The old viscount despised his daughter for lacking the beauty of her deceased mother ...' here Grant's vague thoughts of a convenient match were burst like a bubble, and he understood himself to be shallow indeed. The old man wiped snuff from under his nose with a handkerchief, 'often saying, in my presence, that she was useless to him, that her hair colour was proof of a curse.'

'Hair colour?'

'It is blonde, I should say, but it has a little red in it, and you know all the old wives' tales of red hair belonging to the devil.' Duvall remembered a friend of his father's with just such a hair colour, the rakish Lord Bennet. Perhaps there was more than superstition that made the father dislike the young woman, Grant thought cynically. The old lawyer continued, 'The closeness between the siblings warmed them both and was particularly intense. Neither of them liked their father, I think, although the daughter was very filial. When the old viscount knew he was dying, he *might* have sent Miss Ursilla to live with a kind maternal aunt in Northumberland, who had offered to bring her out in London, but he refused, choosing the Coles instead. After some time I visited the young lady there, and I wrote my observations to the new viscount, and eventually received his reply from Spain that he would return ere long, and that his sister had written that she was comfortably established. However, in light of my concern he undertook to write to his aunt and have his sister removed. I do not know if he ever did so before his death. But unfortunately Miss Duvall is now in a sad state, made worse by the injury from the accident, of course.'

'You seem to like to prolong a tale, sir, pray do not!' Grant had discerned much about the old lawyer. His voice may have the crisp delivery of information from a legalist, but he was a sentimentalist. Rigby-Blythe would have been the one, likely, who had found and contacted the maternal aunt from Northumberland, and he was now trying to evade his duty of legal discretion to help Miss Duvall.

'Miss Duvall was thus with the Coles when her father died, and the new viscount, now her guardian, made the arrangements I spoke of by mail. She ought to have been living a comfortable, fashionable life with her relatives, and the Coles were provided with enough for her to do so. But when I saw her, it became evident that she was not well treated in that house. I spoke to Lady Cole, but she and her son knew that I did not have the power to interfere with her family's arrangements. I was not able to speak to Sir Neil Cole, the owner of the house, for I was told he was from home, and later discovered he does not live there and has little to do with his family.' Grant vaguely remembered a dissolute baronet who must be Sir Neil Cole. He had a rather more handsome and upright son, whom Grant had heard referred to as a prig. The lawyer's tale continued. 'After that, she became injured in saving a son of the Cole family from harm. She had been living there perhaps five months when it happened, awaiting her brother's return.'

'After her brother died too, the current viscount made no provision?'

'As far as I know, he did not see her after the memorial service for her brother.'

'If she saved the son of the Cole family from *harm*, why, as you suggest, do they treat her poorly?'

'I shall speak without discretion. I have found that all the occupants of the Cole house are venal and greedy, and petty in a particular manner. The daughter of the family, for example, complained that Miss Ursilla's vestments were superior to her own and they confiscated her clothes as unsuitable to her *position*. She was kept as a poor relation when in fact she added considerable income to that home. As Miss Cole is at least three inches taller as well as much plumper than Miss

Duvall, she could not profit by *wearing* the gowns, but only wished to see that young lady demeaned in company. This is my speculation only. I cannot see my client often; I do not have the excuse. But I felt that the rescued son, in particular, *hates* Miss Duvall with a passion.'

Grant arched a brow. 'Why should you say so?'

'I was once in their company, and I saw the vile disdain in his eye. It seemed to me ... vicious.'

'You seem to know a great deal of the family business.'

'I bribed a maid,' said the old lawyer briefly, and without shame, 'but the girl no longer works there.'

Grant blinked, but remarked in a detached tone, 'Efficient of you.'

'She told me that much, but I get a feeling she was too afraid to tell me more.'

'More?'

The lawyer did not answer, but said, 'Do you know Mr Hubert Cole, Baron Grant? Four years her senior, a *prince* among men,' he added, with heavy sarcasm.

Grant cast up in eyes in reflection, 'I may have met him. His father is Sir Neil Cole?'

'That is the family.'

'Why did you wish to see me?'

'If I complete the arrangements and Miss Duvall receives the money soon, it will disappear from her within a week, I should suppose.'

'Can it not be put into an account for her use only?'

'Females are not supplied with accounts. Her cousin, the new viscount, refused my appeal to host one for her.' The old man sighed, 'And anyway, she would be persuaded to surrender it.'

'Is she an idiot?'

'No, she is merely ... a woman of no importance who has been conditioned these last years to do as she is bid. To be grateful for her shelter and so on...'

Grant thought about the letters. He wondered if he could grasp her situation better by reading them? But the thought of reading correspondence that was not his own repulsed him.

'It is better, then, to buy an annuity?'

'I believe so. But I am not quite permitted to do so.'

'You could, with *her own* permission. Call her in, rather than see her at the Cole's residence. If she is biddable as you say, *you* may bid her let you do so. Tell her ... that her brother told a friend to look after her interests, and that friend insists she *must* do so.'

'I am not sure she would even receive my missive.'

Grant frowned. This was a coil he did not wish to be embroiled in. But he visualised the concern in his dying friend's eye once more.

'Might *you,* my lord, deliver a message to Miss Ursilla, urging her to come see me alone?'

'I do not wish to meet her.' Grant said.

Mr Rigby-Blythe narrowed his eyes, seeming to divine the reasons for Grant's reluctance. 'Very well, my lord. Then you might *see* her at least. She attends the subscription library today on her own ... I have made it my business to find out.'

'How might I recognise her?

'She is small and will probably be the dullest dressed lady in the room. She generally wears a short cape rather than a pelisse. Her hair is reddish blonde, tied back tightly, her face scarred. She has a very bad limp.'

'You paint a dreadful picture.'

'She is a very pleasant young lady.' The lawyer had been writing and he handed the paper as a note to Grant. 'You should hurry if you wish to see her.'

The baron found he *did* wish to see her. He could at least, with the help of this dusty old lawyer, prevent her from being robbed. Not that this alone would improve her present living conditions.

Ursilla Duvall took her aunt's books to the desk at the subscription library and was rewarded with a disinterested look from the man who had, a few seconds ago, fawned upon a dowager marchioness.

'Whose maid might *you* be?' he sniffed.

'You know who she is, Barker,' said a lady to her left. 'She comes every week.' The glamourous lady turned and smiled. 'It is Miss Duvall, is it not?'

The rude attendant bowed from the waist. 'Lady Faulkes!' Ursilla thought he said.

Ursilla nodded, afraid she would be called upon to speak to this lovely, richly dressed lady.

'You were so kind to get Trixie some water last week,' the gorgeous lady said, snuggling a white ball of fur.

Ursilla nodded again, touching Trixie's woolly head. The lady's smile, and also her manner, was friendly.

'As that rude individual said, I am Lady Faulkes!'

The lady held out her hand to Ursilla, and the young girl hardly knew how to respond, but took it for a fleeting second, and mumbled something that might be *'Pleased!'*

Lady Faulkes seemed disposed to take an interest in her, looking at her strangely. Ursilla was confused and distanced by pain. She had stood still for too long, and she felt she might swoon. From a long distance Ursilla saw Lady Faulkes look a little concerned, then, mercifully, the lady was distracted by the squirming ball of fur. 'Behave!' the dog's owner said, and Ursilla stirred, as though struck.

Then the second strange thing happened then. A liveried servant came and handed Ursilla a note *on which her name was inscribed*. She took it and the sight of her name roused her a little, and she peered at it short-sightedly. She was amazed that it contained a summons to Beltane Buildings *now*. Ursilla frowned at the contents, especially the word *now*. She had to get back home once she finished her commission here, but this letter contained a later injunction, so as usual she would do as she was bid, when she was bid.

'Are you quite alright, my dear?' asked the lady with the dog.

Ursilla attempted a smile, but only one side of her face cooperated. The lady before her looked concerned when she saw it. So Ursilla tried to speak but could not. 'G...go...' she eventually got out and grimaced her regret to the lovely Lady Faulkes.

As she left, Ursilla dropped the note, and a passing gentleman picked it up.

'Clumsy!' he said rudely, but she did not seem able to respond. She took it, hardly glancing at him, and went off toward Beltane Buildings.

Unbeknownst to her, the gentleman followed, while the glamourous lady with the dog looked on, bemused.

Grant followed. He had nodded to Lady Faulkes, whose husband was an old friend, but when she called, 'Edmond!' He merely lifted a hand and left.

Miss Duvall was quite unattended, not at all usual for a gently bred young lady. He had no idea why he followed her, he had taken his closer look at her in the subscription library, watching her progress. She dropped books and hair pins, stumbled over her dress, which indeed seemed overlong, and walked with a very uneven gait amongst the tables set here and there, for the reading comfort of the patrons.

She was thin and small and wearing a dress in a faded maroon stripe, topped by a short cape, and the dress was too long, as though it had not been made for her.

Along with the clumsiness, Grant chalked up another black mark. She was not a woman of taste and industry, or at least she might have altered the dress to something approaching respectability. Her hair *might* be the strawberry blonde described to him, but it was dull as though unwashed for some time, and escaped her bonnet in wavy wisps as *distrait* as the rest of her. Her face was all eyes, and there was a crescent scar just visible on one side of her cheek. He had seen such a scar before, though not on a face. It was from the edge of a horse's hoof. Her gait was also uneven, and it was not until after he called her *clumsy* that he had seen her hand. It bore a large, deep scar that ran straight across the back and towards the webbing between thumb and fingers. Perhaps that hand no longer grasped as easily as it once had. He thought of the dreadful handwriting in the letters to her brother and understood.

He had stood back from her immediately after retrieving the note, and he followed her now with no idea of introducing himself, but only to know the outcome of his advice to the lawyer.

Yes, she was unaccompanied, but in little danger. Her clothes gave no incitement to thievery, neither was she tempting to those who sought to entice ladies into a life of debauchery. She did not look like the kind of female who was ever flirted with, even. A woman of no importance, indeed. She could be a maid or a flower seller, except that her little kid boots were rather better than most. They might be remnants of her life as a viscount's daughter.

It did not surprise him that she got lost on her way several times. It *did* surprise him the number of times she had to halt and rest against a wall or railing. Not exhaustion, but pain, he thought. One hand seemed to go to her left hip without her awareness, her eyes closed, and she breathed heavily. Why on earth she did not hail a jarvey he could not guess. But even unaccompanied, he thought cynically, she need fear no assault. He regretted the thought, for all females were vulnerable on these streets, especially those least able to defend themselves.

But as he watched her gait, it reminded him of something, and he thought to deal with it later.

She entered the building which housed the rooms of the lawyer, and emerged, looking a little concerned, twenty minutes later. Rigby-Blythe was holding her hand and bowing over it as though she were a princess as he saw her off. She smiled up at him — trustingly, Grant guessed. He had already seen, by her gift of pennies in the mean streets surrounding the lawyer's, that she was a fool.

Mr Rigby-Blythe was satisfied with his meeting. Lord Grant was not a man of unnecessary charm, but he *was* a man of decision. If one were to describe the baron, it would not justify his *presence*. Tallish, but not above six feet, a compact set of muscles and powerful shoulders. Brown hair in a more severe style than was popular, being brushed back rather than the forward swept curls that were the prevailing fashion. His face was not pretty, it was harsh, all strong planes with ingrained lines between nose and mouth. The nose was strong, the mouth the most sensuous feature on his face, for it was full, though he tried to keep it stern. His eyes were deep-set, dark, impenetrable. He was entirely masculine, a fascinating man for females, the lawyer imagined. But although he had been reserved and impatient, there was something in his firm handshake at leaving that meant the lawyer had his measure. A gentleman.

Now Rigby-Blythe reflected that he had at least arranged for Grant to *view* the girl. Surely such a man a would not fail to pay attention to her situation. The baron would, at least, investigate. The old man was almost sure of it.

The days passed. Grant had slid back into his life in London as though he had never been away. It had happened to be the Season when he returned, and there were many entertainments to keep him amused. He began to attend private balls, and even Almack's Assembly Rooms, which housed public balls each week. Entry to this establishment was only allowed by vouchers supplied by the mighty patronesses, often stricter in their invitations than any aristocratic hostess. Here, inevitably, his mother introduced him to *suitable young ladies*, from a carefully curated coterie.

But it was at a smaller entertainment (of only fifty or sixty) where some reels were offered after dinner, that he had he danced with the charming Miss Anders, the best prospect of his Season so far.

When he had come back to his sister Dulce and mother, his sister said, 'However lovely Cecily Anders is, she has a very uneven temper.'

His mother, whose hopes of potential marriage had been much heartened by the knowledge that her son had also danced with this young lady *twice* in Almacks last week, scoffed, 'Well, *you* have an uneven temper yourself, Dulce dear, so what is *that* to say to anything?'

Dulce, a rather prettier version of her mama, with dark curls and a much less striking nose, said, 'I do not at all care about a temper used *well and wisely*, Mama, however I myself witnessed Miss Anders *slap a maid* in the withdrawing room set aside for the ladies.'

Mother (dressed in rose satin with similarly dyed ostrich feathers in her hair) and son then looked at the pretty Miss Anders dance them with regret. The young lady had shown him some spirit in conversation with him at least (unlike many simpering debutantes) thought Grant, and she had a beautifully turned ankle, which he once had the good fortune to glimpse as she retied a shoe ribbon. Pity, but treating one's inferiors as medieval chattels was bad breeding, and probably betrayed a viciousness not on display in the ballroom. It was a cautionary tale for him. Society manners could conceal much.

He looked over at the other people whom he had regarded earlier this evening: Mr Hubert Cole, his mother Lady Cole, and sister Miss Susan Cole. He did not much like the view, and believed he would not have, even if he lacked the lawyer's description of them. Cole stood very upright with a pious, rather than sardonic, reserve. He had dark brown hair and a good athletic figure, and the sort of even features that might pass for handsome. His eyes were dark and intense in colour, but this evening he merely looked to be elsewhere, performing a duty, but thinking of something else. His mother had a sharp mean look and wore a surfeit of lace. His sister had less even features than her brother, but might be counted prettyish. Her hair was a featureless light brown, her clothes fashionable enough. She looked a little self-satisfied, but there did not seem to be a plethora of swains in pursuit of her. It was, he judged, her third or fourth Season, a time when looks alone can no longer serve: a lady's character and manners also become the talk of men in their clubs. Adequate portion, he supposed, so there must be something displeasing in her disposition.

Their presence reminded him that he had been meaning to investigate the Coles to assess Miss Duvall's situation, and indeed he *had* begun enquiries, but he had not yet decided how best to help his friend's sister. He had helped stop the Coles from further robbery of her inheritance, at least, but that would not be sufficient to address the unpleasantness of *living with people who do not like her*, as his friend John had said. Remembering this as he looked at the Coles, he felt himself remiss. He should have been speedier in his arrangements. There was an aunt in Northumberland, the lawyer had mentioned. He should contact the aunt. Northumberland, which he had never visited, conjured up visions of bleak weather and dull living to Grant, but , from his previous view of her, that Miss Duvall's present life allowed her access to the many amusements in the metropolis. Contacting the girl's aunt might involve a conversation with the present Viscount Duvall, head of her family, a man Grant in no way admired, and would much rather not associate with. But if the aunt proved willing to house the girl, he might make a push at forcing the viscount to do his duty.

Sight of the family reminded him of his plan. But he had been rather busy lately, taking up his London life again, connecting with old friends. His mother and sister dragged him out at many such an evening as this one. It would be boring, except for the fact that he was *very* fond of dancing ... and young ladies, of course. But dancing as a pastime pleased him. His mother had held his hands as a child and taught him his steps. He remembered it fondly, and as a source of joy — as time when he had his busy mother, all to himself.

Dulce chided him when she noted the direction of his steady regard. 'What do you look at Edmond?' she asked.

'Just wool-gathering,' he replied.

'Well do not do so in a ballroom. That Cole girl will think you interested. She has looked towards you twice already.'

Grant scoffed. Miss Susan Cole's looks, which were adequate, were coloured ugly by what he knew of her treatment of a poor relation. It was not just the casual showing of one's superiority, in Mr Rigby-Blythe's account, but more than that. If Miss Anders' famed beauty was tainted in his eye by a vicious treatment of inferiors, how could Miss Cole's mediocre looks withstand his knowledge of *her*? He looked at her with repulsion.

As he and his party left and stood in the hall awaiting the fetching of coats, he was stopped short as he saw a small figure in a maroon striped dress and shoulder cape, sitting on a chair against the wall, holding a pile of evening coats.

His mother and sister chattered to him as they donned their own, but he heard little.

'What a strange little maid!' his mother remarked as they got into the carriage.

'She is not a maid,' Grant said, in a voice his mother recognised as cold fury, 'she is my deceased friend's sister.'

'Your *friend*?' said Dulce, astonished.

'Viscount Duvall.'

'You wrote of him! His sister's situation must have changed *indeed* when her brother did not... return.' Lady Grant frowned. 'But why was she in the hall? One does not even set one's paid *companion* to hold one's coat in a gentleman's house.'

'I missed something,' said Dulce, interested. 'You mean the figure seated in the hall is your friend's sister? I did not see her closely. If you knew who she was, you ought to have spoken to her, Edmond.'

'I have not been introduced.'

'Whom does she live with?'

'Lady Cole and her family.'

'I do not like Lady Cole. But such shabby treatment of a relation like this must be a new low in her behaviour,' said his mother, the baroness, annoyed. Then seeing her son's cold, cold expression, she gestured Dulce to be quiet.

Chapter 2

Lady Grant's Decision

Lady Grant was incensed. The more she thought about it, the more terrible it was. She herself had been *frantic* during Edmond's time in his cavalry regiment under Wellington's command. That a young lady, who had no doubt been as frantic as she at the fate of her brother, should be reduced to such *insult* as she had witnessed last night had distressed her, and disturbed her night.

Therefore, at the hour of the polite visit, she and her daughter Dulce — the Countess of Drakemire — made a trip to the baronet Cole's abode. Since the countess had driven her new curricle, she wore a carriage dress with a sharp short jacket reaching just below her bosom, with a trailing demi-train to her gown, plus a fashionable bonnet that she removed to reveal black curls. Dulce's pretty face, all dark eyes and cherubic cheeks, could smile amiably, but today she gave only the slightest of smiles and a nod to the ladies present — evidently the Coles' morning callers. There was only one gentlemen visiting, which did not say much for Miss Susan Cole's popularity.

Since Lady Grant found the ladies of the house thus entertaining, she gave the pretext of coming to discuss last night's entertainment, and the baroness took a seat. She was a handsome woman in her fifties, with a patrician nose and dark hooded eyes, plus a coiffure that had been fashionable in her youth: full and high around her face, with a black and silver ringlet on her shoulder. Atop the high black curls streaked with silver, was the tiniest of lace caps. Her dress, too, was of her age, the bodice still high above the waistline, but stiffer than the transparent muslins with short stays worn today. Her dress below had much more volume of muslin than was the youthful fashion (the Greek goddess look, of muslin worn rather slimmer and closer to the form), and it spread about her feet in a manner that took up a large space in the middle-sized salon. Lady Grant held herself regally, for she had business to accomplish here.

Lady Cole, a sharp-faced harpy in an unbecoming, but richly-trimmed, cap was confused but welcoming, however Susan Cole, remembering some looks her way last evening from Baron Grant, swelled a little in faint hope that there was a purpose of acquaintanceship in this unexpected attention from a family they seldom saw.

All of the company (including the Coles' guests) felt distinguished by the visit, especially that of the ravishing countess.

The hostess introduced her guests. Baroness Grant was graciousness itself, and deigned to incline her head to each, but when the introductions stopped, she gestured to a chair by the window where a small figure worked, ineptly it seemed, on a piece of knitting. 'And this lady?' she asked.

Lady Cole said, 'Oh that is Miss Duvall, only. A distant relation.' A form of words indicating a poor, burdensome family member.

'*Duvall?*' said the baroness, apparently delighted and surprised. 'Are you any relation to *Viscount* Duvall?'

The countess smiled behind her hand at her mother's performance, but retained her stiff, superior demeanour.

The poor girl began to say, 'Bro-ther,' her voice sounded muffled, like a servant with toothache.

'*Cousin*, merely,' said Lady Cole in a repressive voice.

'Ah, then you must be the sister of the *former* Viscount, Miss Duvall!' said the countess, also delighted.

The rest of the company looked on, astonished, at the poorly dressed young lady with the scarred face.

The girl nodded; her eyes filled with tears.

'*Sentiment* has no place in a lady's drawing room, Ursilla,' warned Lady Cole after a glance the girl's way.

'My brother Edmond held the previous Viscount Duvall as a *cherished friend*,' said the countess, with cool emphasis, 'I may speak for Mama and say we *quite* see the reason for Miss Duvall's sentiment. Her brother was a hero of our nation.'

'Oh,' tittered another guest, 'yes, a hero!'

'I quite thought you were not ...' started another lady friend of the Coles, a Mrs Driscoll, Lady Grant vaguely remembered. Good, the baroness thought, she looked like a tattletale. '... Daughter of a *viscount*? I do not quite understand why you find yourself ...' the cold eye swept the girl's tense face and her gown of a lower servant and then went back to Lady Cole '...in this situation?'

'Indeed!' said the baroness to the Driscoll woman, 'It *is* strange, is it not?' Lady Cole flushed but did not speak, and Lady Grant's eye turned to the figure at the window. 'Miss Duvall,' she said warmly, 'will you grant us a visit tomorrow at noon?'

The girl's eyes opened, and her hand touched her chest in question, amazed.

'Of course. I shall not invite your ... eh... *relatives*, since I fear we may indulge in too much *sentiment*.'

Ursilla's face was livid, only the crescent scar remained pale, and she nodded forcibly, even while her relative said, 'Lady Grant, the girl has been left little more than an idiot by a sad accident, I fear. She cannot *possibly* visit. She cannot even *speak*. I keep her in my salon as a charity to her only.'

Lady Grant looked at the disappointment on the fallen face of the girl and made a decision, 'Do not fear that, my dear lady. I wish to *speak* to her; it matters not whether she can reply. I will send my coach for her at one.'

'There is no need ...,' said Lady Cole.

'I *insist*, dear lady.' The two nobles stood to make their departure, but the elder paused in the doorway. 'If Miss Duvall should prove indisposed tomorrow, I should be *most* displeased, Lady Cole. My tongue, when displeased, seems to run away with me.'

The hostess quivered, but smiled.

Lady Cole frowned at Ursilla Duvall later that afternoon. Drat her son for being at his hunting box, for she now had no notion what to do except warn the girl to keep her mouth shut. But as it was, the girl *could not* speak. It was probably safe enough for a short visit. But the baroness had terrified her.

What if they were to take an interest in the dratted girl? But it was unlikely to be more than a passing charitable gesture.

When Baron Grant found out that evening what his mother and sister had done, he made the best of it. His mother had talked much of the girl's oppressive situation, (that he had resolved to deal with by contacting the aunt, whom the old lawyer had called *kind*) but Lady Grant had also been shocked by Miss Duvall's poor *physical* condition. Grant, too, remembered her painful gait from his first sighting and the pallor which he had thought must be habitual to her. But it may indicate illness, as his mother feared. So, he might act on *that*, at least, since the girl was to visit. He sent for his friend Southey, a military physician, to come to his house on the morrow, and then called on his butler.

'Which is the friendliest and kindest of our maids, Baker?' he said, but in his usual clipped tone.

'I do not encourage *friendliness* in the staff, baron,' sniffed the butler, 'but there is a kitchen maid who is fresh from the country, my lord. I have not yet quelled her yen for intimacy.'

'Yes, she'll do. Tell her she may be as friendly as she likes. She will chaperone a young lady while a physician attends her, then follow the doctor's instructions.' Since a morning visit to a stranger was turning into a physician's examination, it might be better if the girl had a reassuring presence beside her, Grant considered.

When Miss Duvall arrived the next day, via his mother's coach, the baron kept to his study, but with the door ajar, and so thus observed, with the physician Southey by his side, her evidently painful gait as she climbed the stairs. His mother had ordered that the young lady be ushered to an upper room, as they had planned. No doubt she would be shocked to be led to a bedchamber, rather than a salon on the ground floor.

Southey said, 'I think ... From what I see ... I can hardly believe that she can *walk* if what I believe is true.'

Grant was grim. 'Tell me later. I will await you here.'

'You do not wish to meet her?'

'No.'

Southey came down in twenty minutes. 'The girl cannot leave here for two days at least.'

Grant was as Stoic as ever. 'Very well. Why?

'Her hip was, as I thought, partially dislocated. I have just readjusted it. Then I noticed her jaw.'

'What?' Grant's tone was no longer clipped.

'I set *it*, too. There is also a bone in her leg that was broken and not set properly, or at all, from what I saw. You mentioned the horse accident eight months ago. Probably when she was trampled in that. The bone has grown together ill. Walking on it must be agony.' Grant's face was grey. Southey continued in an informative tone, 'I wish to break it again. It's a method I invented after men were languishing in those dreadful field hospitals with insufficient attendants. But if I do it it, it will mean incredible pain. The broken rib and dislocated jaw are more recent. This week I should say. Some powder had been applied to disguise the bruising on her face. I had the maid disrobe her for a full examination, for I feared worse, and I was correct.' He looked Grant in the eye gravely. 'There are marks on her body, some newer and some fading. The girl has been systematically beaten, Edmond.' He stopped, then added more lightly. 'And now you have another problem. The little maid with her cannot stop her tears. The patient sleeps now, but once she awakes, if the maid does not desist, it will be unbearable, I imagine.'

'Good God!' Grant sat.

The butler entered. 'Lady Cole's carriage has come to take Miss Duvall back home, my lord.'

'Ask someone to hold the horses and bring the driver here.' When this man arrived, Grant said, in an artic tone, 'Inform Lady Cole that her companion has been taken ill this afternoon and cannot return. My physician here informs me it is an *infectious* illness and may be of long duration. I shall confine her with a maid to a room of the house. It is inconvenient, but pray inform her ladyship that all care shall be taken of her relative.'

The man left, his eye shifty, to take the message home.

'I would rather break and reset the leg today, if I can,' Southey said. 'It is best we cause all the pain at once.'

Grant nodded grimly. 'It is the young lady's decision alone. I'll tell my mother to accompany her when she decides.' His mother, he knew, was waiting with Dulce for news. Grant's decision to call in his friend Southey she had agreed the need for, but she was aware that they were rather pushing the girl before they were well acquainted. But while she was a woman of compassion and good manners, she was also quite as practical and high-handed as her son, when needs must. He became aware that this visit had rather larger consequences than any in his family could have foreseen, but it was not time to think of this. Their duty lay ahead. He requested his mother's aid at once to go to the girl while she was informed of the doctor's proposed treatment.

Lady Grant was shocked, and hardly knew how to do more than reassure the girl who had an utterly confused and distant air. She held Miss Duvall's hand as Dr Southey explained, expecting a fearful reluctance to suffer more. But the young girl decided quickly. She nodded vigorously in favour of the operation. The baroness left the room, hollow eyed, and only the maid stayed when Southey began his work.

Any physician of less military experience with broken and damaged limbs might not have attempted it, but Grant was confident. He found himself outside the chamber door, however, and heard her scream once, then twice, with a short delay between. Southey came out some time later.

'I have given her laudanum. She will sleep the day out, and probably more.'

The Baroness saw off a panicked visit from Lady Cole later that afternoon, calling to take her relative , '*... to be cared for at home, where she might be comfortable,*' that lady said, with a simpering smile.

'I could not expose you to the contagion for the *world*, Lady Cole,' the baroness told her, but in a voice of such ice that the lady shuddered.

As the woman left, her feet hardly able to carry her at the knowledge that a physician must have disclosed her family's treatment of the girl, Lady Grant gave orders that all Coles should be refused entry to the house.

'It may not hold,' said Dulce, visiting later that day. She had listened to the tale, shocked to her core by the Cole woman's gall after what they had discovered from Southey that day, but was concerned that the Coles would be frantic to get her back in case of scandal, 'They will still come after her, I fear'

'I will see that they do not,' said her brother grimly.

It was a footman from the Coles who approached Baker, Grant's butler, later that afternoon. The nervous but determined man said that although he knew it was the worst of crimes for a servant to have loose lips about his master's doings, he *needed* to speak to Lord Grant. Baker eyed him narrowly, but he liked the concern on his open young face, and he now knew something of the condition of the young lady visitor, (by questioning the weeping maid) so he led him to his master.

'Well?' said Grant as a liveried individual anxiously entered his study. 'You are William, Baker informs me, who is employed at the Cole residence?'

Baron Grant's delivery of this enquiry was cool, and hardly welcoming. However, the footman, young for his position, was pulled along by his heightened state of panic and began at a rush. 'She is his *madness*, my lord, since she saved his life...!'

'Pardon?'

The young man tried to calm himself and speak rationally. He had begun in the middle, he knew, but now tried to find the start. 'When miss was walking in the park with the Family eight months since, she threw the young master away from a carriage that had runaway and fell under the horses herself instead. Before that, my lord, the young master had ignored her, usually, said some cruel words, mebbes, but *after... well,* it were like he weren't grateful at all that she saved him, but he *hated* her for it.' The eyes of the footman, dropped as they should be, now sought Grant's own. 'No doctor was fetched to her injuries, your lordship, and she lay moaning for three weeks in a high fever, with naught but water and porridge ordered served.' He shook his head, but receiving no reply, he continued, as though mustering courage to speak about what he should not ...the doings of the Family, those whom he served. 'That were bad, but it were *after...* Miss learned to walk herself, I dunno how, and then she came downstairs again three months later.' He shuddered. 'After that, whenever the young master were in a bad mood, my lord, he would call her to this little attic room and beat her...!'

Grant was shaken, but his voice remained cold as he asked, 'Did he despoil her...?'

'No, no, your lordship! The young master said she were too *disgusting* for him to touch, and he only laid his crop on her, never his hands. Once he beat her with a chair, Matthew told me, and once I witnessed him kick her senseless. There was always a footman present, usually me or Matthew, for we was to drag her out after.'

Good god—! thought Grant, though his face remained stone, *A monster! He will pay.* Then aloud, he said to the footman in a crisp tone, 'What of Lady Cole, his mother? Did *she* have nothing to say?'

'She knows, my lord, but pretends not to. But she once passed me carrying the poor miss and would not look at her broken body.'

'But *why?*'

'I think the young master be *mad*, my lord, though he talks so pious at other times. And something else...' The young man flushed and looked into Grant's eye. 'Can I be frank, my lord?' Grant nodded briskly. 'He were *crazed* when he looked at her, a lunatic, I think, my lord. But there was ... He did not touch her in that way, but I *think*...'

Grant was sick to his stomach. 'Do you wish to change employer?' Grant asked.

'Oh, Your lordship! I did not expect ... I just ... I thought you should *know* as soon as I heard you were her brother's friend. In case you sent her *back* to him, my lord.'

'You need not worry. Miss Duvall will never return to that house. You may go there now and get your things and come back here tonight. Can you disappear without Cole knowing?' The man nodded. 'Good! I do not wish him to find out you have entered my house. For the moment at least.'

'My lord, one thing.'

'Yes?'

'I do not think he will give her away so easy. He is *fixed* on her ... I do not know how else to say it, but it is not in a good way. My young master hates her, but it is as though she is *his* to torture. The butler says he asks him about her doings each day, especially the days she is sent on errands. She is only let out once a week these days, since he shouts at his mother and sister if they let Miss leave the house.'

'Does your master harm his servants?'

'No more than most, my lord.' The footman replied cynically. Then, mindful of his place, added, 'Begging your pardon, my lord.'

'Yes. Get away with you.'

Grant had to wait until the evening before he could look at the girl unfettered. She lay there, asleep: pale, thin, scarred face, broken limbs, pain and fear etched in her twitching body. She was as far from pretty as one might be. Dull, dirty blonde hair, even one hand was scarred. Though he knew this injury was also because of the carriage accident, like the scar on her face, he was able to put it squarely at Cole's door, for he had sought no treatment for a girl who may have saved his life. He remembered every mark on Southey's outline drawing of her body, front and back. He was grim as he looked at her from the doorway, glad that the maid held her hand protectively. 'What *monster* would treat a young girl so?' he muttered to himself. It was as though she stilled in her sleep. He left abruptly.

Grant's visit to the new Viscount Duvall was at their mutual club. The baron joined his card table, and the flabby viscount looked at him idly, wondering, no doubt, why Grant had strayed so far from his friends. It was difficult to see a resemblance to the handsome former viscount in this older, plump individual who was combing his hair carefully to cover his loss. His face too, was loose, and his expression looser. Not a man who met your eye like his cousin and predecessor, honest John.

Grant said, with little attempt at charm, 'Gentlemen, apart from you, Sinclair,' he gestured to a simpering gentleman on Duvall's right, 'I wonder if you might move along after this hand? I have some business to discuss with the viscount.' It was clearly a command, couched in cool politeness, but the viscount's overblown dandified friends recognized the threat of arguing with the baron's fabled cold temper, nodded assent, and finished the hand ten minutes later, the table rather subdued by Grant's icy presence.

The viscount, nervous, nevertheless attempted a sardonic tone, 'Pray, what business might you have with Sinclair and me, Baron?'

'It is business of the *late* viscount's.'

Duvall flushed, his puffy jaws flapping somewhat by the memory of the younger man who had once stood in his position.

'Ah, John! He was a friend of yours?'

'He saved my life.'

'The viscount hero!' said Duvall unpleasantly, 'I am aware of his glorious war.'

'War is never glorious, viscount, but I did not come to discuss this, but your cousin's commission to me.'

'Oh, yes?'

'Are you aware of the situation of Miss Ursilla Duvall, your cousin, and the sister of my friend?'

Duvall seemed to twitch but waved an airy hand and looked as though he had difficulty in recalling something so unimportant. 'She is being sheltered by family friends ... distant *relatives*, I should say.'

'Ah, *friends!*' Grant threw a card on the baize with force enough that it skidded across the table to the viscount's hand.

Sinclair, a figure as florid as the primped and pampered viscount, protested the violence in voice and action in a mildly complaining tone, 'Here! Steady on!'

Grant threw him a look that closed his mouth. He moved his attention back to the viscount. 'Let me enlighten you as to the situation of Miss Ursilla Duvall. The sum she was allotted for her keep by her brother was given directly to the Coles and I doubt she has seen a penny of it.'

'Well, I suppose it costs a deal to keep her, ye know,' said Duvall off-handedly, but Grant watched him perspire.

'They had been supplied for that separately.'

'Girl's too young to deal with financial matters, I expect.'

'Really? And need they confiscate her belongings, too?' said Grant, throwing another card. 'Her clothes, her sketching equipment, her books...'

'Why must a companion sketch or read?' tittered the viscount, looking anywhere but in Grant's cold eye. He shrugged, with an assumption of faux sympathy. 'It may be unfortunate, but her situation in life has naturally *fallen* ... that is hardly unusual.'

'Her *clothes*. Miss Susan Cole objected to her wardrobe.'

The viscount tried looking unconcerned, but he was nervous. 'I expect they were rather superior to the Cole girl's; you could not expect her to stomach *that* in a girl of unequal situation!'

'You *knew*?' The tone caused Sinclair to drop his cards.

'Lady Cole mentioned it. That she would dress her more simply, that is.'

'As a lower servant. Very well, viscount, if you can stomach this, then what about the *physical condition* of Miss Duvall. A lady, I remind you, who bears *your* name.'

'I have not seen her. Is she ill?'

'You heard of her being trampled in the park?'

'The Town has heard of it.'

'Good then, they might be interested in what happened to the heroic young lady after the event.'

'Eh?'

'No physician was called for her broken body. She was left in a fever for days, pain for months.'

'*Well...!*' Duvall's tone now sounded aggrieved, as though unjustly accused, but his fear was rising as he avoided Grant's eye.

'The son of the house, whom she rescued, took to beating her when she eventually rose from her bed. Breaking her ribs and dislocating her jaw.'

'*Good God!*' exclaimed the powdered Sinclair, sounding less effete.

'These are the *friends*, the *family members*, you have left your cousin with, viscount. When appealed to by her lawyer, you even refused to stop them taking her inheritance.'

'It is her own affair, not mine,' whined Duvall.

'She is a member of your *family*, Dickie,' warned Sinclair with disgust. 'If this got out, it would be...!'

'It will *certainly* get out, sir, if the viscount does not now do as I say.' There was silence until Grant began again. 'It would be your just deserts, Duvall, to experience the physical pain that your cousin goes through. A dislocated jaw, a dislocated hip untreated, a broken leg, broken ribs, repeated beatings. Since you lack the empathy to appreciate it, I should school you.'

Sinclair shook and his hand dropped the cards again. Duvall was looking into the cold dead eyes of Grant, all blood draining from his face.

The viscount's breathing was heavy; his friend was utterly silent. 'What is it you want, damn you?'

'You will write a letter, this evening, telling the Coles that you have made other provisions for your cousin. That you, as the head of your house, have agreed that Miss Duvall will now reside with Baroness Grant, mother of her brother's best friend. You may thank them for their care, if you wish, but inform them that there is no more need for any member of that family to address Miss Duvall, either in public or in private, ever again.'

'Is that it?' said the viscount.

'At the moment.' The viscount blanched. 'Trust me, I do not wish to see you again, either. As Sinclair is your intimate, I trust this information stays here. If not, you may look for *him*, for I will not mention it. But if you were to warn Cole that I know, Duvall, or irritate me in any way that *reminds* me of you, you can trust that I *will* harm you. Not only by scandal, but in the *precise way* that Miss Duvall has been harmed.' The viscount's breath was coming thick and fast now, his righteous indignation completely subsumed by panic. Grant added in the same tone, 'Sinclair, you may be his witness if such an event were to occur, so that the viscount may take me to the law.'

'It is *Cole* whom you should threaten, not me!' hissed the viscount, cravenly. 'I knew nothing of it!'

'You were negligent, always jealous of John, and took it out on the sister he could no longer protect. You are a snake, no, a worm.'

'You will *marry* that cripple?' sneered Duvall.

'I have not even been introduced to Miss Duvall. I simply am repaying an old debt to her brother.' The baron looked down at the creature beneath him with contempt. 'There are some people, viscount, who are moved by honour. *You* would not understand.'

Grant began to leave but halted, turning back. 'I just heard you say *you knew* your cousin was crippled. Did you send her aid?' At the viscount's utter silence, the baron nodded. 'I shall add that to the list.'

'My lord,' said Sinclair, with great formality to the shaken viscount. 'I will leave, too.'

'Corky?' protested Duvall.

'Rest assured I shall not speak of what I have just heard, viscount, but that poor young lady ... your *cousin* ...!' Sinclair stood, and now made a grave bow. 'I will not attend the race meet tomorrow, I fear, my lord. I am otherwise engaged.'

Chapter 3

Avoidance at All Costs

It was not truly inconvenient to house Miss Duvall at the moment, but Grant supposed it may become so. Once she was well enough to come downstairs, he intended to avoid her as much as possible, especially initially. But an eventual meeting would come. He thought of her aunt, and perhaps the young girl might wish to go there at a later date, but for now her home was here. When he thought that she had been beaten recently, even since his arrival in London, and he had left her there, his self-disgust choked him. But now he must be practical.

He told his mother to grant her the maid from the country. Now that Sadie had ceased to cry, the physician opined that the naive maid was good for the young lady. Miss Duvall, shocked and incapacitated, could barely speak one word at a time and the effort cost her dearly, but the young maid's constant chatter seemed to soothe her.

'The poor young lady is like a dog that has been kicked his entire life, a cowed and shaken thing,' remarked Southey, sadly.

'But once she was the daughter and then sister of a viscount. She has known a different life.'

'That would have made the abuse she suffered even more shocking, I must suppose. And her suffering now dates from eight months ago, you say?'

'I believe so, although she had probably, by my mother's account, been bullied by the Cole family since she went to live there, but that might have been in the more *usual* ways.' Grant looked down, 'If I had not delayed my return home perhaps...'

'It is useless to say so, my lord.'

'I have been home six weeks now; I might have inquired of her sooner. Spared her some beatings, at least.'

'You *might*. And the horses *might not* have trampled her eight months ago, and Hubert Cole *might not* be a madman.'

'I seldom speculate about *what if*. However my lack of urgent action in the face of her suffering stings me.' Grant tossed off a brandy, self disgust in his face. He looked into the physician's eyes, 'I have never heard of such a madness before. One that focuses on one person. But I take my time before I act towards him.' Grant added grimly.

'Actually,' said Southey, sipping at his own brandy in a less desperate manner, and stretching out his long legs, 'it is quite common for people to make another their scapegoat, someone to focus their anger on. It is usually a family member. You said the footman discerned more than a *violent* inclination towards her?' The physician raised his brows, then leant forward a little to make a point. 'You have described the villain to me as a sanctimonious prig in his public personality. What if Hubert Cole met a young lady ... one he considered beneath him in position, appearance, and every other thing, but *felt enamoured of her* just the same?'

'You mean his pride is hurt by his own inclination?' Grant seeing it, nodded.

'An inclination so strong as to overpower him. But instead of *courting* her, or even *violating her secretly*, he strikes her — to make her *less and less* — thus something he might *cease to desire*.'

'I have heard that he spouts Bible verses regularly and moralises at every chance he gets. I admit I admire Christianity best in compassionate action rather than in empty, self-serving proselytising.'

'But possibly Cole sees his inclination for her as the devil's temptation.'

'But since she has proved her nobility of spirit, her quality, by getting injured in his place, it made him angrier still.'

Southey nodded. 'Every *good* thing she does puts the light on his own depravity. She is *not* the devil's daughter, but an angel. But he can hardly admit it, since he also values status, and hers has fallen. So he sees her as the snake in the Garden of Eden, perhaps, come to corrupt him with temptation.'

'That is why the beatings started *after* the accident, although probably the contempt and other bullying behaviour started before.'

'Then he must *physically* destroy her worth,' Southey said, 'As he beats her, I believe he beats away his own desire.'

The baron sat back in his chair after this, and said, more prosaically, 'We speculate wildly, I fear, but it somehow fits behaviour that is otherwise unbelievable. There are plenty of sadists in the world, but according to the footman, his sadism is reserved for Miss Duvall alone.'

'Men in love are at their most insane, and if one is already a twisted personality…'

'I remember hitting my head against a wall at the failure of a first romance,' mused Grant. 'A lady who had danced with me *twice* became betrothed to another.'

Southey laughed, 'The Cruel Inconstant!' Then he said more seriously, 'But that is it *precisely*. Cole's anger and frustration is turned *outward*, however: towards its *cause,* in Cole's warped mind, at least. It is as though *you* had hit your *dancing partner's* head against the wall, and not your own. But it is your wall-butting taken to an insanely cruel and selfish extreme.'

'Many people's desires turn to hatred, but good manners decree it usually only results in cold looks in a ballroom, or some acid remark in company,' said Grant cynically.

'It seems that Cole has transgressed the norms of society months since.'

'And he found the perfect victim, a woman whom no one notices or cares for.'

'How much will you tell Lady Grant?'

'Everything. My mother is not a fool, and she has guessed something of it already. Also, our new footman has said that Cole will not give her up so easily. So, we must all be on our guard.'

'Yes. I believe Cole thinks that she *belongs* to him, in this lunatic way that he permits himself.'

'Well, my mother must be alerted in case Miss Duvall is ever well enough to leave the house.'

'Yes. You may be right. But there will be some time before that is possible.'

URSILLA AND THE BARON'S REVENGE

Lady Grant cried bitter tears when Grant coldly told the tale. But soon she wiped them and went upstairs to the girl's room.

She sat on the edge of the bed and took Ursilla's hand in hers. The girl was not fully conscious, she was still in a deal of pain, but the apothecary had recommended decreasing the number of doses of laudanum in a day so that she might begin to recover her wits.

'I hope you can understand me, dear Miss Duvall. Might I call you Ursilla?' The girl nodded, searching the elder lady's eyes for some hint. 'I wish to say first that *you will remain with this family* in the future. My son has seen that the annuity your brother granted you will be sent here by your lawyers. You will be neither a companion nor a poor relation, but a *family member* here.' The girl looked as though she would refuse this huge generosity from strangers, but Lady Grant was imperious. 'There is to be no argument about this. Your brother saved my son's life, and thus could Edmond return safe to us.' Her eyes glazing a little, she reached for Ursilla's cheek. The girl recoiled like a frightened dog, but Lady Grant's firm but gentle hand persisted, cupping her chin. 'No person with the surname Cole shall enter this house. We know something of what you have suffered, child, and you need have no fear.' Again, the girl shook her head, still terrified. 'We have a new footman, his name is William, so you need not deny it.' The young girl frowned, taking this in and looking questioningly at the baroness, who nodded. *The same William.* 'It will be his job, along with your maid's, to accompany you when you leave our doors, and he has assured me that no one, *of whatever rank*, shall accost you when he is with you. What I wish to say to you, Ursilla, is you may begin to release your fear. My son, Baron Grant, is very busy and will not visit you but wishes to offer you his assurance that you are henceforth safe and are very welcome to our family.'

When the lady rose, the little maid with the apple cheeks and curly head came to the bed and said, 'How about *that* then, Miss? You is safe and sound here, all you need to do is to get well.'

The little maid left when Ursilla slept off another dose of laudanum, and she appeared in front of her ladyship, ushered in by the butler.

She stood before the lady with her hands clasped in front of her, saying. 'Miss is sleeping, my lady, and I just thought I'd come to you with an idea, like.'

The butler rolled his eyes behind her.

It was certainly unusual for a maid to come with an *idea*, but Lady Grant was amused, and said, 'Very well.'

'Well, since that dress, if you could *call it* a dress, my lady, is too long for Miss, I was going to take it up for her, as I do not have enough to do when my miss is asleep.'

'Is *this* your idea?' asked Lady Grant. 'You need not have informed me.'

'No, but *then* I thought, after I heard what you said to my miss just now, that it might be better to order some muslin and have me make some pretty things for her to wear once she is well enough.'

Lady Grant looked down her nose. 'I will, of course, have Miss Duvall go shopping with me when she has recovered somewhat.'

'Well, but you don't want her to be wearing that *fright* when you take her, do you, my lady?' the maid sniffed. 'Even the scullery maid would turn her nose up at it if she were offered it.'

'Excuse me, my lady, I'll take her away,' said Baker apologetically.

'No, no, Baker! She — Sadie, is it? — is a trifle dramatic, but upon reflection, she is quite correct. I cannot well invite seamstresses here when Miss Duvall is in her present state,' she looked back at the maid. 'Can you really sew?'

'Oh, yes miss. M'mother took in grand lady's sewing, and I helped her since I was a li'l 'un.'

'Well, take down Miss Duvall's measurements, and I shall give you two lengths of muslin to make her first gowns.'

The butler nodded Sadie out, but she stood her ground and said, 'Pink and amber, my lady.'

'I *beg* your pardon?' said Lady Grant, surprised to be still addressed.

The butler jerked the maid's elbow, but she continued in her confiding manner, 'I think them colours might be best for her, my lady.'

Lady Grant's eyebrows were disappearing into her hairline, but she only said, 'You may be right!'

'And shifts, my lady, if you'll allow.'

'I shall. One shift at present. I have already donated my own nightwear. I shall order more shifts when I have her measurements.' Her ladyship nodded her head as dismissal this time, but the maid's eye had reached a side table, and she did not move. Lady Grant sighed, a little exasperated. 'Why do you tarry?' her ladyship followed Sadie's gaze and found the side table. 'The ladies' journals?' she inquired.

'If I could just have a *look*, my lady,' said the little maid greedily, 'maybe I could make her a real *good 'un*.'

Nodding to the butler for Sadie's dismissal, the enthusiastic maid left with the journals.

'I apologise, my lady,' Baker came back to say, 'She is but newly arrived from the country and wholly untrained. She was to work in the kitchen only, for the present, but Lord Grant asked for a *friendly* girl, and ...'

'I *quite* understand. She will learn how to comport herself, no doubt. But I confess I liked her. Your master is wise, it needs an affectionate presence such as that little maid to accompany our guest at present. So, do not scold her *too much*, Baker.'

'Yes, my lady.' Baker said, but his eye said otherwise.

Grant met the maid outside the door of Ursilla Duvall's chamber. Her head was down, and she wiped at some tears. Grant, who had been on his way to the stairs, said, 'What ails you, girl?'

The girl looked at him dumbly, dashing away more tears.

He realised that she had no idea who he was and said, 'I am your master, Lord Grant. You must be Sadie.'

'Yes, my lord,' the maid replied with a watery sniff.

'Why do you cry?'

'Who would *not* cry, my lord, when they tend my young lady's wounds? Her poor broken body.'

'She is young. She will become strong and well' the physician informs me.'

'Yes, my lord.'

But the girl still looked miserable, so Grant ventured, looking at her coolly, 'Do you know why you were chosen as Miss Duvall's maid, when you have no experience at all?'

'No sir, I had not thought of it. Perhaps because the young miss is not important enough in status to merit a better maid?'

'No. I asked Baker to find me a girl who was kind and cheerful to keep Miss Duvall, *a very honoured guest* of this house, company while she is here.' He handed her a handkerchief, 'but if you continue to weep, what comfort can you be? Perhaps I chose the wrong person.'

'Oh no, my lord. Dr Southey has already warned me to be cheerful and I do not let Miss see me cry. But it is just today ... she will not take the laudanum dose, and she suffers so much.'

'Why will she not?'

'She says it induces dreams, my lord, nightmares that *I* fink are prob'ly memories of what was done to her ... I want to ask Baker for a truckle bed in her chamber, so that I can be there when she cries in the night.'

'Good.'

'I'll take her linen to be washed. There's them that will be angry with me for not washing it meself, but I don't want to leave her ...'

'I'll tell Baker to make it clear below stairs.'

'It weren't a complaint, my lord.'

'I know, it was a worry.'

Sadie looked at him, becoming more decidedly cheerful. 'Well, just you stand here, then, while I go down. I'll make the door ajar so's you can hear her.'

She patted his arm in a shocking manner and disappeared on her journey to the back stairs. She had brothers, Grant concluded, as he stood doing *the maid's bidding* in the hall. The figure in the bed was sleeping fitfully, he could see through the gap, but a cry from the bed made him enter.

Her thin sleeping face showed terror, and Grant lowered himself to tap at a bunched-up fist with one finger, and say, as his mother had to him as an infant, 'There, there!' *What on earth did these foolish words mean?* he reflected as he said it, but the figure on the bed quietened and slid into a deeper sleep. He stood over her before he backed out of the room. He recalled the outlines of the body that Southey had drawn him, front and back, with each injury he had noted drawn in. The physician used it to keep a log of her injuries and treatment, and perhaps as evidence later. Grant had yet to decide if his best recourse was the law. He wished very much to have Cole pay *right now*, however, there was the delicate issue of Miss Duvall's reputation that his mama had reminded him of several times. He would not leave her open to gossip for the world. If Cole's actions were made public by his arrest, who in the Polite World would not question *what else* Mr Cole had done to Miss Duvall? The *on dits* would inevitably stain her.

Sadie returned, finding her master still in the corridor, and Grant inquired politely, 'Might I leave now, *madam*?'

Sadie, taking the irony as a joke, smiled and said, 'It's fine now.'

The result of this was new instructions delivered by the butler to the little maid. Sadie could *ring*! This colossal privilege made her crow, and her young miss, who was awake when Baker informed them, give a faint smile at Sadie's response. The butler pulled the maid from the room to repress her. But the essential remained: in matters relating to her mistress Sadie might ring, night or day, and the maids or footmen would fulfil her needs. Disposal of chamber pots, linens, bringing of refreshments, medicines or bathing water — all could be done by others. Sadie's only job was to accompany the young lady, nurse her, and report to the physician on her progress.

Her lady slept less and less each day, and Sadie had done what she could to entertain her. She had ordered a set of cards, some ladies' journals and some novels for her, but the patient was still restless and unable to focus. Her miss picked up a book again and again, only to discard it after a few seconds, a hand to her temple, as though in pain or confusion.

This Sadie could not help her with, for she could not read. She had chattered about the gowns in the fashion-plates, but she could tell that her lady was not too interested in fashion. It was still difficult for her mistress to speak, and it was usually in one word, 'Water!' she would say or 'Thank you' perhaps. It seemed to require much of her, these utterances, as though there was an invisible cord about her neck, strangling the words in her throat as she made them emerge.

Sadie, escaping her lady's chamber for a moment by dint of leaving Mary the maid in charge of her while asleep, crept down the stairs and waited until Baker the butler left the hall, to stealthily enter the salon where her ladyship, so kitchen gossip informed her, read until she heard her son's carriage wheels in the street, and then went to bed before he entered the house. A concerned mother, who did not burden her son with her concern. Sadie approved. The maid slid into the salon before George the footman could catch her.

'My lady,' she said.

Lady Grant looked up, surprised by a female voice. 'You!' she said.

'I have an idea, my lady.'

Lady Grant sighed and closed her book. 'I thought you might. Speak!'

'Yes, milady. Well, I hear that you like to read, Lady Grant, and it seems to me that it is silly, my lady,' the baroness recoiled at the word silly, 'that you are reading *here* while my own miss is *trying* to read and not managing it, upstairs. So I fought you could just read your story aloud to her upstairs.'

'*Indeed?*' said the baroness with haughty sarcasm.

Sadie nodded. '*I* would, but I don't know how, my lady. Give me a cow and I'll milk it, or a horse and I'll saddle it, but give me a book and I can do nothing but look at the plates.'

'Oh,' said Lady Grant. 'Very well!' She went back to her book, and in a minute, with huge exasperation she said, aware that the maid had not moved. '*What now*, girl?'

'Yes, *now*, my lady,' said Sadie, misunderstanding her mistress again, 'Miss generally wakes up around now, and tries to read.'

'You wish me to go *now*?'

'Yes, my lady, as you guessed.'

The second aristocrat of the day did the maid's bidding. They passed the butler in the Hall, and Sadie could feel his eyes boring into her, ready to have strong words at another date. She dropped her head and pattered swiftly away.

Chapter 4

Cole's Discovery

Hubert Cole had returned to his house with one thought in mind. To see her and make her pay. When his mama, trembling as she looked at him, handed him the viscount's letter in lieu of telling him her news, he read it and crumpled it up in rage.

'How *could* you let this thing happen, Mama?' he hissed at her. He came towards her and raised an arm, and her squeal had the butler enter, asking in a nervous tone if there was anything that her ladyship desired?

Cole strode to the fire and looked therein, the crumpled letter in his hand behind his back.

'Nothing, Jenks,' said his mistress faintly. When the butler left, she began, voice shaking, 'My dear boy ... perhaps it is better ... that ugly girl made you so angry ... it was not like you!'

'Angry? Her very existence disturbs my peace. But that Baroness Grant should *take* her...!' He looked over his shoulder. 'If the girl talks, your reputation and Susan's will suffer.'

'But she *cannot* talk.'

'Are you *sure*?' He balled his fist. 'After all the care I have taken to restore this family's respectability when that whoremonger of a father had ruined it, it might be broken by a worthless girl's sorry tale. She is a snake, I told you so. Did she write to them? The Grants?'

'You know I do not permit Jenks to forward her correspondence. She daily awaits news of her aunt, but I destroy both her letters and the girl's, as you wished, Hubert. It was only correct. She should no longer correspond with family who might encourage her to give herself airs.'

'Those *airs* she shows us every day. Has she ever complained to you once? If she had, I should have been glad to know she knew her place. But I told you, she holds herself above us.'

'Yes, yes, I saw it my son, when you pointed it out. Even her obedience was an insult to those she should have grovelled to.'

'But you *let her go to that house*. Why?'

'You were not *here*!' cried his mother. 'The baroness said, *in front of my friends*, that she was amazed to find a viscount's daughter in such a condition. Then she said her carriage would call to bring her to a visit the next day and that if the girl were to be indisposed, she threatened she would talk of it,' since his rage was still palpable, his mother added in an appeasing voice, 'And you wouldn't have wanted *that*, Hubert.'

'Both you and Susan are fools,' he said bitterly. 'It was the *clothes* of course. Had the girl been dressed as she came to us, the baroness would have paid her little attention.'

'But Susan was *right*, dear. Her clothes were much too fine for her position.'

'And you replaced them with servants' clothes that did not fit. Thus, showing yourselves up as cruel and parsimonious.'

'But it is *your fault* she *stayed* at the Grants…,' his mother said defensively, '…for they brought in a physician.'

'*What* did you say?'

His mother trembled anew. 'I only mean, the carriage accident, her injuries…!'

He gave a derisive scoff, laced with rage. 'They will make her a heroine, won't they? Those Grants. Like her *hero brother*. Little did they know that she behaved so only to make herself *admired*. Well, I cured her of that wilful pride.'

'I am sure no one could admire her now,' said his mother, 'not even Lady Grant.'

'She will be displayed as a *charity case* again, this time in Lady Grant's drawing room, not yours. She cannot talk, and she will be too afraid to write any account. But I *will* have her back!'

'But *why*, Hubert?'

'Because she may not come and go as she pleases, or even as the great Viscount Duvall pleases. She was *your* responsibility, Mama. You must fetch her back.'

Lady Cole jerked at his tone and whined, 'You do not know what Lady Grant *said* to me or her *manner*. If I insist again, she will start a *scandal*, I know it.' This word, she knew might be the only one that could stay her son. She pulled at a tassel on her shawl and whined. 'I *tried* to visit again, to warn the girl to say nothing, but I was refused entry. The butler was haughty, as I fear he had been instructed to be.'

Cole kicked a log on the fire, and sparks flew. '*I* will find away.'
It was a deadly promise, and his mother looked at him fearfully.

Hubert Cole locked himself in his study and thought of her. He remembered, as he tried not to do, the first time he had seen her. It was at a large Duvall family occasion, large enough that even the outlying family members, such as his father and his family had been invited. Old Viscount Duvall had just been honoured by the Crown for something or other, and so the family were lauding him, the dry old stick. Duvall had his children by him, his handsome son John who looked, thought Hubert Cole, so very relaxed and confident. His sister had looked a little young, and shy to be at the party, but then her brother lent down and said something in her ear and Cole had seen the fifteen-year-old's face light up in a smile he could never forget, laughing back at her sibling. Cole's father had, by this time, moved forward with his family to felicitate the viscount, who looked much too old to have such a young daughter. Sir Neil Cole's compliment had been met with the minimum of civility.

Hubert Cole had found his eyes on the girl, whose strangely coloured hair had glinted under the lights, and the viscount, noticing this, had given him a distant look and did not introduce her. It was quite deliberate, Cole had known, smarting. No doubt he judged the son of Sir Neil Cole with the reputation of his father, or possibly he was too proud to consider these distant cousins worthy of attention. Warmed by candlelight the Viscount's immediate family sparkled together: an old-fashioned emerald on the viscount's hand and his star on the King's sash across his body, a diamond pin on the son's muslin stock, glowing pearls at the ears, and a silver butterfly in the hair of the girl-child who was named Ursilla. He did not see much in affection from the father, but the siblings were close, and gave the scene some animation. John Duvall was charming to the guests, and the girl seemed to answer questions prettily.

The Cole party were once more on the outskirts of the room, his parents bickering and his sister complaining. Cole felt the sting of inferiority. But his eyes returned to her again and again. He guessed she would not come out for two years at least, he caught her eye as he thought so, and his face smiled before he could control it. She looked through him as though he was not there, her eye moving on. It was possible that she had not registered his gaze, but when, after her father's death, he had seen her again in his own house, she had given him a vague look and distant smile and he, who had known a moment of joy at the new encounter, had felt smirched once more. Well, he was no longer tarnished by his father's presence, he was now a respected fashionable gentleman who was single-handedly restoring the Cole family's reputation, and who was much sought by fashionable ladies. And he was master in this house now that his father had left it. He would make her feel his superiority!

But to all of his mother's compliments about him, spoken before Ursilla Duvall, she had only agreed in a faint voice, or said, 'You must be proud, my lady,' in the same tone and smiled that vague smile once more. She had not, for one second, shown him the deep gratitude and respect he deserved. She had not once, in those early days, seemed to *notice* him particularly. She mouthed grateful platitudes to his mother each day, and accepted his parent's admonishments, but she had never sought his support, even. Had she done so, looked his way for help, perhaps he might have deigned to play her protector.

He loathed her, loathed her indifference, her acceptance of her fate. When her brother had died too, she had been grief stricken, and he had relished her misery and been stung by it, also. So, she *could* care so much for someone — and yet be completely indifferent to *him*. Well, now that she did not even have the protection of her brother's name, she would be made *not* to be indifferent. His mother and sister took away her clothes and other affairs and made her feel her place. She was accepting, resigned, but protected from the full humiliation by the thick fog of her mourning. She did not trouble herself to beg for the restoration of her possessions, or for mercy. She did not curry favour. He loathed her more.

Then there had been the accident. She had pushed him away from the trampling horse and fell below it herself. For a moment, he had crawled to her and taken her broken body and held it. He had whispered his thanks, but she had opened her eyes and said, 'No, it was nothing!' *Nothing!* It was no compliment to him, no scrap of affection from her, just *nothing*. He hated her then, had thrown her from him.

It was *she* who was nothing. No real beauty, uglier by the day, no *firelight sparkle* any longer. No smiling affection. Once he had seen her give a smile of thanks to a *footman*. He had sent the man off without a character that night. He began to show her, then, what she was. Nothing more than a punching bag he could use for sport. But she was so vile, so dirty, that he would not touch her with his hands. If he once used his hands on her ...! He closed his eyes in a wave of self-loathing. He could not ... not with *that*! He was not his vile father, subject to his basest desires. Such feelings he strangled at birth. But tonight, he had come back dreaming of the beating he would give her to relieve the ache that he had felt at being apart from her, from the delicious fear he often saw in her eyes that at last replaced her indifference ... and now ... she was out of his grasp. He swilled the brandy, but it did not help.

He left at night, cravat untied, and very unsteady on his feet, Jenks told her ladyship later. He did not come home till dawn.

'Susan,' Lady Cole confessed to her daughter, 'I am *glad* that girl has gone. Hubert was the most sober of men before *she* came here. Everyone remarked how different my son was to that creature I married. So strict in his morals, so philanthropic, so dignified and polite. But after *she* came, something happened.'

'She is a vain and wicked woman. *Poisonous*, Mama!' Susan Cole said. 'See how she lured away Mr Paul from my side. He does not look for me now at all.'

'She must have made him pitiful eyes. It is her way to entrap men!' agreed her mama.

'Even *Hubert*...!' suggested Susan.

'*Nonsense!*' hissed Lady Cole with venom, 'Mind your tongue.'

'Yes Mama. She is not even here and is causing destruction. I *never* liked her.'

Chapter 5

Settling In

Sadie was out of the truckle bed and had opened the door in a trice. Grant stood outside, looking guilty, as though he had been found out in a transgression.

'I *knew* it were you,' she whispered, '...my lord,' she added as an afterthought. 'It is always around this time that I hear you. She's sleeping.'

Grant pulled himself up, a neutral expression on his face. 'How does Miss Duvall go on?' he asked, his tone lowered.

'Well, she don't complain about the pain in the day, my lord, but I reckon she still suffers a lot, even after all these weeks. The nights is the worst. My lady comes and reads to her before sleep, and it calms her greatly, but after a half hour she begins to wake in the night, and it takes a deal to comfort her when she's in them nightmares.'

'How do you do so?'

'Well, I talks, my lord. It seems to get into her to hear a voice ramble on about normal fings, and then I get someone to fetch warm milk, in case I need it.'

'She stirs!' Grant said.

The sleeping figure cried out and tried to curl herself into a ball, causing her obvious torture from the splinted leg.

'It is a warm milk night, for sure,' said the maid, sadly. 'It is faster if I get it, my lord. Just you stay and talk until Miss quietens down.'

With this she whisked herself from the room. Grant wasted ten seconds on exasperation, then entered the room, drawn by the agonised moans. Ursilla Duvall had stuffed her fist in her mouth in an effort, he thought, to stifle her cries. Is this how she had behaved in the attic room where she had been assaulted by Cole? Her body jerked, as though she was reliving blows, and Grant sat on the bed once more, and tapped her tight fist again, as he had on the first occasion. He began to speak.

'My mama reads to you, I hear. I wonder what books you would wish to read if you were given the choice? Novels, like mama? I will tell Sadie to have you write me a list of your favourites.' It seemed as though she heard his low voice and was comforted by its steadiness. She twitched less and breathed deeply, but occasionally seemed to revert to her nightmare. 'Mama is very intelligent and kind, but rather shallow I feel. A typical fashionable female, like my sister. You have met her, I understand. Dulce has a very happy marriage, but connubial harmony is relieved by her daily visits and outings with Mama. And poor Drakemire, who is rather a slave to my sister's stronger personality, then has time for his own pursuits. Dulce too, is a fashionable lady, and she laughs a great deal. You will be happy here, Miss Duvall, happy and safe. Just wait and see.' He was silent, believing her to be calmed, but in five minutes, the twitching began again, as though images appeared in her dreams, the eyes under her lids moved frantically, and he began again, continuing the taps on her bunched-up fist. 'Sadie is a strange maid, but Dr Southey and my mama have told me that you have taken to her and that she cares for you well. You must stop these unhappy dreams now. That life you lived, the one where you are not safe,' she twitched her semi-clenched hand and grasped at his finger that tapped on it rhythmically, 'is gone now, all in the past. Your new life will be like the one you had before John went to war. You may seldom see me, but I will protect you, as I would my own sister.'

Sadie entered, glass of milk in hand. She regarded his finger, still clutched by the sleeping girl,

'Your feet are bare,' he remarked, standing and disentangling himself. 'Knit yourself some short night stockings.

'Yes sir.'

He had passed her, but stopped at the threshold without turning. 'Do not tell her I was here.'

'Can I ask you why, my lord?' said the bright voice of the maid, which might have been considered pert, if it was not for the fact that she had no notion of the rules of subservience that she constantly transgressed.

'No, you may *not*.'

'Oh!' the maid said and blinked. 'Very well, my lord.' But her tone was that of one doing him a favour rather than obeying a decree.

In the first days of Ursilla's stay, when the Countess of Drakemire had visited the girl for the second time, she had noted much. Ursilla, in and out of consciousness, was comforted by her maid's presence and was glad of the sympathy from Lady Grant, but rather overwhelmed by it all.

On the way downstairs she had told her mother, 'I shall not visit her every day, Mama.'

Her mother said, 'You shall not?' for it was a rare day that Dulce did not come to her. It was an unusual thing, she found, and unexplainable, that mother and daughter were best friends as well as relatives. Edmond, too, was close to both in his way. The baroness supposed that it might be because their family was so small that they held on to each other more than most.

'I think she has sympathy enough from the excellent maid and you, Mama. Any more might be mawkish,' Her mother frowned, but Dulce added, 'I mean to be a different kind of friend to her.'

As they entered the salon where chocolate awaited them, the baroness squeezed her arm, 'I'm sure you are wise, Dulce dear.'

'I shall go upstairs once a week only, and I will be myself and whitter on, as Edmond calls it, about fashion and the latest scandals and so on, and not seem to notice her injuries at all.'

'I see it!'

Dulce's eyes filled. 'And anyway, Mama. I can hardly bear it. When I *think* of what she suffered I am torn by the desire to embrace that poor girl and cry, or to find that evil man *immediately* and feed him to Drakemire's hounds!'

Her mother embraced her, and they hugged and cried a little together. The baroness pulled away, regaining her dignity, and said, 'You have let me see that burdening the poor girl with sympathy may be inevitable at the moment, but cannot continue for too long if she is to recover. She will be part of our family, and she must not be made to feel a *charity case*, as I heard that dreadful Lady Cole refer to her. And *this* about a girl who may have saved her son's life by her bravery!' The baroness's eyes narrowed dangerously, 'If it would not bring unwanted chatter to Miss Duvall, I would set her ladyship's dreadful behaviour as the talk of the town. See where she could show her face then!'

'It is a miracle that Ursilla's virtue remains intact!' said Dulce. Then, 'I suppose we can be sure of that?'

'Yes, yes. The brute did not touch her with his hands, the footman was sure.' Lady Grant looked at her daughter, 'But even if it was not so, I would merely cling to the girl even more and keep her safe, and let no bad words reach her ears.'

'I know, Mama, I know!'

Ursilla Duvall was beginning to emerge from the fug of pain and confusion that had marked her stay here and was becoming more and more grateful and wondering. She was really safe, was she not? When she came for 'the visit', she had been sent upstairs to this bedchamber. She had been confused, but docile, and eventually Dr Southey who said he was a physician, had come. A little maid came too. A girl with rosy cheeks, brown curls, and a smile. The physician said that Lady Grant wished her to see *him* first, since her ladyship was concerned for Miss Duvall's health. Ursilla was afraid and ashamed, but the maid undressed her and held her hand during the exam. She had made no demur, for it had been a long time since she had felt she had the right to protest anything. Her confusion deepened.

Suddenly, Dr Southey had grasped her leg and twisted it, holding down her hip bone. She screamed, but it was a good pain. All the sharper agony she had felt for some time now seemed gone in a moment, and only a dull ache of bruised muscles and tendons remained. Her hip had been put right after eight months, then her jaw, injured a week before. She had known it did not work as it did, but now she seemed to understand that it, too, had been dislocated. She had felt the swollen face before, but such swellings were not unusual. Then, Lady Grant had come and cried a little, and the physician had asked if he could reset her leg, but explained that it would be painful since it would first have to be broken again. She was confused and upset, but she trusted the three pairs of eyes that had looked at her for her decision. She had nodded firmly. In her clouded state she wondered what Lady Cole would do when she did not return this afternoon. But soon there was too much pain to wonder for long, and then laudanum sleep.

Since waking, Sadie's presence reassured her, and once William the footman had stolen in to see her, too. This had set her screaming for a minute, but he had gone to the threshold and said, 'The young master is not in this house, miss. You need not fear. My new master in this house bids me guard you, and I am happy to do what I could not do before for you. I see now I should not have come to see you yet. But do not fear me, Miss, *please.*'

'No,' she just was able to croak. 'Thank ...'

She did not know why she could not speak. It just terrified her to communicate, so she did not. What was safe, and what was not, was a mystery she could not fathom. Except Sadie. She knew Sadie was safe. But still, her throat constricted when she wished to speak, even to the sweet maid.

Since she had once woken up to find her maid kneeling beside her bed, holding her hand and weeping over it, she had realised that Sadie was something both precious and terrible for her. Ursilla had only been able to survive, for the last months at the Coles, by living in a distant place in her head, cutting off what feelings she could, becoming numb. But the maid's grief for her, coupled with her cheerful face in the daytime, cried out to her. She was being called back to *feel* once more, and it was terrifying.

A baroness and a countess came to visit her, the elder reading to her each night. This last calmed her terrible anxiety about speaking. She only had to listen. The countess was warm and friendly, but hid tears. Ursilla could not think why the pretty, elegant, lady cried. There was the terrible shadow of the son and brother they mentioned. A *man* lived in this house. It was terrifying. But he was, they reminded her, a friend of John's. *A friend of John's*, she breathed, when she panicked at the thought of him. She sometimes thought that there was a male voice in the night. But it was the nightmares, was it not?

She was with Lady Grant, she remembered when she became more lucid, whose son had served with her darling brother *John*. Lord Grant's name was Edmond, she had heard his sister the countess, say so. Edmond had been frequently mentioned in John's letters. Edmond had saved him from a fatally aimed rifle ball, Edmond and he had drunk and revelled in a Spanish town. Edmond beat him at cards. Edmond and Townsend were his best friends. Edmond was a *devil with the ladies*. Meaning he was attractive, she supposed. This last made her breathe more easily. Since he was popular with the ladies, Edmond would hardly be interested in *her*. He would not be like HIM. It was a while since she had used a looking glass herself, but she remembered how awful was the sight therein. It would send a normal man in the opposite direction.

He, who hated her, had let her know how ugly she was. She could see his leering jeer, his hot gaze while he spat out his insults, telling her how hideous she was. Why he had brought her to him again and again she could not fathom. She had hidden from him whenever possible, had striven not to annoy him when she could not — as when she must sit with his mother, and he entered a room. She had strained herself not to meet his gaze or do anything to draw attention to herself, but his mother sometimes complained of her to her son. Once, when she had looked and seen the *satisfaction* on his face at this, she had looked back at Her Ladyship and had surprised a look of shame on her face. All of it confused her, but she knew that in the son's satisfaction at the mother's complaint, there was the promise of her being called to the terrifying attic room again. A room she dreaded, not just for the pain and suffering, but for the fear of more ... what, she did not know.

Cole had not been good with the young females who visited the house with their mamas, trying to vie for his attention. He had been too cold and harsh to ingratiate himself, despite his dark good looks. But he was the eligible heir to a baronetcy, and many persisted. He liked to make his contempt for Ursilla clear before them. It had seemed to her that he used them *only* for this purpose. She felt always that *she* was the centre of everything for him, though it did not make sense. Even in company, she could feel his quick disdainful glances, his concentrated angry energy, directed always at her. She knew it, and never understood it.

She had borne this humiliation ... it was nothing to the rest. His assumption of superiority, or that of his mother and sister, had never much troubled her. It was unpleasant, that was all. She had not previously lived in a home where rank was much flaunted or taken into account. She had simply been waiting for John's return. That was her only reason for existence. Until the day when she discovered he was *never* going to return.

Now, in the Grant house, she was told several times a day that she was *safe*. But any sudden noise still made her jump, and she could not express to anyone that Hubert Cole visited not just her nightly dreams, but flashes of him looming over her came many, many times a day. She felt no hatred, only fear. *Why* did he hate her so? Why would anyone? She had wanted only to live a useful life. Her further fall in status when John had died had not concerned her greatly, only the loss of her dear brother and friend held sway over her.

Now she knew that even at the last, John had asked his friend to look to her — he had thought of her, Lady Grant had told her, in his last moments.

She would like to meet his friend at least once, but she could guess, even through her fog, why he might not choose to meet her.

William the footman took to bringing up Miss Duvall's washing basin himself, or sometimes her chocolate or other refreshments. On these occasions he was able to speak a little to Sadie outside the room or inside it and thus Sadie probed what had happened in that house. Apart from the ubiquitous butler, the other servants only knew that their new permanent guest had had an injury from a carriage accident that had not been sufficiently well cared for and their master had sent for the best surgeon to make it right. It seemed that the young lady was the daughter of a hero of the great battle who was a close friend of the baron. Nothing else was known, and all the maids or footman who had reason to enter the bedchamber wished the poor lady well indeed, for she smiled her thanks whenever she was awake, and was much to be pitied. If there was talk below stairs it was, at the start, about whether the lady might survive, for as Mary, a chambermaid who fetched and carried said, she looked close to death, a ghost already, and moaned when under the morphine something terrible.

So, it was only Sadie who knew. Because she had been there from the first, because she even now wiped down miss's body, checking the progress of her healing. But it was Sadie too, who heard her in the night, the cries she sometimes stifled by putting a corner of the sheet in her mouth. And now, with William's limited account to her she understood more. Of course, the man responsible (Sadie would not call him a gentleman) could not be strung up right now, as she wished and hoped for with a passion, and of course the young lady's sufferings at his hands could not be fodder for general talk. Who would believe he had not done worse than beat her sweet miss? Her reputation would be sullied indeed.

So, Sadie worked on at cheering her lady and sewing her the most beautiful dress that she could. One day, Sadie was determined, her lady would have a new life of health and happiness and every good thing. It was not only duty, or even pity, it became deep affection. Once, when

Miss's sleep had been much disturbed, Sadie had yet again knelt by the bed, holding her hand. She fell asleep once more in this position and awoke to Miss stroking her curls affectionately. She had hugged Miss Ursilla time after time, when she had awoken in pain or fear, and the young lady had clung to her. This was not the affection of lady and maid – instead, they had taken each other into their hearts.

Dr Southey visited only once a week now, not every day. Ursilla Duvall's hip hardly pained her at all after the day he had manoeuvred it into place. Like the jaw, it had not been broken. After three days for the jaw (a newer injury) and two weeks for the hip, the ligaments healed and there was little pain. The re-broken leg was bad, but ribs had been the worst. However, she had had broken ribs before, once even spitting blood for a fortnight afterward. Cole had been in a kicking frenzy — caused, she believed, by a casual remark addressed to her from his sister's gentleman caller.

This gentleman, a Mr Paul, had inquired if there was a draft at the window where she was seated, and she had answered in the negative. She had seen Hubert's eye change and had sat out the rest of the visit in terror. When she remembered this scene, she thought of the change in Mr Paul's eye when Miss Susan Cole informed him that *he need not address Miss Duvall*. The man, who simply had ordinary good manners, had a cool eye to Miss Cole thereafter, and had given a brief sympathetic look to Ursilla Duvall.

Now, Ursilla said to Sadie one day, doing a mime of circular motion with her hand, 'Cro ...chet!'

'You wish to crochet, Miss? I thought your hand couldn't hold the hook?'

'Learned...!' Ursilla held up her left, uninjured, hand and wiggled the fingers, smiling.

Sadie laughed. 'You learned with your left hand! How clever.'

Her mistress smiled even wider.

'What colour wool will I fetch for you, Miss?'

Ursilla frowned.

'How about if I fetch some fine white cotton and you can edge a cloth?'

The young miss nodded, happy.

As the maid sewed, showing her mistress the new gown in its series of construction pieces, Ursilla sat, propped in bed with pillows, crocheting an edge on a crisp linen cloth, suitable for covering a picnic basket, perhaps.

Her actions were a little clumsy, but she was succeeding, until Sadie came and changed the hook to her other hand.

'Try a few stitches with your right hand, miss. Who knows but it might improve a little.' The hook slipped through Ursilla's fingers and Sadie put it back. At Ursilla's sceptical look, Sadie said, 'You never know until you try.' After a few attempts dropped off the hook, which Sadie chortled at so that her mistress joined in, Ursilla eventually made some stitches, that she and the maid pulled at to make uniform, and then Sadie pried the hook from her hand and changed it once more. 'A little every day, Miss, that's the way!'

Ursilla laughed at Sadie's unconscious demeanour. She was a trifle bossy.

'Have ... siblings ... Sadie?' Ursilla managed to ask.

URSILLA AND THE BARON'S REVENGE

This was almost a sentence, and Sadie glowed. 'Eight sisters and two brothers, Miss. I'm the eldest.'

Ursilla seemed to laugh a secret laugh at this and gave a look and a nod that said *I thought so!* better than words. Miss could make a *joke* at her! Sadie tipped up her chin in mock offense, and they both giggled.

Grant, passing the room at this precise moment, heard it and wondered. She *laughed*.

In a flash, he remembered something. On leave, he was obliged to bring his friend, then The Honourable *Mr* Duvall, back to his London home, drunk. He went into the foyer with John draped around his shoulders, and a young girl had catapulted from a room in her nightwear and cap and said, 'Oh John, is that you?' Then, taking in her brother's sorry state, she giggled. The exact noise he had just heard in his own house. He remembered her youthful, schoolgirl enthusiasm, her merry eyes, and not much more. She had become aware of her attire, it seemed, and excused herself, running up the stairs as two footmen took Grant's cheerful burden.

She once had merry eyes. He wondered if, behind the thick mahogany doors, her eyes were once again merry. The impudent maid, he thought ... what a fortunate notion he'd had when he asked for someone kind.

At dinner his mother said, 'I read for Miss Duvall last evening. I shall call her Ursilla henceforth, since she is to be part of our family. She has begun to crochet, and said 'tatting' to me, and I suppose she wishes to keep her fingers busy. She even *smiled* to me and said *Lady*

Grant! — though it was in a poor, rasping voice. I think her throat, too, may have been damaged by that cur. I was so *touched* when she said my name. She is better each day.' His mother laughed. 'That pert maid Sadie had *another* idea. She pulls and pushes at Ursilla's legs each day, so as to keep them strong, she says — but I fear she is somewhat clumsy with the broken leg. There will be a scar on that leg, I suppose, but no one will see it, after all. I asked Dr Southey if there was aught to be done about her face, and he said no, he feared not. But I believe that if I were to have her hair cut differently and had some ringlets on her cheek it would barely be discernible.'

'Her face with her hair back is becoming enough, I think,' said Grant. 'One grows accustomed to the scar.'

'I thought you had not seen her?'

'Only when she is asleep.'

'*Ah!*' said his mama insinuatingly, but jokingly, 'You visit in the *night*.'

'Once or twice only. And I had seen her in the street previously, remember.'

'Really...?'

Seeing something in his mother's eye, Grant said. 'I mustn't tarry tonight. *You* do not go to the ball because Lady Stuart bores you, mama. But I must run to get the first waltz with Miss Charlotte Parris.'

'You think you can steal a march on her suitors?'

'Well,' said Grant suavely, 'one must try.'

'Do you like Miss Parris?'

'She is very lovely ... and amusing. There is a quick brain there too, though she has been schooled, like all young ladies, to disguise it.'

'Yes, indeed!' agreed his mama, 'I hid it well myself. No gentleman in *my* age wished for a clever woman. Your poor papa did not realise until it was too late for him.'

'You ran rings around him.'

'Yes, an enjoyable dance,' smiled Lady Grant reminiscently. 'So, you do not visit Ursilla tonight?'

'I do not. It is not a *habit*. It was just that the maid asked...!' Lady Grant laughed, but her smile was rather commiserating. She had followed the lead of the maid a few times herself. 'Anyway, I shall be late for Miss Parris.'

'I trust you have the address to defeat your rivals,' said his mama, archly.

'Mama! Am I not your son?' He quipped as he left the room.

His mother looked after him, raised her eyes to the ceiling, then sighed. She wished he would visit Ursilla, but she knew what he feared. But it was absurd. For all Lady Grant's affection for the girl, she could not wish a broken woman upon her son, it was true. Who knew what damage had been done to the poor child internally? But she was so very fond of Ursilla already. She wished for her protection, and there was no one better to make it so than her son. But Edmond *would* protect her, even if not as a suitor. The strong and beautiful Charlotte Parris might be good for him, indeed. As long as she was not unkind to Ursilla. Lady Grant had become a tigress as far as her new family member was concerned. Even a foul remark would not go unchallenged. It irked her that Hubert Cole still strode the streets. But she did not believe that Edmond had forgotten Mr Cole.

***

The baron had another chance to hear Miss Duvall's giggle. As he passed the invalid's room one afternoon, he heard the maid say chidingly, 'Who told Sally to bring up that basin?'

'Me!' croaked the mistress, with an apparent amused pleading.

The door was ajar, and he stopped, looking through the gap. The girl was holding up a bunch of her hair, looking comically pleading.

'I said it is too soon to wash it, miss, the whole bed will become wet, and you will be uncomfortable.'

The girl pulled all her hair to the side and dropped her head sideways in a mime show.

'Don't bend! Your poor ribs.'

The girl's hands met in a prayer-like motion.

'You mean we should wash it over the edge of the bed?'

Miss Duvall nodded, smiling widely, and Sadie sighed.

'Wait until I pose your legs better.'

Grant moved on, going down the stairs, then stopped halfway. Perhaps he had forgotten his handkerchief. Perhaps. He turned, to the butler's surprise, and walked back upstairs, quite slowly.

He paused at the gap in the door and saw that Miss Duvall was now draped sideways on the bed, with her dull hair hanging over the side of the bed into a basin balanced on a chair. Her maid was pouring water over by means of a jug, then took her fingers and splashed her mistress's face lightly. It was as though she were bathing a child rather than a lady, but Miss Duvall giggled again and flicked some wet hair onto the maid's brown apron. Which Sadie greeted with a girlish shriek.

Chapter 6
A Life of Luxury

Everything, she simply loved *everything* about being here. The first days had been hard, but even then, the kindness with which she was treated seeped into her from a long way off. There was the formidable but kindly baroness, the pretty countess, the warm and winning maid, the doctor, brisk but gentle. He had made jokes to amuse and distract her when he must poke her in uncomfortable places. He had not warned her when he relocated her hip, just talked to her about nothing very much, and suddenly jerked it into place. The pain had been piercing, but then relieving. She had felt herself, for one horrible moment to be back with *him* in the attic room, suddenly attacked. But then she had seen those sympathetic eyes and felt the relief to her hip and *realised* that she was not there, no longer facing the malice of a madman.

Though she had been falling asleep and wrapped in nightmares for a while, when she awoke, she found the cheerful little maid with tender caring arms and hands, and was comforted. Then too there was the things: soft pillows that reminded her of her old home, the feel of smooth fine linen against her cheek, and covering her head to toe. Food was delivered and though she first felt she could not eat, soon she smelt and saw and began to eat for more than necessity. The walls of the room were clad in a silk moiré that was the colour of her favourite rose. It made her remember the garden of Duvall Court, which she had once loved so much.

There was a painting opposite her bed: a happy sylvan scene of a pretty shepherdess and her sheep, walking in pasture in the dusk. There was a cottage behind her, whose windows showed lighted candles as though she was assured a warm and cosy home at the end of her labours. When Ursilla was fit to do little else, she gazed at it often: the foamy white linen fichu at the girl's neck, her petticoat beneath her blue gown, the mob cap that kept her curls in place. She knew that this was a more glamourous shepherdess than she had seen in life, but she cared not. The shepherdess was like she now, with a comfortable place of rest at last. She wondered if the girl had fought wolves to protect her sheep. There was also a dark forest behind her, and a tear in the blue gown that was kilted up to protect her skirts. Possibly, the shepherdess had met some dreadful things in the forest, but now she had emerged, safely on her way home. Ursilla, too, felt suddenly free of the wolves. This pink walled haven with the comfort and the view of a back garden promised both safety and liberty at once.

Now, she was consistently asked what she would *like*. She had no answer, her voice would not work, but neither did her brain. It was too long since she had been asked what she wanted, or permitted an opinion, and therefore she had ceased to hope or desire. She found that Sadie the maid, when confronted with no answer made intelligent guesses.

'You'll like this soup Miss, and I've asked Cook to make you a custard after. Or rice pudding perchance?'

Ursilla smiled. And she smiled too, when Sadie brought the cards and tried to play with her, at first merely complying. But Sadie was loud and squealed when she won, and was darkly suspicious when she lost. Once she insisted on searching her mistress for hidden cards and ended by tickling her shamelessly.

Sadie was precious. With Sadie she had found her smile, and then her joy, and then her own naughtiness. She had never, even in the days when she still lived at Duvall, had such a friend. Sadie was her constant companion, when she cried in the night she awoke to Sadie's arms about her, cradling her like a baby. She feared Sadie cried too, sometimes, although she tried to hide it. How could the maid care so much for someone like her? Sadie was alert to everything about her. If she wished to move position, Sadie was there before she had time to ask, making it easier. She sensed Ursilla's moods even when she hid them behind her smile. And then, too, the little maid's mother's wisdom was constantly imparted to her.

'A pig's a pig, even when it puts on a moustache.'

'Thinking on the bad things don't peel no potatoes.'

'Roses and thorns go together, but 'tis the rose we remember.'

Ursilla wished she had had such a mother. Once when they were starving, Sadie reported, her mother had taken the scrags from the vegetable sellers in the market, plus a chicken neck, and made the best soup in the whole world.

Tales of Sadie's family, tales of this household that the maid gleaned from her infrequent soirees below stairs, were like children's stories for her delight. It was evident that Sadie was fresh from the country. She told her mistress that Cook bemoaned that she had not had the schooling of her, for she did not qualify for an upstairs maid at all, with her mouthy opinions and her not knowing how to show due respect. But Ursilla, when she was being persuaded, or even lovingly *bullied*, by Sadie to do something for her own good (eat more, rest when she was frustrated, have her hair dressed, practise her drawing even when it was so bad as to make her despair) thought she was the perfect maid for her. A God-given presence, indeed. Even the dreadful attempts at drawing did not seem so tragic when greeted with Sadie's hilarity. 'That's me nose miss?' she giggled. 'No wonder Seth Clutterbuck didn't favour me when I was batting me eyelashes at him.' She felt her appendage, 'what a conk! Is it really so lumpy?'

But Sadie's jeers were delightful and so Ursilla nodded gravely, saying, 'Xactly!' which produced another explosion of giggles from them both. But wise Sadie put the charcoal back in her hand, a put a fresh sheet on the board and adjured her to start with the fruit bowl instead.

The world beyond was calling, too. She smiled at William, the footman's, attempts at serving her with cheerful complements on her health whenever he arrived. He was, of course, a tie to the past, but even though seeing him sometimes brought back waves of dread or memories of her fear, she knew that even in those days he had wished to aid her. Even after Polly was driven off for sending her a breakfast roll when she was being 'confined to her room for rest' (with no food permitted) he still managed to get her fresh water, or a blanket from the servants' quarter when she was shaking with cold. So, she smiled at him these days, and tried to keep her occasional shaken response hidden.

She looked forward to the baroness's extracts from her rather lurid taste in reading material. Since the raving success that Lady Caroline Lamb's *Glenarvon* had produced, with all its use of real fashionable personages in scant disguise, other novels on the same lines were now written and read. Though there were plots of a kind in these novels, their chief interest was in who the renamed characters could be, and what scandal was being suggested in the plot that referred to them. Obviously, Ursilla had no clue as to whom these referred, but she enjoyed being told by the baroness.

'Lord Galashields turned to the pretty Countess Evesham and said, "Now that your husband is in my hands, you must yield to me in all my desires!"' read the baroness, 'Oh, how shocking! I should not at all read this to you,' her gaze returned to the page however and then she leant forward in a confiding way, 'I suspect, though, that Galashields in this tale is in fact Sir Rupert Ballantyne, you know. He took Romney's whole fortune at play but was rumoured to have seduced his wife to allow them to retain the London house at least. But now the two Romney's reside in London all year round, which is not at all healthy, I fear. I should feel sorrier for them but Lady Romney tried to involve Edmond in an entanglement when he was only eighteen years old, and I have resented her ever since.'

Ursilla's eyes had become quite round.

'Oh, she did not succeed, however, but only think how awful to be mentioned in this dreadful scandalous novel.'

'Oh, *yes!*' Ursilla managed, with feeling.

'Shall I continue? I understand that the Italian lady in the next chapter is really Mrs Prendergast, who is blonde, but shall we see if she is like?' Ursilla smiled at the baroness's avid appreciation of the tale and laughed to herself. '*Signora Lucia Fabriano said to her daughter, "You must marry Galashields whether you will or nay Adriana, for your father would cast us both from his gate if he knew I was the man's mistress! You must put all thoughts of Giovanni from you ... his family are beneath us."*' The baroness nodded, eyes narrowed, enjoying herself. 'That must be Mrs Prendergast *indeed*. Selling her daughter to a rake such as Bromley to protect herself from scandal! But poor Mr Tippen!'

Since there was no Mr Tippen in the novel, Ursilla's brows asked a question.

'Oh, he is a young physician who is making a name for himself. I understand he was courting poor Miss Prendergast before she married Sir Rupert. He must be Giovanni in the tale.' The baroness flicked the pages forward. 'I wonder if there is any mention of Dierdre Lawson, whom I believe is Bromley's latest flirt?' She hit upon a page with her finger. 'Oh yes! She must be Desdemona, for she too has red hair.'

Ursilla pulled a sheet over her mouth to hide her somewhat sad amusement. Sadness for the tattered lives of the fashionable persons mentioned by Lady Grant, and amusement at Her Ladyship's love of scandal.

'Oh, perhaps not! It says here that Desdemona throws herself from a cliff because of Gallashields' abandonment, but I saw Miss Lawson eating a hearty helping of that tasteless pudding they serve at Almacks.'

It seemed that Lady Grant was rather disappointed that Dierdre had not thrown herself from a cliff like Desdemona, and Ursilla laughed more, hiding it as best she could.

'I did not read it straight through, as usual. I am sorry, my dear Ursilla. I seldom peruse novels in order, I am not your best reader.' She had leant over to touch Ursilla's cheek affectionately. 'I shall try to do better tomorrow, my dear. Goodnight!'

In the next days, Ursilla began to stand, and then walk on her damaged leg, opening the door of her room at last and walking the corridor, even to the gallery that gave a view of the hall. There she saw him, the dreaded gentleman who lived here. *John's friend*, she reminded herself. She began to spot him traversing the hall sometimes, and she became calmer. He walked not in the stiff proud manner of another she knew — he who had adopted the manner of a king almost, and which did not ring true. No, *this* man's walk and manner was energetic and decided, but in no way pretentious. The baron had the air, she thought, of a military commander, someone who spoke and had others listen and obey. He was a fine figure, but she could not quite see the face, but she heard the voice, not quite stern, but definitely matter-of-fact, rather than smooth and charming. Was he harsh? His servants seemed respectful, but not afraid as their counterparts in the Cole house had been, in the presence of their master. Baron Grant was the son of the kind baroness and the brother of the lovely countess, and thus also the benefactor of her recent comforts. It was he, the baroness had confessed, who had thought to ask the butler for a *kind* maid. So, he was too, the donator of the most precious gift, Sadie.

Chapter 7

Out of Darkness

'What are you wearing?' Grant said to his sister the countess when he saw her in the hall donning a green crocheted shawl.

'Hush!' said Dulce, 'Ursilla made it for me, and so I wear it today with my yellow gown to complement the green, as you see.'

'It merely dulls your lovely satin, my dear.'

'Hush, I said! I wear it because Ursilla might come downstairs today. She has been marching the corridors above, you know, and may appear any day now.'

'Someone should have told me to avoid mama's sitting room.'

'Why *do* you avoid her? She is a guest, no, a family member here. It will be increasingly awkward if you continue.'

'I will not do so for ever. But I think she should become more used to her surroundings, more at home here, before I see her. If she can feel at ease first, she may not then fear a male presence.'

'Oh!' said Dulce. 'I did not think. You are more sensitive than you seem, Edmond.' She sighed. 'It is a shame I am not acquainted with Hubert Cole, or I could have given him the cut direct last evening at the Cowper's. I could, at least, ignore his mother.' She sighed again. 'It had no effect, however, since she was avoiding me, and no one knows that I am acquainted with the Coles in any case. I *would* tell tales, but I must not, for Ursilla's sake.' She frowned. 'Will you leave him unpunished, Edmond? I cannot bear to think so.'

'I have my own plans for Hubert Cole.'

'Oh, no!' cried a voice from the stairs. He looked over his shoulder to see an amber muslin gown descend in a manner that was reckless and she almost tumbled, breaking away from her maid's supporting hand.

Grant, frozen for half a second, got there in time and caught her waist in his arms. Sadie ran down and he surrendered her immediately, turning away.

'***Please** ... not* go to Cole.' Miss Duvall's throat was fighting to get out the words. '*You do not know.* Must ... not ... hurt ...you!'

He looked down at a person much improved than he had last seen her. The eyes were no longer in a skeleton face, her hair was styled simply, but as a fashionable young lady, but her blush showed the white crescent scar in contrast. 'I do not *know?'* he said to her cynically, but in a lowered tone to avoid being overheard by servants in the hall, 'who, with a knowledge of your injuries, could *not* know what Mr Cole is capable of?'

Dulce, seeing the fear and distress in Ursilla's face, took her arm and turned the girl towards herself. 'Edmond will not approach Mr Cole, I assure you, my dear,' she said soothingly, casting her brother a glance that conveyed promise of a sister's retribution. She added in a brighter tone, 'And today is the day you come downstairs. We must *celebrate*, dear Ursilla, and not think of things past.'

Ursilla tried to smile, but as her breath evened, she turned back to grasp Grant's sleeve. *'Promise!'*

Grant was not accustomed to being ordered in his own home, but her eyes were raw, and her maid sidled to him and whispered, 'Just *promise*, my lord, and then do as you wish.'

He almost thanked her for her permission to break a Commandment, but as she winked at him, he knew that his sarcasm would hit a brick wall. 'See to your mistress, you!'

The hand that grasped his arm squeezed, and he looked at it significantly. Miss Duvall did not withdraw it, however, and he gazed into those panicked eyes.

'Cole cannot hurt me,' he assured her, coolly.

'Pro—' her eyes were almost crazed.

'I promise that *before I inform you*, I will not approach him.'

She sighed, her hand fell from his coat sleeve, and Sadie led her away into his mother's sitting room. It was after the hour of callers. As she walked off, he saw her rear view. Pretty amber muslin with a satin sash beneath her high bodice, red-blonde hair in a simple topknot, white kid slippers, somewhat large for her, he thought— Dulce's perhaps. From here, she looked like any fashionable young lady. He thought John Duvall would have been happy to see her so.

But even as he thought so, he remembered what she had suffered in the months when he had delayed in his promise to his friend. The broken bones he might have saved her, the comfort he might have offered her sooner. But he knew guilt was useless, so he quashed it, and went to his club to drown it in cognac.

Ursilla gravitated to a window seat in the salon, but neither Dulce nor Lady Grant would permit it, granting her a seat by the fire. She was given a handsome workbox of her very own, which was placed on a table, and her basket of work projects, which Sadie had brought from the bedroom, sat at her side.

Lady Grant looked at her from the other fireplace seat and beamed. 'You look *perfect*, my dear!'

'Oh, she *do*, my lady,' said the impudent maid Sadie, from the back of the room.

'*You here?*' the countess sniffed, to depress pretension.

Ursilla said, rather desperately, 'Sadie... st-stay!'

'Of course,' said Dulce, good-naturedly, then turned a mock-stern face on the maid, with whom she had had some altercations before, '*if she is silent.*'

Sadie closed her lips, but her eyes danced. She caught the eye of the butler, who had brought a message on a silver salver, and subsided, lowering her head.

'Why is that girl more afraid of you, Baker, than our family?'

The butler's face was inscrutable, and her ladyship laughed.

Sadie was working on a sash for the second gown it seemed, and after twenty minutes she got up from her chair and approached her mistress, who was crocheting. She put the sash beneath her arm inelegantly, swapped the crochet needle into Ursilla's other hand without preamble, as the other ladies watched, amazed, then cast an eye about her, turning to the countess, as the only person without work in hand.

'Could you hold this, my lady?' she inquired, offering her the sash. Dulce, Countess of Drakemire, took it automatically, as her mother looked on astonished, and the maid was thus able to turn the strangely cut sash inside out, so as to finish off the middle stitches in closure. The maid went back to her place to do so, and Ursilla watched, smiling as the other ladies stared, open-mouthed.

Sadie's lack of concern, and her obvious ignorance of having crossed lines of subservient behaviour, made it impossible to think of a quick retort.

After that first visit to the salon, Ursilla came often. Sadie was allowed to stay and sew, and her stitchery (as displayed on some pulled work that edged the new amber gown) was such that Lady Grant gave her a pile of mending to help with. The aristocratic mother and daughter had agreed not to challenge the maid too much at the moment, since it distressed their dear Ursilla, and to allow her to remain. They had tried, indeed, after a few days to banish her, but Ursilla was duller and depressed, and the pert maid was granted entry once again. Her presence brought peace to her mistress, and so the ladies were content.

***

Dulce was complaining about Drakemire again, and Ursilla twinkled at Lady Grant, raising a humorous brow. Her ladyship relished this exchange. It was part of the coming alive of Ursilla. After two months downstairs, Ursilla now could talk a little more each day, but it was this humour that showed the spirit returning to her, and her security here. Ursilla must have been a vivacious little thing once, never the most beauteous perhaps, but pretty — and with a vibrancy (Lady Grant guessed, seeing these hints of it) that would have made up for any little lack of classical beauty.

Ursilla still refused to dine with her in the evening, in case, Lady Grant intuited, that Edmond wished to do so. This meant, on the evenings she was not engaged for dinner and Edmond was, that the baroness dined alone sometimes. Soon she would insist. Edmond had worried, Dulce had told her, that Ursilla might fear him as a male. But her ladyship thought them to be past this, and wished to try at least. She would orchestrate something. On two days when she knew Edmond engaged, she would insist on Ursilla joining her, then on the third night, she would trick them both, only warning Edmond belatedly, inviting the earl and countess, too, to make Ursilla more comfortable. If she could not bear it, or seemed distressed, she would have Sadie take her to her room. But, Lady Grant considered, they really must stop floating around each other like ghosts, with Edmond avoiding the rooms that Miss Duvall might be found in.

Grant did, indeed, avoid the rooms that Ursilla was in. Entering them, at least. Baker, noting that the baron occasionally lingered near the door of the drawing room where the ladies were to be found, quite early on took to leaving the door ajar, and that of his master's study across the hall.

The baron made no remark upon this slight dereliction of duty, and so he was able to hear, with increasing regularity a little laugh. His mother came into him one night and asked if he even wished to *know* of their new family member's progress.

'I imagine you will inform me if there is a problem, Mama.'

'So cold Edmond! Do you not feel for her?'

'I saw her walk across the hall the other day, not discernibly lame. Therefore I assumed all is well.'

'Oh, her *physical* health is good, but it was the damage to her nerves that worried me so dreadfully. But now she, who could only jerk out a word occasionally, speaks a little more each day. But even from the first, she spoke volumes with those lovely eyes of hers. Do you not think them lovely, Edmond?'

'I have seen her so few times Mama.'

'I suppose. Well, long before she could make little jokes, as she did today, she could make them with her eyes. She raises her brows at me in the drollest way when Dulce complains about Drakemire again. I think, before the years with the Coles, Ursilla must have been an imp.'

'I believe so,' Grant said, remembering the child who dashed out so impulsively and joyously to see her brother. His mother raised her brows. 'John mentioned it.'

'Ah! Well, you should spend time with us in the drawing room sometime, my dear, and see how her spirits have improved.'

But Grant knew that, however well she appeared, Ursilla's night time terrors had not ceased.

'By the way Mama, I remember the viscount used to collect seeds for his sister. Perhaps, if she cannot yet leave the house for the streets, she might be interested in the garden.'

'How did you know that she still fears the outdoors?'

'If you had taken her on a visit to the dress establishments, I imagine you would have mentioned it.'

But his percipient mama gave him a knowing look.

So, he was more and more careful of being seen as a spy. But it seemed essential to keep daily abreast of her progress. One day Baker, seeing his master cross the hall to depart the house, swung open the door fully, allowing the baron to have a full view of three ladies in conversation — and Grant witnessed himself the ironic eyebrow that Ursilla threw towards Dulce, over some remark of his mama's. It really *was* impish, he thought. And it showed, above all other things, the understanding and sympathy between the girl and his family. The baroness, catching the arch look Ursilla and Dulce exchanged, pretended to chide them, but he saw his mother's eye after Ursilla looked back to her stitching, and it was ... doting.

It was a good thing that they had bonded in this way. *Pity* would only have taken them so far, but Ursilla's evident playfulness was unifying them into something much closer.

His mother's wicked notion was put into practice, and so Grant found himself at last at a dinner with Miss Duvall: he stone-faced, Ursilla embarrassed. The Earl of Drakemire, a good-natured man of burly build, was also present, and he tried some heavy jocularity to lighten the mood. Unfortunately, these large hints did not aid the discomfort of Ursilla, or the bad humour of the baron.

Grant was attempting to be polite, but he was hardly warm. His sister Dulce kicked him beneath the table, a feat that required her adjusting her seat to reach him. He looked at her and frowned, but the evil look he encountered from the countess's eye caused him to say, in Ursilla's general direction, 'Your leg is quite healed, I hear, Miss Duvall.'

'As we are now family, Edmond dear, we have all agreed to dispense with conventionality and use our given names,' said his mama.

The baron remained silent at this and continued to eat.

'Is that so?' said the bluff earl, 'very good, very good!'

He looked at Grant, who did not look up, having done his duty with a remark addressed directly to his guest. He did not seem to notice that she had not managed to answer him but had reverted to silence.

'Eh, well, Ur*si*lla — pretty name that, I have a cousin named Urs*u*la, of course, but no one called Ur*silla* have I previously encountered. I wonder what it means? *Ursula* means *bear*, ye know, and I have always reflected that my cousin *is* rather a female bear. She has a sturdy form, I call it, and a fiercer handshake than her brother's. But you, now ... I wonder whatever *your* name may signify? You are more like a nymph or a fairy in form.' Ursilla blushed, but the earl, unaware, continued heartily, 'I am *Michael*, you may use my Christian name at will you know, *Michael Willoughby*, I was named at birth, though most of my friends just call me Drakemire, you know. Even my dear wife calls me Drakemire. I wonder if that is because Michael means 'gift from God' and...,' here he chortled, 'poor Lady Drakemire no longer sees me as a gift!'

'Drakemire!' said Dulce in a warning tone.

'Oh ... er ... yes!' he smiled at the young girl who had the good manners to smile at his joke, 'but ... what does *your* name mean?'

'The ... same!' managed Ursilla, and her voice croaked in the attempt. Lady Grant, divining that since the throat damage was past, the croak was due to nerves, looked sympathetically at the young girl. But it was as well she practised among gentlemen, she *must*.

Good old Drakemire continued, slapping his leg in amusement, which made Ursilla jump. 'You don't mean to say *bear*? Anyone *less* like a bear than your tiny ...'

'*Drakemire!*' warned Dulce once again, but Ursilla giggled.

The earl was silent now, and Lady Grant, determined to fill the pause said, 'Ursilla kindly made Dulce a shawl, did you see it, Edmond?'

Grant's eyes were dragged back up from his plate at this, as though through mud. 'I did. It was well achieved, I suppose, but it does not wear well with my sister's delicate muslins.'

'Oh, for *goodness' sake* Edmond—!' Dulce snapped.

But Ursilla smiled at him, rather sunnily, and ventured heavily, 'Country ... wear!'

He was taken aback by the smile and paused, staring at her. Then he said, 'It might do for that, certainly.'

Dulce, who seldom dressed differently in the country, not being a person given to exercise except on horseback, and who even if she *had* been would never have worn a crocheted shawl on her walk when her chest held several fine cashmere weaves, said, 'Just the thing!'

But the mother and daughter gave up trying to entice the baron into the conversation, in case he said anything else of dispiriting bluntness.

Grant and Drakemire talked horseflesh a little, Dulce, the baroness and Ursilla talked of the meal, and the fashionable ladies talked a little scandal, also.

Before the ladies left for the withdrawing room after dinner, Grant stood and bowed at Ursilla, who stopped, surprised. His tone cool but grave, 'I am happy to see your health much improved, Miss Duvall.'

'Thank you for ... *everything*, Baron!' Ursilla managed, tears brightened her large eyes.

He turned from her, and the ladies left the room.

'I apologise for my son, dear Ursilla!' he heard his mother say.

He could not quite catch the reply, but he thought it was, 'At least I had the chance to thank him.'

Chapter 8

Gentlemen Conspire

'Titus!' said Grant to the tall, handsome figure of Viscount Gascoigne, a gentleman with a mane of autumn coloured hair on his head and a careless, but much copied, line in fashionable dress. The viscount was passing by his table at their club, going to the exit. 'Want a word.'

'Don't owe you anything, do I Grant? Did you find an old, lurking IOU in a drawer?' Since Gascoigne had a fortuitous marriage to a very rich beauty a year ago, the paper would have been old indeed. There *had* been a day when Grant had franked him, but Gascoigne always repaid, even in the days before his marriage. The viscount took a seat at Grant's deserted table and waved off a gentleman who was asking to join them. 'Play cards!'

They did so, and eventually Grant said, his face grim, 'What do you know of Hubert Cole?'

'Is he a member here?' said Gascoigne vaguely.

'You know he is ... or was. Who gave him the blackball?'

'Now, how would anyone know *that*?'

'I considered, after a little digging, that it might be you.' Gascoigne played on. 'I was wondering *why*.'

'It is not my habit to gossip, Edmond, and neither is it yours,' the viscount said musingly.

'That is why I will not tell you that I know the blackball was totally appropriate.'

'Mmm,' said Gascoigne throwing down a jack of spades. He looked up at Grant with hard hazel eyes and said, 'You know Wilbert Fenton's nephew Benedict?'

'Sir Ranalph's son who makes the ladies swoon?'

'That's him. Fenton told me that Benedict had come upon Cole in an alley and prevented him from beating a person to death.'

'A footpad?'

'No. A young wench from the tavern they had both been in.'

Grant arched an eyebrow. 'Where can I find young Fenton?'

'I suppose at his home, Sumner House, in Russell Square. He married the widowed Lady Sumner, you know.'

'I think I heard. Childhood friends?'

'That's it!'

'I'll go now.'

'Something I can help you with, Grant?'

'Perhaps. Can you let your beautiful viscountess wait long enough to come with me?

'Now?'

Responding to the urgency, Gascoigne got to his feet and followed him.

They were fortunate to find Mr Fenton at home, having just finished dinner with his wife, uncle and his uncle's wife. They were shown into the dining room where uncle and nephew sat alone savouring some cognac, Grant guessed from the colour of the liquid.

Fenton senior raised a brow at their entrance at this after-dinner hour, but nodded to Grant as Benedict Fenton was introduced to the baron by Gascoigne. They were passing acquaintances, of course, but the young Fenton's lively, handsome face was now alight with interest as to their purpose.

'Do you wish me to leave you, gentlemen?' asked Mr Wilbert Fenton, a suave individual of forty or so, with a deeply sardonic expression.

Grant, forever blunt, said, 'No sir, you may be some help.'

'Enchanted!' Fenton said faintly, drinking his cognac.

'I wanted to ask you, Mr Fenton,' began Grant, turning to the younger man, 'about the night you saw Hubert Cole outside the tavern.'

Benedict looked at Gascoigne.

'Grant's not a slack-jaw,' Gascoigne reassured, 'I believe he has a reason to reveal to us.'

'I do,' asserted the baron. 'But first I would like you to tell me....'

Benedict gestured to a waiting footman, 'Tell the ladies we are delayed by visitors, George, and then do not come back in. First, fetch two new glasses. No, we can serve ourselves.'

The footman left and the gentlemen sat, Gascoigne by the elder Fenton and Grant on the other side by Benedict Fenton. Fenton was handsome in a way ladies admired, with arresting dark hair and chiselled features. He looked a good deal the junior here, but Grant thought the open, youthful face might disguise a slightly greater age than his appearance.

'I was drinking with some friends in the *Master's Den*,' Fenton began, referring to a well-known tavern not far from fashionable haunts, frequented by gentlemen and commoners alike. 'I recognized a gentleman at a nearby table whom I had seen at White's a time or to, though we had not spoken. He was alone, drinking a good deal, but on one of the occasions my eye caught his table, I saw his gaze

follow a serving wench with a particular look I found ... *unpleasant.*'

'And then?'

'You understand, she was an attractive girl, and even some of my drinking fellows were crass enough to flirt with her in passing, but were held back by the more sober of our number. She stood out from the other serving girls because she sported a bright plaid apron. It set her apart, and she exchanged banter with the customers quite gaily. But then I saw that gentleman speak with her, and she pulled away from him quite violently.'

'I must suppose, from her position at such a place, she must be used to the attentions of gentlemen,' remarked Grant casually, but his eyes were keen.

Benedict raised two brows in a knowing look of understanding, 'Yes, normally a ... *friendly* girl, by all accounts.' He looked at Grant, whose eyes were intense in concentration, 'but I could see why she might pull away from *him*. There was something strange in his look, something ...' he could not seem to find the words.

'And then?' Viscount Gascoigne prompted.

'And then I continued drinking with my friends. My wife was from town, and it was an excuse to be more indulgent than usual.' He looked over as his urbane uncle scoffed and smiled in acceptance of his jest. 'But I regretted it afterwards, for I did not notice the absence of the serving girl or the man I had recognized, not for some time.' He looked from one visitor to the other. 'My fellows and I were seated close to a window, and I began to hear scuffling sounds that I disregarded at first: a deep voice hissing, a cat meowing. At least, I thought it was a cat. The privy was full and so I stepped into the alley to ... and I saw it, that man kicking the cat, only it wasn't a cat, it was the poor girl in the plaid apron, hardly able to breathe.'

'So, you cried out?' asked Gascoigne.

Benedict Fenton scoffed. 'I would not give him the warning, I threw myself at him, kicked him to the ground and we fought. The girl crawled away, and I shouted to my friends to see to her. Cole ran off, and we took the girl to safety. She was barely alive, with broken ribs and arm. I think he placed something below the limb to make a good job of the break.'

'Could she talk?'

'She said that she had refused him, but he lay in wait for her when she came to the alley to wash the tankards in the old trough there. He began to violate her, but she struggled, and he gave it up and tried to throttle her. There were marks at her neck. She passed out and when she came to, he was kicking her viciously and because of her throat, she could barely cry out for help. He is not a man.'

'The girl?' asked Grant.

'She lives above the tavern. The landlady fetched an apothecary. We left them a guinea for her keep and in lieu of wages, so that she might keep her room.'

'You are a good man, Fenton. Did you talk of it abroad?'

'No. Even my friends do not know her assailant, for he ran away. Uncle Wilbert happened to visit me that evening, very late, and found my bruises.

'On the neck, especially,' said Wilbert Fenton in a drawl, 'strangling seems to be a habit with Mr Cole.'

'How did you discover his name?' asked Gascoigne, but amused, for Fenton's reputation was knowing.

'It was *quite* simple ...' said the elder Fenton, playing with a fob on his gold edged brocade waistcoat. 'I have since been considering how to *deal* with Mr Cole.'

'You already had him blackballed, Uncle Wil!' said Benedict breezily.

'The first step. But not *nearly* sufficient for harming my nephew.'

'I am before you, gentlemen,' said Grant, with decision. '*I* will mete out justice to Mr Cole.'

'May one inquire *why*, my lord Grant?' that drawling voice again.

Grant looked at the ceiling. 'First, might I attempt to describe the girl in the plaid apron to you, Fenton?'

'*Pardon?*' said Benedict. 'Were you present?'

'No.' said Grant in a clipped tone. 'She is slight and small in height.'

'Yes!'

'She had russet blonde hair and very large eyes.'

'Yes!'

'So I thought!'

'How on earth can you know that? Have you *met* her? Do you recognise her because of the apron I described?'

'No.'

Gascoigne, too, was showing an unfashionable display of amazement (which for him was merely a raised brow), as was Benedict. However, Wilbert Fenton was eying Grant narrowly. 'He knows *another* like her.'

The other two frowned, but Grant met the perceptive dandy's eye and nodded.

'He has done this before?' asked Benedict.

'To a lady under his protection.' Grant paused. 'I need not say this must—'

'Of course!' cut in Gascoigne irritated, 'But when you say "under his protection"...'

'I said a *lady*. A young girl, a relative, in fact, given into his mother's house to be cared for.'

'He did so to a *lady*... in his mother's house?'

'Repeatedly.' Grant said in a hard voice.

'My God,' said Benedict, 'is she safe? Is she alive?'

'She now resides with my mother. She was the sister of the last Viscount Duvall, my comrade in war. He died at Waterloo.'

'Good God!' said Gascoigne.

'I did not admit to your prior right to act against Mr Cole,' said the smooth voice of the elder Fenton, 'but now I concede it. Deal with him mercilessly, Grant!'

'I will. And since I want his destruction to be complete, I may come to you gentlemen for aid.'

'Anything!' swore the gentlemen.

'We should leave you to your wives,' declared Grant, standing.

'A moment,' said the drawling voice of Wilbert Fenton. But it was his intelligent, considering voice. 'You have described the girl to Fenton, since you believe that Miss … *Duvall* is it? … to be the source of his obsessive brutality.'

'Correct. I have discussed it with a physician who deals with conditions of the mind occasionally, he believes it a kind of mad obsession. It is probable that Cole desires her, but he detests his *craving* because he thinks she is unworthy of him. He holds himself ridiculously high, it seems. Then there was an incident where she pushed him away and saved him from a horse and was horribly injured herself. Unbelievably, it seemed to increase his hatred of her, and his obsession, both.'

'I see,' said Fenton, 'She shows herself noble, and he finds himself more loathsome…!'

'I did not quite think of it like that. But you may be right. Anyway, when he was displeased about anything at all in his life, he had footmen take her to an attic where he beat her…'

'He did not *violate*…?' asked young Fenton, anxiously. Then in a contrite tone he added. 'I am sorry, I should not have asked.'

'He did not,' Grant said in his cool tone. 'The footmen were witness to that. But one told me that he nevertheless leered at her as a lecher might.'

'Yes, *a leer* would be the word to describe his look to the girl at the tavern,' interjected Benedict Fenton.

'He beat out his own demons, as the medieval monks did to their own bodies,' mused the elder Fenton, 'But he used the girl.'

'The coward!' Gascoigne growled.

Grant nodded.

'The poor young lady!' ejaculated Benedict. '... is she well now?'

'She is doing better ... but she is still rather afraid of company. She could not talk at first, but she improves now. My mother wants her to go out a little, but she is too afraid to meet the Coles, as yet.' Grant remembered the girl he had first seen in the street, enduring more than he knew as he had gazed at her then. 'Possibly, she was braver before, or merely accepting, when she lived with them. But a place of safety has allowed her to *feel* more, and it has made her fearful of return.'

'Indeed, she must have felt so hopeless, the little soul.'

Looking at the sympathetic faces did not change Grant's clipped tone, but it did make him a trifle more loquacious. 'That and the pain she has had to endure having her leg broken and reset, and other operations have resulted in a kind of breakdown from which she only now emerges.'

'I see why she is afraid to go out.'

'Nevertheless,' said the elder Fenton, 'she must begin, before she becomes trapped by her fear.'

His nephew ventured, his handsome, open face sincere, 'We live close enough to your townhouse ... if we tell our wives, might we not invite her out slowly, first with the ladies, and then with a dinner, perhaps ...?'

Benedict Fenton was a kind young buck. Grant had done horse business with his wife, the blunt Mrs Genevieve Fenton, and liked her very much. Gascoigne and his wife were a superior pair, in beauty and bearing, and Delphine, the viscountess, was regarded as cold, but Grant had friends who had eaten at their table and said that her warmth became apparent. The fashionable couple would be good practice in socialising for her in time. Lady Aurora Fenton, Wilbert Fenton's wife, was elegance and kindness both, a visit from her would be a boon.

'I think we should plan this a little with my mother and Sadie.'

'Who is Sadie?' asked Viscount Gascoigne.

'A maid,' said Grant shortly, ignoring the general surprise. 'Well, we should take our leave.'

Two ladies came in as he said so, and Genevieve Fenton, some few years older than her husband, said, 'They told me it was you, Titus, and you, baron. If you are here to discuss horses, Grant, you had much better do so with *me* than my husband.'

Benedict protested, 'Here, I say! I am *renowned* for my mounts.'

'Says the man who bought Merivale's roan!' she sniffed. 'Your mounts are renowned because *I* choose them.'

'Save me *some* dignity, Jenny, I pray you!' her husband protested, but merrily.

'Are you leaving, baron?' asked Genevieve to Grant.

'Yes ladies, we had come to consult your husbands,' here he nodded to the divinely lovely Lady Aurora Fenton, 'on a private matter. No doubt they will tell you of it when we are gone.' This was implicit permission to do so, for these ladies were not tattle-tales. He took Genevieve's hand. 'And I am not deficient of wits, dear lady. If I had come to discuss horseflesh, I should *certainly* have applied to you first.'

Genevieve shook his hand in a manly fashion and said, 'Quite right!'

Benedict made a sound of protest to amuse her, and after a few parting words, Gascoigne and Grant went out to be handed hat and gloves in the hall. Wilbert Fenton followed them.

'As I was saying, Grant, if, as you guessed, Cole found *one* replacement for his obsession, since Miss Duvall is still kept from him...'

'There might have been another...?' Grant frowned, considering.

'It seems possible!'

'Then how can we find out ...?' Gascoigne said.

'It depends how careful he is. But an alley at an inn argues for a deep impulsion. He may have been rash more than once...!' Grant's eyes narrowed.

'The magistrates at Bow Street may have some knowledge of women attacked lately...' Gascoigne ventured.

'Some women, like the tavern wench, might not have reported it, but the Runners have their ear to the ground everywhere in London, and might have heard things,' the elder Fenton offered.

Grant nodded. 'Yes. I'll apply at Bow Street.'

'I may know a *quicker* way,' drawled Fenton.

'The excellent Mr Mosely!' said Gascoigne, catching on to the reference.

'Yes.' Fenton smiled at Gascoigne. 'Mr Mosely can find out what the Runners know in a trice, since he was once senior at Bow Street!'

'Very well, since you both know him, I shall depend upon you gentlemen.'

They left and Grant was very thoughtful in the hackney on the way home.

The dinner with the hapless Earl of Drakemire and Baron Grant had not been so dreadful as Ursilla had supposed.

Drakemire had been so under the thumb of Dulce, so completely harmless despite his bulk, that it was impossible for even so nervous a lady as Ursilla to fear him. Indeed, she pitied him a little and he made her smile a great deal.

Grant, on the other hand, was a distant individual, cold in demeanour, it could be said, but somehow…! Ursilla could not understand why, but she was not afraid.

His voice was sometimes curt, and made her jump, but his stern delivery, which might have been said to resemble the man whom she did not want to think of, seemed, by contrast, to soothe her. She thought of the male voice in her dreams and was astounded. Could it be he? He was not friendly, but she did not expect, or even wish, that from him. Male advances, even of friendship, held terror for her. But the baron did not quite like her, and she was reassured. She watched him with his sister and mother and thought, that while he was still dry, there was humour there, and warmth beneath the irony. She knew why John would have liked him.

John had been open (as she had once been, too) but had not quite the *force of will* of Baron Grant, she thought. Her brother was a friendlier, but less strong, character. Taller, more amusing, more handsome in a youthful way than Grant. But Ursilla could imagine that John would have relied on this man, lent on him even. For the baron was a powerhouse, though in a neater package than her tall brother. Just above average height, but broad shoulders and narrow waist spoke of muscle beneath his fashionable coats, as did the energy he exuded, even at his most urbane. He had been described, by her brother, as a philanderer. Ursilla imagined that he could turn on the charm to ladies when required. But she doubted Grant's seduction method would include a surfeit of flattery or fawning. No, this man would give a hint of appreciation, she thought, enough to keep a woman waiting for his next rare gesture. How or why she imagined such things she did not know. But she knew that in an assembly of people, with her handsome, friendly brother, and the compact, powerful figure with the harsher, masculine face, which would have been the one that most ladies would gravitate towards.

Grant, fashionable but not flashy, only harshly handsome and reserved rather than charming, still exuded such masculinity that would make a woman's knees weak.

She thought of the day she had first come downstairs, the moment his hand was around her waist and *her own* knees had been weak, and then shook it off.

Sadie, folding her mistress's gown after the dinner, asked casually, 'What did you fink of the baron then, Miss Ursilla?'

'He is ... strong.'

'Were he nice to you?'

'Not ... exactly!' but Sadie saw there was a smile around her lips. As the young lady moved herself in bed to read (releasing herself from the baroness' taste in literature) she said, 'Was the baron ever ... in this room ... at night?'

Sadie considered that it might be best if she obeyed her master on this matter, and kept her trap shut. Not because she was ordered, but in the young lady's interest. It was certain that the baron were a match for any villain, in Sadie's view. But it were better, after all, if miss placed her dependence on the *ladies* of the family. She had noted herself, since the new footman William had arrived, and came to ask after Miss frequently, that young girls could start to have fancies very easily, and it would no more be useful to Miss Ursilla to think too much of the baron than it would Sadie to think about William. She had started to, after all, and it was annoying when a face crept up on you, or you thought too much of how a boy said, 'You're a champ, Sadie!'

If Miss thought the baron as concerned as he *were*, Miss might go thinking things that wouldn't happen. By all accounts he were a right Jack with the ladies, and with molls that weren't no better than they should be. But that might just be old Mrs Hart's opinion. The Cook claimed to know everything about The Family, but she was a gab, and Sadie didn't know if she knew what she was talkin' of. Anyway, the master was interested in Miss like he would be a wounded creature, and now she were going downstairs and was better, he probably never asked after her at all.

This was not quite true. Grant did not *ask* his mother or sister how Ursilla got along, but he did not *stop* them when they prattled on about her, which he was quite capable of doing, if bored.

He put the matter of Lady Aurora and Genevieve Fenton visiting (at the hour when Ursilla generally came down to sit) to the baroness. For it was now the custom that his mother, Dulce if she was there, and Ursilla Duvall met to talk and to work a little together each day. Lady Grant, mentally reviewing these excellent ladies, agreed to the visit, but only if Ursilla would permit it.

Ursilla was somewhat reluctant when the idea was broached. Lady Grant said airily, 'You will never find such strange friends as that pair, you know. Lady Aurora is charming and the most stylish lady in London, whereas Genevieve Fenton is horse-mad and has no conversation other. She does not care a whit, I believe, about fashion.

The countess, who was present, said, 'But there is a great improvement to her style, you know. And it is due *solely* to Lady Aurora.' She descried some interest in this on Ursilla's part and added. 'Genevieve Fenton was married before, you know, and was pressed to wear gowns with a great deal of trim. Fussy, Drakemire called them. I should say *hideous*.'

'When one saw her riding in the park, one saw her real self: a simple, rather shabby habit, her curly nest of hair everywhere, and a happy look upon her face.'

'She sounds ... nice!'

'But at social functions her hair seemed bullied into submission—' Ursilla gurgled at this description and her maid laughed.

'That's a good 'un!' the maid approved, from her seat in the corner.

Lady Grant frowned her down, 'How often must I tell you to be invisible, Sadie!'

'Sorry ma'am.'

'But Dulce is correct. Lady Aurora has worked *wonders* on Genevieve Fenton, she has her own style now.'

'Just as well, since she is married to one of the most handsome men I have ever seen.'

Ursilla's eyes glittered.

'If you want to see them, you must agree to have them visit!'

'Oh, miss!' Sadie interjected again, 'It is Lady Aurora *I* wish to see. The most stylish woman in London will know how I can finish these sleeves!'

'Sadie!' cried the countess, but she subsided as she saw Ursilla give way.

'Is that so, Sadie?' she said, including her maid in manner beyond etiquette, 'I am more interested to see ... the other Mrs Fenton.'

Chapter 9

Female Wisdom

And so it was that Ursilla saw others beyond the occupants of the Grant house.

Lady Aurora entered first and Sadie, who was engaged in changing Ursilla's crochet hook to her weaker hand, whispered to her, 'Oooooh, lookie there Miss!'

The vision of loveliness stopped Ursilla's heart. A lady in the prime of her life had entered, her luxuriant hair piled high in the most interesting coiffure Ursilla had ever seen, elongating the line of her neck which reached down to the barely discernible bodice of her gown. It was a day dress, but the sleeves were falling from her shoulders of their own volition, the silk mousseline was coloured the sea-green of dreams. It was simple, this dress, so simple in line, and it moved about her willowy form as she glided forward, smiling. It was an open smile that denied the walking definition of sophistication, and Ursilla found herself addressed, and taking the proffered hand in a dream. She stood a little straighter in the ladies' presence and muttered something in reply to her greeting.

The second lady visitor could not be more in contrast, though still elegant of dress. She was wearing a day dress of simple muslin with a closer fitting skirt than the flowy profusion of Lady Aurora's. It had a twill bodice, made like a short waistcoat with a stand-up open collar, giving her a mannish look that suited her rather definite features and longish nose. Her hair was very wiry and curly, and the sides had been cut to display it a little, the little ringlets softened the simple coil of her topknot.

'Hello!' she said in a clipped, but not unpleasant, voice, holding out her hand, 'Genevieve Fenton. Pleased to meet you!' she shook Ursilla's hand briskly. Suddenly her eyes narrowed. 'Did a horse do that?' she said directly, referring to the crescent scar on her face.

Lady Grant gasped, but Ursilla smiled — much preferring Mrs Fenton's directness to the sidelong looks of those ladies who affected not to notice, like those whom she had encountered in Lady Cole's morning room.

'Accident!' rasped Ursilla.

'It did not,' said Mrs Fenton, frowning, 'give you a fear of the animals?'

'Not ... much!' rasped Ursilla, and Mrs Fenton smiled.

'Well, we shall dispel any such thing. I have a quiet carriage horse for the first, to drive in a gig, you know, and then I shall find you a pretty mare to ride that will make you no trouble.'

Ursilla looked scared at this, and the little maid piped up at her side, 'I shall veil a hat, miss, so that you will be quite unknown as you take the air.'

'Oh yes, Ursilla, and one of us will always be with you,' reassured the baroness.

'*Can* you drive?' continued Genevieve Fenton.

'I used to ...'

The words were coming hard at the thought of leaving this room, and Ursilla faltered but Sadie interrupted again, finishing for her, '... drive a phaeton at her old country home.'

'Did she tell you so Sadie?' said Lady Grant, surprised.

'There was such a carriage depicted in a journal plate, milady, and she said *green!* Which I understood as the colour of her phaeton, miss.'

The company looked to Ursilla, who nodded.

'A phaeton it shall be. Lady Grant has a fine phaeton, but your horses are too spirited, my lady, for a first turn. I shall borrow a quiet pair from my neighbour.'

Ursilla had begun to quake a little, but she was grateful, too, and looked to Sadie for help. But unexpectedly, the little maid said, 'This afternoon, Mrs Fenton?'

Genevieve understood the maid's quiet determination as she put a hand on the shaking girl's shoulder. The less anticipation, the better. But Ursilla looked up at Sadie as though she'd been betrayed.

'I'll bring them round at two.'

Ursilla, out gunned said, 'Bonnet!'

'I have some heavily veiled, fear not,' said Dulce.

Lady Aurora, who had not uttered a word since the greeting, was surprised at Genevieve, often silent in company, taking the lead. The subject of her conversation, horses, was not so surprising, however. But she was utterly shocked when Genevieve said to Lady Grant,

'Might I have a private word with Miss Duvall in another chamber? We will not be absent long.'

Directness, often lacking in the fashionable drawing rooms of England, rather floored the baroness, but she said, 'The yellow salon is on the left, Mrs Fenton!'

A footman led the way; Ursilla was strangely unafraid of this mannish lady. Her whole being was brutal honesty. She was rather swept away in fear at Genevieve Fenton's plans for this afternoon, but of her person, not at all.

Mrs Fenton marched ahead into the salon and gestured Ursilla into a seat on a gilt legged sofa, as though it were her own home. For some reason Ursilla could not decipher, she was amused by this woman without artifice. But Mrs Fenton's next comment wiped the amusement from her face.

'Myself, Lady Aurora and probably now Delphine, Viscountess Gascoigne, know the outline of your trials at the hands of a villain.'

Ursilla stiffened, wanting Sadie, wanting to leave the room. Mrs Fenton sat down abruptly beside her, taking a trembling hand in two of hers.

'*My* suffering was not so bad, I think, but I, too, was once the victim of a brute. I was married to him, but fortunately, he died.' Ursilla's eyes met Mrs Fenton's pitiless ones. 'But I managed to get free of him *before* his death, and I learned to live my life well, with the help of friends.'

'Yes!' said Ursilla, riveted.

'Lord Grant is *your* friend.' Genevieve said, and suddenly Ursilla knew she was right. 'His mother and his sister, your intelligent little maid—' Ursilla smiled warmly at this strange lady's understanding of Sadie's importance, 'and us. Lady Aurora seems only a fashionable dress mannequin, perhaps,' Ursilla found herself inwardly laughing at this blunt judgment, but listened on, 'but really is the *kindest* friend one could have.'

Ursilla could not know, but *felt*, that this lady did not usually talk a great deal but was making an exception.

'Few people know of my past, Miss Duvall. I tell you because you have already been brave and come so far, but you are still afraid. There was a day, you know, when I realised that that man could no longer hurt me. My gratitude to a friend, who risked his life to punish him, showed me what I should have known before. My husband was *pathetic*, not all-powerful. When I saw it, I saved *myself*.'

Ursilla looked off, remembering a night when Cole used his feet on her, and shuddered.

'You think of the power he used against you. But soon you will see *other* things.' Mrs Fenton jerked the hand she held a little. 'The power you might have used against *him*.'

Ursilla looked confused and doubtful.

Genevieve Fenton shook her head wryly. 'You think I do not know him; I cannot imagine ... and indeed his madness seems to be beyond even my late husband's. But I know enough to understand that *all* such men are pathetic. Somewhere, *you* know it, too.'

Ursilla thought that she was right, this female. She had always, in some part of her that was not occupied by trying to avoid or stop his violence, looked down on Hubert Cole. Had descried the weakness in his rage. Her eyes were fixed on Genevieve Fenton now, as a fount of all truth. '*Yes!*' she managed again. Ursilla wanted to tell her how wise she was, how grateful Ursilla was, but she did not have the power yet.

'I wanted to tell you...,' continued her instructress, 'that it is possible and even, you will one day know it, *easy* to live without fear. *I* did so. *You* can too!'

Ursilla glowed at her. But suddenly the other thing arose in her, and she wanted to reach out to this amazing new confidante for understanding. 'The Grants!' Ursilla managed. 'Too good to me.'

'You are overwhelmed by their generosity? Do not be. Receiving is a gift, too. Though I admit *that one* was hard for me, also.' She nodded her decisive nod. 'The best thing you can do to thank them is to be well and happy.'

Ursilla nodded too. She stood to go back, squeezing Genevieve's hand, and looking her earnest thanks and admiration.

But Genevieve still delayed. 'My husband was also in the great battle.' She smiled. 'My second, wonderful husband and lifelong friend, that is. My Benedict.'

Ursilla saw that now Genevieve's eyes sparkled with tears.

'It changed him from a joyful boy to a true man. He was hurt by war, dreadfully. But he heals himself, is able to laugh once more, by being of service. Now, whenever there is *anything* he can do for the family of his fallen comrades, it is his honour.' Ursilla knew that this had a point. Mrs Fenton, she realised, *always* had a point. 'You understand, Miss Duvall? Not his duty, his *honour*!' Ursilla saw it then, and this strange lady had lifted yet another burden from her heart, that of being undeserving of the Grant's bounty. 'Lord Grant is the same. And for his closest comrade, how much more so? Help him by accepting his gift of a home and a position in his family with *pride*, not shame. It will also heal *him*.'

Genevieve smoothed her skirt and stood with her no-nonsense facade back in place. 'Now you know more about me than the rest of the world combined, excepting my dear Benedict and his sisters. But I trust you with my secret, as you may me.'

Ursilla, for lack of the ability to speak her heart, kissed Mrs Fenton's cheek, an action that shocked Genevieve enough to make a faint squeak. Ursilla laughed at her, and with all the naturalness in the world, threaded her arm through Genevieve's — and thus they re-entered the drawing room.

Seeing them so caused a moment of consternation, which Lady Aurora covered by saying, 'I have admired your gown from the first, Miss Duvall. What *modiste* made it for you?'

The little maid entered into the conversation again, sending the baroness's eyes skyward for divine aid, 'That were me, milady!'

'Really?' said Lady Aurora, amused. 'I have never before seen such a falling twist on a sash before. Was it an accident?'

Sadie got up and came forward. 'Oh, no, my lady!' Ursilla was about to sit again, but Sadie grasped her shoulders and turned her around. 'See, the sash is flat at the back, my lady, but I cut it so that it would spiral at the front.' Sadie manhandled her miss opposite to Lady Aurora again.

'Sadie! Take your hands off your mistress, girl!' said Lady Grant, incensed.

But Lady Aurora had risen too, and touched the spirals of sash between her fingers, 'Oh I see the cut now!' she cried. 'How clever! Did you think of it yourself?'

'Yes, my lady. But it *did* come of a mistake I made on me sister's sash on her Sunday best years ago.'

'From accidents comes innovation!' said Lady Aurora. 'It must have been difficult to turn.'

'Oh, the countess helped me, milady!'

Aurora looked towards the stately Countess of Drakemire with amazement, and Dulce sighed.

'The amber is just right for you, my dear,' said Lady Aurora to Ursilla.

'*I* told Lady Grant to pick amber!' said Sadie smugly.

'Sadie, sit back where you belong,' instructed Lady Grant.

'Yes, my lady,' said Sadie meekly, but she turned to Lady Aurora, 'But now you mention cut, milady, how does it look like your bosom is encased in two blue tulips? I ain't never seen that done.'

'I'll show you the cut, if you will undertake to show me your designs for this dress.'

'Oh, I cannot draw, except patterns, my lady. But when I see something, it becomes a pattern in my head.' She frowned. 'And then I change it. For fun, like.'

'You have a genius of design under your roof, Lady Grant.'

'Do not encourage her,' said Lady Grant, but with that resignation and not true anger that the countess and she seemed to apply to Sadie. The maid did not know her place, it was true, but she was very amusing.

Ursilla, at first overwhelmed by Lady Aurora's magnificence, liked her for liking Sadie, and the rest of the visit went on well. Lady Aurora told some amusing London tales, and Ursilla relaxed. Nothing was required of her, but eventually she showed, by her laugh and a naughty look in her eyes, her appreciation of Lady Aurora's more wicked observations on the great and good. She found a voice, too, before they were gone, to say a genuine thanks to Mrs Genevieve Fenton.

'I shall come back at two with the horses. Be ready.'

Ursilla stiffened her back and nodded, wishing to please.

Though she dreaded the outside, Ursilla went to the hall dressed in the same amber gown, over which she wore a short cape of green velvet that the baroness remembered she possessed, and that would look well with the amber. She really needed to get Ursilla to the dressmaker, to purchase riding dress and pelisses as well as more gowns. The first visit beyond family had gone well, but of course the ladies had made no inquiring remarks, since they knew the situation. The baroness was surprised at her son organising the visit, but it had proved his wisdom. Ursilla had seemed happier.

Now, though, Ursilla was in shock again. Sadie stood on her tiptoes and placed a driving bonnet upon her head — a little confection of Dulce's in green, with the addition of heavy black veiling. The baroness saw Ursilla's shoulders go down a notch, whether because of the hat's gift of anonymity, or the touch of Sadie's arm on her shoulder, she did not know. Suddenly Ursilla looked at her scarred hand, appalled. Lady Grant gestured Baker to hand Ursilla her own kid driving gloves, and again the girl relaxed. There was now no identifying mark, Lady Grant was sure this had been Ursilla's concern, for she had displayed little self-consciousness about her scars before. Her ladyship's heart ached that the young girl should have to consider it.

Genevieve Fenton would attend her on her first drive, and even if they went to the park, no one would be surprised if that lady ignored a hail from friends, or from a gentleman looking, in the most roundabout way possible, for advice about horseflesh from a lady. Mrs Fenton was well known for doing what she liked.

But Genevieve had not given Ursilla the direction towards the park, but to a common on the edge of the fashionable world, and Ursilla had been glad. At first, she had looked from right to left, in terror of seeing *him* and being recognised.

'Remember,' said Genevieve dryly, noting this, 'that you have a *whip*.'

Suddenly, Ursilla was grinning, regarding that implement with the dawning, absurd notion that she might use it on a person, and then she was soon tooling the calm horses through the city streets, avoiding obstacles with some skill. Her injured hand seemed to hold the reins with ease, and in her surprise, she thought of Sadie's crochet hook. She was elated, and enjoyed the anonymity of the common, driving her pair a little faster, the wind blowing her veil to her skin, displaying her wide smile to Genevieve.

They returned in an hour, and Genevieve let her down. The terror returned. It was only a pavement to traverse, and some steps up to the door, but Ursilla felt adrift and heady, as though she was in a vast universe, abandoned.

'Alright there?' said the crisp voice of Genevieve Fenton as she adjusted the reins.

Ursilla heard the concern and did not want this lovely afternoon to end on this note. She looked over her shoulder and said, but with humour. 'I no longer ... have the whip!'

'Then I'll have Benedict gift you a pistol!' Genevieve said briskly. To every problem, Ursilla thought with a smile, a solution. Her friend left then, without looking back, and Ursilla walked up the steps with resolution, looking neither left nor right.

She spent the evening in bed, Sadie declaring it so in her definite manner. She was taken to a bath and bathed (not so difficult now that she did not have to drape her leg over the edge), and Sadie put her in her night things, and urged her to bed.

'It is too early!' Ursilla protested.

But Sadie, taking away the stew she had just eaten, and cleaning Ursilla's teeth with toothpowder, ignored her. 'Just you lie there miss. It has been a big day today, and you are tired.' The maid touched her cheek as though she were a child, and as she sunk beneath the covers Ursilla's thoughts still protested, but she was asleep almost before Sadie had raised the sheet beneath her chin. *Safe!* Was her last thought.

Grant was headed to his room when he saw Sadie sitting on a chair outside Ursilla's chamber.

'Why are you here?' he asked. He frowned. 'Is this chair not from *my* room?'

'Is your room the one four doors along, my lord?' Sadie enquired airily 'Then yes, it is.'

'Who gave you permission...?' he began. The maid's blue eyes looked guilelessly back at him. 'Oh, never mind. Why are you here?'

'Well, Miss has gone to bed early, my lord, and I was squirming around because I'm not yet tired, and I got out so as not to disturb her. But I can't *go* anywhere until I know she's settled, and so I looked for a chair. This were the first light enough for me to carry.'

'I am so glad to have accommodated your needs, Sadie.'

'Well, you don't want me to wake her, do you? I'm a squirmer when I'm bored, me mother tells me. I thought of an idea to help with that, but I must wait here a bit before I can ask the baroness.'

Grant sighed. 'What do you wish to ask of my mother?'

Sadie waved a dismissive hand, 'Oh lady's things. I won't bother you with them, sir.' She looked at him and he knew she was about to be outrageous again. '*You* can calm miss as good as *me*, me lord, so hows about you keep watch on her, and I'll go the baroness now, and then you can get your chair back. Now that's fair, ain't it?'

Whatever advantages this pert little maid provided Ursilla Duvall, it was nothing, Grant was beginning to feel, to her lack of schooling in the art of service. She was *negotiating* for revolutionary fairness with her master, whose commands she should abjectly obey, and had no notion of her insolence. But he only said, with the sigh she inspired in all his family, 'Off with you, then.'

He opened the door. He was not at all sure that his leniency with Sadie was not for this glimpse of the patient, for he was engaged in avoiding her in the day, especially after the disturbing dinner. He had no wish to be thanked by her, or to be considered her rescuer, when it was clearly his mama who had brought her here. Yet he had almost *smiled* at her during dinner, when he had seen her vast improvement, which would have been fatal. His concern for her must not be noted, by his family or by her. It was a commonplace thing, after all, to be concerned for his friend's sister. But the circumstances of Miss Duvall's situation that had caused her removal here could not be seen as casual. The situation was charged. He did not wish her to think of him. It was best for all.

A candle burned near Sadie's cot, which had rumpled blankets as though she had indeed tried to sleep. He lifted the small flame nearer the sleeping girl and gazed at her. She seemed peaceful enough, and Grant considered taking up the seat outside to wait for the pert maid to come back, leaving the door ajar as Sadie had, in case Ursilla cried in the night. But instead, he watched the sleeping girl, though he held the candle high aloft so that it might not disturb her. The bones of her face had more flesh now, he'd noted that at dinner some days since. But today there seemed to be a light bloom on her cheek, possibly the action of the air and the sunshine from her first outing. He tried to think if the energetic child he had met in Duvall's house all those years ago had rosy cheeks, but he could not recall. It seemed, looking now, that she might have had.

He blessed Genevieve Fenton in his head. She had left Ursilla Duvall no time to think, had just taken her outside. It was best. His Mama had said Sadie had been the deciding vote. She said it without thinking, for when had the baroness ever sought counsel from a *maid*? Grant smiled, thinking of it, but it was true that Sadie was their expert on the tolerances of Ursilla Duvall. Sadie was pert and interfering, perhaps, but she was sensitive and noticing, too.

Carefully putting down the candle, Grant sat on the bed in the same manner, continuing to gaze at the sleeping face.

'Your sister is returning to us, John,' he murmured. 'Little by little, she returns.'

Sadie entered the baroness's sanctum, where she sat at her book.

'Do not tell me!' the baroness declared, with a long-suffering sigh, 'You have an *idea!*'

'How did you guess, my lady?' said Sadie amazed.

'What,' said the baroness, keeping her temper, 'can I do for you?'

But as Grant has discovered already, irony was lost on its target.

'Well,' said Sadie, accepting this as her due, 'I was thinking ... at least *one* evening gown, my lady, if you was to send for some silk. I was thinking green would be best. But not grass green, but more blue-green. More bluish than Lady Aurora's, but towards that colour, like.'

'There is no need for you to worry yourself about Miss Duvall's gowns anymore, Sadie, I shall take her to Oxford Street in the next days.'

'Oh, *good* milady! You could take Lady Aurora, too!'

'Do you doubt my taste?'

'Now, don't say *that* baroness, you look very fine indeed!' said Sadie, indulgent. 'But Lady Aurora has *the eye*, now ain't she?'

That there was no denying this meant that the baroness could only look balefully in the maid's direction.

'But about that green silk, my lady...' Lady Grant eyed her awfully. 'Or it could be fawn, if you like. Or gold satin. But I think miss would balk at gold satin as being too showy, don't you?'

Lady Grant continued to eye her.

Sadie continued, 'So, a greeny-blue, on the warmer side, is probably best.'

'I have already said that *professionals* will make Miss Duvall's gowns henceforth.'

'Don't you *like* the gowns I made?' asked Sadie, a trifle hurt.

'As to that, they were well done,' said the baroness with dignity, 'but I do not need you to make another.'

'That's because you haven't *thought*, my lady,' Sadie said.

This was outside of enough. 'Sadie, go to your mistress *at once*!'

'Oh, don't fear nothing, baroness. I set the baron to watch 'er!'

'You set ...!' Lady Grant was bereft of words.

'He's done it afore, milady, no fear. He can calm her nightmares as good as me. Taps on her hand and talks nonsense! I seed him!'

This knowledge distracted the baroness from her goal of putting Sadie in her place. 'He *does?*' she asked.

'Oh, yes, milady. But back to the matter in hand, as you ses, baroness. It's the silk. I can give you lots of good reason you need to buy it, milady.' This was said cheerily.

'Oh, yes?' said the baroness sarcastically. But the blue cloud of sarcasm burst before the large eyes of the maid, never to be seen again.

'Yes. The first is *practical*. You don't want to be paying a maid in your house to sit on her hands, now *do* you, my lady? But that is what I do sometimes, now miss is getting better. I can't take up any duties like laundering or such, since I cannot leave her in *case* she is overtook with one of her spasms, but I am twitching with nothing to do now that she can read and sew and crochet. And me *second* reason is practical too. You don't like me talking in the drawing room.' The maid smiled kindly at the baroness. 'Don't you be embarrassed, my lady, I *did* notice. But what with one thing and another I open me trap and ses me piece from time to time, as though I was at home. But if I was to be *really busy* making a lovely gown, say, well I'd be too *occupied*, likely, to talk.'

This was too much, and Lady Grant drew herself up stiffly.

'Are you *bargaining* with me, Sadie? How dare you! I am looking forward to the day when you go back to the kitchen and are taught how to conduct yourself in this household, from start to finish! A few blows from Cook's hand and you might improve immensely!'

But Lady Grant was now confronted with a tear-stained face of tragedy. *'Leave my poor miss?'* wailed Sadie.

'Stop that!' said Lady Grant, disturbed. As Sadie evidently tried and failed, wailing again, her ladyship conceded, 'No, no! You shall not leave her yet…' when Sadie's eyes searched hers, she added desperately to stop the floods of tears, 'Not for a long time yet.'

Sadie stopped, smiling radiantly, 'Oh milady!' she chided, 'You *did* frighten me!'

'Go!' said Lady Grant, testily.

'And the silk, baroness?'

'What makes you think *you* can do better than a town modiste?'

'Well, Lady Aurora said I was a *genius* milady.' Sadie laughed, disparaging, 'but I'm just jesting. Them dressmakers can make her any number of gowns better 'n' mine, I'll be bound. But it keeps me busy and happy…' and as Lady Grant wondered what business of hers it was to keep a maid happy, she added, '… and that keeps me cheerful for Miss Ursilla. She can't bear it when I'm sad, ye know!'

There was nothing to say to this. 'I shall do my best to fulfil your requirements, *miss*!' said Lady Grant frostily.

'Oh, milady!' said Sadie as she left the room, smiling. 'You are a one!'

URSILLA AND THE BARON'S REVENGE

The next morning, Lady Grant described the event to her daughter the countess, who laughed. 'And I could not even argue with her, because Ursilla is devoted to her.'

'You cannot rend them apart for now, it is true!' Dulce laughed again, 'but when she told Lady Aurora that I had helped her turn the sash ... quite as though she was sharing the honour with her handmaiden...!'

Lady Grant laughed too. 'She is outrageous. I wonder why we do not dislike her?'

'She enters the heart stealthily. And from what you say, she even orders Edmond, the most arrogant man in England.'

'Do not say so of your brother! But you are right, my dear girl! As my proud son shares our defeat, I feel much less affronted.'

'But...' said Dulce musingly, '... *he sits with Ursilla at night*...?'

The ladies exchanged looks, wondering what this could mean.

Chapter 10
The Stalker Stalked

The marvellous Mr Mosely was quick with his report. There were, in fact, two girls who fit the description of the tavern wench attacked. One was violated by a man in a mask — Cole careful, perhaps? Or was the mask related to the act itself, Grant suggested. Shame. One girl was in hospital, throttled, and with multiple broken bones. Southey, who Grant called on to discuss this, agreed. It was, he said with horror, likely the same man.

Mosely was following up on other trails, one a missing maid ... with strawberry blonde hair.

It was the elder Fenton who delivered the news. 'Can you call in the footman you acquired from Cole?'

William came in and stood in the middle of the study looking nervous as three grave faces regarded him.

'We find we must consult with you, William,' said Mr Wilbert Fenton noting the boys flush at his use of words. 'Can you think of anywhere that Cole might hide something?'

'I, eh ... what kind of thing might that be?'

'Something fairly large,' Fenton's voice might be careless, but his eyes were piercing.

'No, I ...' the footman looked strained, then frowned, 'Well .... once me and Fred took out a trunk of used clothes. He told us to chuck it in the river at night, but we was worried about the river wardens, and well, we just laid it at the edge of a common, like, in the woods.

The baron stood. 'You can take me there, William.'

'Yes, my lord.'

'It may be nothing,' said Southey. 'Was it a particularly heavy trunk, William?'

'Heavy, but not *particular*, sir.'

'There is nothing in that,' said Grant dispassionately, 'a slight figure would not weigh more than a pile of gentleman's old driving coats.'

William looked pale. 'Figure, my lord?'

'How long ago was this?'

'About a month before I came here, I reckon.'

'Was there,' said Fenton, 'anything wrong with Miss Duvall at that time?

'Eh?' said William. 'I don't know, sir. But it might have been the time when Miss was kept in bed for a week or so when she got a fever because a wound was infected. There was a new maid that tended her, even though she were told not to.'

The men exchanged glances. 'Order the carriage, William. We'll all go.'

What remained in the trunk was not a recognisable person, but some poor clothes including a cloak, rather loudly striped in blue, remained to identify it as female. And there was hair of an unusual colour. It was evident that animals had attempted to get inside, but it was locked and corded, and the gentlemen had had a job to open it.

The doctor stared for longer than the other three, and said, 'I must go to the hospital and record that other poor girl's injuries. And see if I might find the second.'

'If you cannot find her, Mosely will. Let me know!' said Fenton.

In the carriage back to the fashionable streets, (with William on the box with the driver) Grant, his chin resting on a fist said, 'Is it too awful that I am glad?'

Fenton seemed to understand, and Southey said. 'Not for the girls, I'll warrant.'

'No, I pity them truly. But for Miss Duvall ... this might be the way to punish Cole while nothing stains *her* at all.'

'But *three*...!' Southey said.

'That we know of,' said Fenton, cynically.

'You gather the medical evidence, Southey. When we take this to Bow Street, I want it to be more than speculation.'

'Someone must have seen the girl smuggled *into* the house.'

'And I cannot see him cleaning up after himself. Might there have been blood?'

'A maid then, or a footman. William might be able to lure a friend from the house and get some evidence.'

'I am going to follow him tonight, I do not think that the young ladies of London, those with red-blonde hair, at least, are safe.'

'However, I think we must give thanks that Miss Duvall has red-blonde hair. He must take time to find her replacements, since it is not a commonplace colour.'

'Still, I think Grant is right. It may be unlikely tonight, but any risk is too great. The sooner we hand this to Bow Street, the better.'

'Well, they have the trunk. But we need to piece together more evidence before Cole is taken in.'

'I sent the report anonymously,' said Grant. 'It seemed to me that while the magistrates would interview Cole, they would more likely be interested in the footmen who carried the trunk.'

'Yes,' said Fenton, 'When in doubt, suspect the servants.'

'In truth,' said Southey as he stepped down in front of the hospital, 'if we did not know the whole story, we too would doubt that a respectable heir to baronetcy could be responsible for such a thing.'

'I think our dear doctor is more innocent of the ways of the world than he looks,' said Fenton to the baron as the door was shut upon them.

'You feel no amazement?' asked Grant.

'None at all,' said Fenton, stretching his long legs. 'The unhappy result of age and experience, my boy.'

But it was said, *en passé*, and Grant, looking at the lounging dandy, was glad to feel Fenton was on his side. He would make, Grant intuited, a bad enemy.

Well, so would he. As Hubert Cole was about to find out.

During his last night time visit to Ursilla's room, Grant knew that he had looked at her too long. It occurred to him that Ursilla Duvall took up more of his thoughts than he wished. Until Cole was punished, until Miss Duvall was quite well physically and in control of her nerves, in short, more like the excitable girl he barely remembered, perhaps it was normal that his thoughts were so engaged with her. Once all was well, and Cole crushed to a e, then he might concentrate on his quest for pleasure, and soon perhaps, a wife.

He longed to crush Cole with his own hands, as he had crushed the body and spirit of his friend's sister, and only the consequences of scandal for the innocent girl had held him back. If an inkling of the cruelty inflicted on her were to be discovered by The World, it would be assumed she was also *despoiled*, and her reputation ruined. He did not suppose her to be seeking a husband any time soon, but she must at least be treated with respect in society. At the play, or the subscription library or other such entertainments she should be able to attend — with no insults around her.

Miss Lucy Bretton, a lovely blonde baron's daughter, had promised him a waltz at a ball this evening when he had met her at a musical evening three days ago. It had been her own pert suggestion, but he had declared himself honoured at the possibility. But now he had his work cut out and would not attend. He toyed with the notion of dashing her off a note to say so, but decided this was too much of a marked attention. Instead, his sister, who was also to attend, could casually drop the news that her brother had pressing business that precluded his attendance. Pretty Miss Breton could wait.

He had been surprised by a note from Benedict Fenton, declaring that he would join him in his surveillance of the evil baronet.

Grant had no idea why females admired him. He knew himself to be a rough sort of man and not winning in his ways. Charm and flattery were base skills that it was beneath him to learn. Yet, he had been castigated by friends for diverting the attention of this or that lady with merely a glance. He did not affect it, but he was aware of female attention since his extreme youth, and hardly thought of it. He liked women, perhaps because he liked the women in his family, but he did not fawn on them. However, he received everything from the shy hopeful glances of young ladies he danced with, or the warm looks of others, to the hot demands of some (usually married) females. He had his methods of dealing with each. Young ladies did not much interest him, but he was kinder than usual to them, avoiding them if they seemed disposed to linger. He would not inveigle himself in an affair with a married woman no matter how beautiful she was or how amenable was her husband. He liked intelligent, forthright ladies, somewhat confident in their charms: these matched himself.

Dulce had told him that Miss Breton was too like the others he had spent time with during his life before the military. Therefore, Dulce had no confidence in his boast of thinking of marriage. His Spanish mistress was lovely, intelligent and forthright too, but his sister did not know of her, of course. But because it was true, Grant considered it. Did he have a *type*? He rather thought, remembering the charms of Miss Breton, Miss Parris and Miss Anders, that he did.

Benedict Fenton was already there when Grant arrived on the street outside the home of Hubert Cole. The baron knocked on the roof of closed carriage and picked him up, the coachman already understanding that he must park at the corner of the street, so as not to be noticeable to the windows of the Cole house. Grant saw a different Fenton tonight, the good natured, open face was no longer on display. Fenton, for the first time, resembled his uncle, the cool, sardonic Wilbert Fenton. He was dressed in black, and the coat may have belonged to his groom, for it was made of rougher stuff than his fashionable attire. A hat had been pushed low on his brow, and his face was closed and concentrated. He nodded, rather than smiled, his greeting and Grant did the same. William was on the box with the coachman, and the footman jumped off to go to the kitchens for a discreet visit to the Cole staff, but really to find out for certain if the young master was home.

The footman returned in ten minutes and told them Hubert Cole was dressing to leave right now. Fenton left to keep an eye on the mews, in case the gentleman would simply ride out, and Grant sat alone in the carriage. He was surprised when a head poked in.

'Hello, me lord!' a chirpy voice issuing from a sharp face said.

'Mosely?' said Grant.

But the man had turned the handle and entered, and was seated opposite before he answered, 'The viscount told me your plan for this evening, and I thought that I'd join you in the first place and take over in the second.' He tittered. 'Me, I likes the viscount, though standing in a room with all that muscle and good looks takes an inch off me legs and a chip off me confidence every time.'

'Take over?' asked Grant, concentrating on the facts.

'Well, this face,' he pointed to his sharp goblin features comically, 'can go most places and not be remarked, my lord, but *you* might be someone that there gent that put a gel in a trunk and dumped her, might be looking out for.'

'He doesn't know me, I don't think. Or only vaguely.'

'Well, that might have been so in the past, my lord, but I doubt if it is so these days. *You* have his prize ... he will certainly have had his peepers out for you, to see what a threat you might be if he's planning to recapture her.'

'He must know she's protected now.'

'Aye, he will that. And though he's bigger 'n' you, I think I'd know who to put me money on,' said Mosely running an appraising eye over the baron's form. 'But will that do? I think he's itchin', me lord, itchin' to get her back. Planning the ways. Hope you got her window secured, if it be at the back of the house.' Grant frowned. The little man's eyes narrowed, 'But until then ... there are the others ...'

'We have speculated so...'

'The viscount told me. A fancy speculation but...' Mosely hit a finger to his nose and tapped it, '... and so we must be careful. Killing you, for example, might suit his humour.'

This made Grant shrug, 'He could *try*.'

'Oh, he don't have to do it hisself, me lord. There's roughs I know would do the job for two gins and a penny. Best keep to the fashionable streets until we nail him down.'

'You seem very sure we will manage it.'

'I don't hold wif putting gels in trunks, meself ... it makes me angry. And so, we'll have to put a stop to that.' The little man cocked an eyebrow, 'About that fancy theory of yours. It must have infected me brain-box like, because I've got a bit that *adds* to it.'

'Yes?'

'Did you know that there bag-o-bile has a father?'

'Don't we all? But I do know him — Sir Neil Cole.'

'And do you know he don't live in that house there, but in Percival Street?' Grant frowned. 'Wif the governess that used to instruct his daughter.'

'Well, if my mother is to be believed in her description of his wife, I can't say I'm surprised.'

'But don't it add to your fancy theory, me lord?' Mosely pulled on his earlobe in a cogitating manner, 'or am I all about in me head?'

Grant drew his brows. 'The father leaves the house to live with a female *inferior to him in status*. I suppose, though it is not shouted about, that the World has discovered it, and chatters.'

'And for a man of pride, too much pride if you ask me, the shame for his family would be enormous. His father parading around Town wif 'is mistress and their young 'uns, which I heard he does.'

'Yes,' Grant nodded, seeing it, 'If Hubert Cole looked down on his father, and believed himself more virtuous than he, if he prided himself on his superior rectitude, then to meet another lady whose station was no longer high, then fall for her, just as his father did...'

'It's all ridiculous, me lord!' said the little man with a shrug, 'I mean, you and me ... well we can tell there's a difference, can't we? It's easy. I was born to me station, and you was born to yours, and that's that. But for a young, gently born lady to be judged so harshly jis on account of her brother died a hero in the wars, well, that's just bull's-pizzle, ain't it? Workin' folks ain't so severe on each other as that.'

'Yes, *them aristos need beheading,* Mr Mosely.' Grant said in the vernacular with a sardonic look at the investigator.

The little man chuckled, 'Now, that's for them Frenchies, not me, me lord. It don't matter that Hubert Cole is heir to a baronetcy to Bow Street, I hope. They overlook a thing or two, p'rhaps, for the Quality, no doubt of it. But they stop short at murder. As a Runner *I* treated a man by how he behaves, not the station he was born into.'

'Quoting the Scottish poet, perhaps, Mr Mosely ... *A man's a man for aw' that.*'

'Now *he* sounds like a cove wif his noggin on straight.'

'You are correct. What Miss Duvall suffered in the house of her relatives, beyond the beatings from a madman, is not only suffered by her in the fashionable World. It is why a great house without a son can be a *tragedy* in our society. For women who have been cossetted within those houses are often thrown off to a very reduced life, sometimes to live with relatives like the Coles. But my mother, and many other decent women, would never stoop to behave so to a member of our family who required shelter.'

'Ah well, now I thinks of it, there's many a woman who marries into the house of a labourer only to be scolded by his mother for the rest of her life, while some others are welcomed, so class don't make a bit o' difference there!'

Benedict Fenton ran swiftly but stealthily back to the carriage, keeping to the shadows. He opened the door and said, 'He's out on foot, but not by the main road. He's not dressed for his club, either.' His cool voice was decided. 'I'll run and catch him in a minute.'

A cheery voice said, 'I'll do that, Mr Fenton, sir!'

'Mosely!' Benedict's voice lost some of its cool in his delight, 'you here?'

'I'll get going, sir. And I'll take the young lad and send him back to you if there is a problem. Best get off!'

He was gone in a moment, William following, and the carriage inhabitants sat redundant and disappointed.

'It *is* true that Cole might recognise you or me if he looked back,' sighed Grant.

'William, too...!' protested Benedict, like a schoolboy not chosen for the cricket team.

'Not in that greatcoat and hat. He's used to seeing him in livery.'

'I suppose so!'

William ran back. 'Mr Mosely ses as he'll send a note to your house, my lord.'

'Very well.'

Benedict Fenton said, his cheeriness returning, 'Well, Mosely has a way of making me feel useless.'

'I might say the same!' murmured Grant. 'But everyman to his trade. Let's wet our whistles instead at the club.'

'Not dressed for it.'

'No. You look more like a Runner than Mosely tonight. *Cribbs's Parlour*, then!'

'Well, Mosely told Gascoigne we should look out for you. In case you should encounter Cole.'

'Yes. I could do with a bodyguard,' said Grant sardonically.

Benedict scoffed. 'Well, I think it is to save you from a charge of murder, also. *I* am angry enough to kill the villain, but *you*, who know

Miss Duvall, must be worse. Genevieve would never say so, but she worries about you.'

'She is a good woman, and you obviously adore her,' Benedict did not shy away from Grant's description of his feelings but smiled. 'You give marriage a good name, Fenton.'

'Oh, that's to Genevieve's credit!' he said easily. He looked off, musing, 'I've loved her all my life, I think. Her letters meant everything to me when I was with the regiment. And I could tell her anything.'

'I have never,' said Grant, 'been truly friends with a woman in that way. My closest confidant was John Duvall.'

'He sounds like a fine man.' The close cocoon of the carriage, and the shadows of the night seemed to have created a safe space for sharing. 'I lost a friend at my side in that battle.'

'So, you know.'

'I do. And it is a great thing you do for his sister.'

'I should have looked for her sooner ...' Grant did not know why he voiced this to the younger man. But he felt his goodness, and he too had been there at that final battle. And so he understood that the victory was not the whole story.

Fenton put a hand on his shoulder, 'I think, after Waterloo, few of us could return to a fully responsible life all at once. I know I couldn't.'

Grant thought about this. Perhaps it took an edge off his guilt. The stay in on the continent, his preparations for his lover, his delay in going home to a mother and sister who were waiting for him to return, no doubt assuming that he would be the same man as he had left them — perhaps it had been necessary, as Fenton suggested. Certainly, if he had known his friend's sister's suffering, he would have returned, but as Southey had said, he had not. One could not account for the actions of a madman.

Benedict and he had a swift drink at Cribbs' and got a tip on a horse race into the bargain, but they did not long delay since Grant wanted to await news from the investigator at home.

When he got the note later, it was to say Cole was now back at home. The man had visited a number of low dives, and Moseley's note suggested he had not yet found what he sought.

So, thought Grant, Cole's itch *was* strong. He was hunting – but thankfully, a rare species. If Miss Duvall had happened to be a brunette, Grant thought balefully, perhaps many *more* would already be injured or dead. After some consideration, Grant told Baker to arrange for a team of grooms and footmen to watch Cole's every move from now on. But not William. He might spot William.

'Plain clothes, my lord?' suggested the butler.

'Not the footmen. There are enough footmen running around London to make them inconspicuous. And he shouldn't note the same one twice.'

'We have the old livery, my lord. We might change coats in case the green is spotted too often.'

'I knew I kept you for a reason, Baker.'

'Yes, my lord.'

'Send a note to Mosely regarding the same.'

'Yes, my lord.'

It was not to be supposed that while his wife and nephew were so engaged, Mr Wilbert Fenton did nothing for the cause. And so it was that at a club he belonged to, but seldom visited, he was enjoying a brandy and cards with Sir Neil Cole, head of the house of horror. Had he but known it, it was rather like the evening when Grant had interviewed Viscount Duvall in White's.

By the kind of luck that Wilbert Fenton thought himself blessed with (made of information, intelligent supposition, and blind chance) Sir Neil Cole walked into Chadwick's only ten minutes after he did. Fenton had already spoken, in a languid way, to various acquaintances, favouring none of them with the courage to invite him to play (for he could be a remote and intimidating figure when he chose), but when Cole came in, a lackey whispered to him. Fenton turned to the gentleman to his left, Rodgers, to have him invite Sir Neil for a game. Rodgers, honoured to oblige Fenton, brought Cole over to the small table Fenton now chose, and was about to join them, but obeyed the lazy white hand that moved him off.

Sir Neil Cole looked rather better than when Fenton remembered seeing him, about four years since. He had been a man who was as overweight as Fenton was, at that time, *pretending to be* (in his bid to keep his plump friend the Prince Regent from the jealousy he was rather prone to among his cronies): Cole had once had a soft and slack looking body, was flushed of cheek and nose, and had a permanently blurred, moody look on his face. Nowadays, well, he still looked like a man who became regularly fazed, as tonight's rheumy eyes demonstrated, but he was a trifle slimmer, and with much more good humour in his look.

The baronet sat, a trifle nervously — because the doings of Wilbert Fenton were not such as a peace-loving man like himself wished to be part of. But since he hadn't seen him recently, Cole felt he could not have offended, so he tried for hearty, 'You look well, Fenton. Slenderized on the wedding trip, I heard. Wish I could!' Fenton said nothing, 'Lady Aurora well?'

'She is. And you, too, look better, Cole.'

'Ah well, I have someone who keeps me in order these days.'

'Not your wife, I hear?'

'That harpy...?' Cole slurred, then cursed. 'You won't repeat that, I'm sure.'

'Mmm. I have heard that you no longer reside in Brook Street.'

'I still give it as my address. Dammit, it's my demmed house.' They dealt cards. 'You don't come here much...'

'Only for news,' drawled Fenton, 'One likes to be *first* in knowing scandal.'

'Well, there ain't much to mine. Went to live with m'mistress, is all.' He looked at Fenton direct. 'She ain't a doxy; she's a good gel.'

'I see. And you do not go home?'

Cole dropped his voice, 'I don't know why you should care, Fenton, but it is like this. I married a vicious-mouthed harridan who gave me two children ... she claims. I admit Susan is mine — a drunken night explains her existence — but her mother could never convince me that that vicious looking upstart is mine. I mean have you seen him, Fenton? All the Cole men had the nose, ye know' pointing to his own exaggerated Roman appendage, 'and his ain't there. And where does the black hair come from? Not from his mother or me. Bloody entail means he'll inherit the lot. I have a fine little chap in Percival

Street, looks just like a miniature my mother had painted of me as a child. *He* should get what's mine. And Hubert's a prosy bore to boot. Calls himself upright, but *I* know the places he visits. He's no bishop! *Bad blood*, though God knows whose! Butler keeps me informed of his doings.' Cole has no idea why he spilled all this, but Fenton's intelligent eye seemed to urge him on.

'*Does he?*' said Fenton. 'Are you quite sure you know what goes on at your eh, *demned house.*'

'*You* know? Don't tell me if you don't want me to *fall asleep*. Callers and a lot of female nonsense and that stuffed-shirt Hubert coming in and putting a damper on things among visitors with that long face of his.'

'It might *not* put you to sleep, Cole.' Fenton looked at him narrowly. 'Did you know of the relative that Duvall entrusted to your wife?'

'To Edwina? No one would entrust anyone to *Edwina*. The woman's a snake. You mean foisted on her, because that fool Duvall calls himself the head of our house?' He shrugged, 'Forgive me for running my tongue. Is the esteemed viscount a friend of yours?'

'Hardly!' said Fenton with hauteur. 'We were discussing the sister of the late viscount.'

When Fenton remained gazing at him, Cole coughed. 'Never met the girl. Got a dashed rude letter from Duvall, though, telling us not to visit her at Grant's house.'

'I expect it was at the baron's dictation.'

'What problem could Grant have with *me*?'

'The problem that *anyone* might, who knows of the treatment Miss Duvall received in your home.'

'Good God!' said the baronet, looking mildly shocked, and, thought Fenton, uncomfortable that a man who could exude threat like Lord Grant should have an issue with him. 'I *told* you that woman was a witch. Susan is going the same way. Cruel tongues, and judge everybody around them. Mean spirited. If Susan had married early, she might have escaped it ... she was a sweet little thing once, ye know...'

Fenton judged it time to end the parental reminiscence. 'She is not now.'

'Why do you say so?' when Fenton just looked at him, he said, 'Did they give the girl the life of a midshipman? Treat her like a servant or some such thing?'

'You clearly know nothing of what happens in your own home, Cole. But you can expect there to be *consequences* to your wilful ignorance.'

'What ... Grant means to make it *known*? Paint them as a pair of harpies? Well, it won't matter to me much. Don't go to Watier's or White's anymore. Play is too deep, my Amanda says. And I have two families to keep.'

'She sounds like a sensible woman.' Fenton sighed. 'There is nothing to be got from you, except ... you say you know his past haunts.'

'Whose, Grant's?' the baronet looked confused.

It was difficult, Fenton reflected, conversing with idiots. 'Your son's!'

'Oh him? Some of 'em.'

'Scrawl them down for me.'

'Now?'

'Yes. And get your butler to give you his complete list. Tonight.'

'Why should I help you make trouble for my name?' The baronet tried some low cunning. 'If you stop Grant's tongue, I might.'

'We are so far past that now, Cole. Your name *will* be in the mud and there will be no avoiding it. The, eh, *cuckoo in your nest* has seen to that.' Cole was beginning to lose his air of disinterest and looked anxious. Gazing at the baronet, Fenton feared he was becoming too empathetic since he had met his Aurora, but even so he added, 'You have other children, don't you? Take them to live a quiet life in the country. Or sell up and go to Europe.'

'Not much to sell. The cuckoo's portion is entailed, of course. Makes me mad to think he'll inherit ... !'

'I should not think he *will*...'

Cole sat up. '*Fenton? What...?*'

'Stay ignorant, Cole. I'm telling you this not for you, but for the woman good enough to reform an old libertine, as my wife did me.' Fenton stood, taking the paper he had gestured for, which Cole had written on. 'You might want to get drunk a time or two in White's or Watier's and start spreading the word that Hubert Cole isn't yours, but your wife's by-blow.' The baronet looked shocked at this. 'Trust me, she well deserves the insult. I'll do so too, if you give me permission to speak of it.'

Cole was totally sober now and looking confused but grave. 'As bad as that?'

'What Hubert Cole has done you want no part of.' Fenton began his elegant ambulation away, but turned, 'Don't warn him, Cole. Or you, too, will face the law.'

The baronet was sober. 'I'll send you the rest of the list.'

Fenton nodded.

As he left, the groom shut the door on Wilbert Fenton's closed carriage, and Fenton said to himself, a germ of urgency overtaking him, 'No, I need it *immediately!*' Then, to his groom, 'Brook Street, Jed!' The groom drove the few streets and parked when Fenton knocked. 'Do a back door visit to the Cole establishment, Jed. Tell the butler that his master wants to see him secretly, in the mews.' There was a slight chance Fenton might run into his quarry, but he played the odds. Fenton pulled his coat revers over his silver waistcoat and walked to the mews, Jed the groom running ahead, leaving another groom to walk the horses.

A tense, middle aged man in a black coat and knee breeches came out, holding aloft a torch against the gloom. 'Sir?' he said, confused to see a stranger and not Hubert Cole.

'Do you know who your master is, man?' drawled Fenton.

'Mr Hubert Cole, sir, but ...'

'No,' corrected the cold voice, 'It is *Sir Neil* Cole. And he desires that you complete this list.' He took out the paper and handed it to the man. 'You will receive instructions to that end tonight, but there is some urgency, I feel, and I am *seldom* wrong.'

The butler was reading the paper with the help of a torch he had brought out with him. The flame flickered as he held it.

'You know what this is a list of?'

'I do, sir. I think.'

'And...'

'And I only know of three other establishments. One in Brick Lane, another in Cat's Alley and a third just on the outskirts. I think it's called ... *The Pot and Kettle*, just off Kensal Green.'

'Do *not* tell the occupants of this house that I enquired. Your *master* will say the same. If you do ...' Fenton, misliking this man's shifty eye, and remembering that he had not informed the baronet about the plight of Ursilla Duvall, '...I *will* come back for you, make no mistake.'

The flambeau shook in the man's hand. 'Yes sir!'

***'

Seven servants were dispatched, and seven returned.

And so it was that evening that Wilbert Fenton, before he joined his lovely lady in bed, knew more than any other man in London about Hubert Cole. But that, after all, was usual.

Chapter 11

Accustomed to Her Face

Ursilla did not like to look in the mirror, of course, but as with the crochet hook, it was something that Sadie required of her without argument. The maid would dress her, and her hair, then demand that her mistress should assess her work before she headed out the door of her chamber, or Sadie would not be content that she had done aright. After a few days of this, Ursilla tried to tell the little maid that she now trusted her skill, and that there was no need for her to look again, for her eyes, as ever, were drawn to the crescent scar that deformed, she thought, her face. But Sadie looked so hurt that miss wouldn't see the result of her ministrations, that Ursilla reluctantly looked each day and said, *well done*.

And so it was that Ursilla became accustomed to her face. There were many occasions to look in the glass these days, after all. The two pretty dresses that Sadie made pleased her, as did the others that Sadie's careful measurements sent to modistes allowed, and she looked at herself in a little awe. She had not dressed so since her days at Duvall Park, and her hair was made very pretty by Sadie. Ursilla insisted on a plain style, but Sadie seemed to make her curls tumble in an interesting way at the back of her topknot, even when she had asked for a coil. Sadie would *begin* with a coil, it was true, but some curls would escape at the back and arrange themselves in a casual, but charming style. 'Ooops!' Sadie might say. 'But there miss, these loose curls might stay, *unless* you wish me to remove all the pins and start *again*.' Sadie would look put out by the thought, and once again Ursilla would consent.

And so it went on. Sadie admired the double ribbon pulled round the top of the head and then wrapped around a lower knot at the back, as in the portraits of Greek and Roman ladies that the maid had seen depicted in paintings on the staircase wall of this house. These females were otherwise wearing only lengths of silk, looking more like nightrails than gowns, Sadie reckoned. But the ribbon effect was pretty, and Sadie tried it on her miss. When Ursilla objected, Sadie protested, 'It is just a bit o' ribbon miss, not a diamond tiara!' and so she gave in ... *again*.

Since Sadie had got the ribbon past her mistress, she used it in other places too, some days. To form a simple bracelet, or to put a bow at her neck, or to suspend the cameo that Lady Grant gifted her.

A great deal of things were gifted from Lady Grant, Lady Aurora and Dulce, who all said they did not care for them ... a cashmere shawl with silken fringes, a silver butterfly for her hair, a velvet reticule, a lace peignoir that was too small for the countess, *she said* (though there was acres of it, said Ursilla to Sadie later.)

'But too *short*, miss, for the countess. It's out of fashion to be *too short*.' Ursilla felt the victim of a plot. But the plot was well-intended, and the conspirators so pleasant that she was warmed by it all.

In addition, Sadie heard her lady talk of her few pieces of jewelry, left to her by her mama. Ursilla had not seen the box for some time, but it contained a pearl collar and hair ring, a miniature of her grandmama, and a pair of tiny diamond droplets. All this Sadie conveyed to the baroness, whose terse note to Lady Cole brought the box by return.

Also among the gifted items there was a dressing set, which belonged to the baron's grandmama, a brush and comb and mirror, all in chased silver.

When her pin money arrived from Beltane Buildings, with a sweet note from the old lawyer, Rigby-Blythe, trusting that she was happy in her new home, the girl, who had never before held such a sum, gave it to Lady Grant, to keep it for her and to defray the cost of the muslin she had bought. The baroness looked about to refuse the money, but then thought better of it, saying, 'Yes, dear, I will take charge of it. It is a great sum and will likely pay for all your new wardrobe once we visit town.' The girl trembled at the thought of leaving the house, but for once the baroness ignored it. 'Take these two guineas for trifles, and we will send the bills here to be dealt with.'

Ursilla began, in a far room of the mansion, to practise the pianoforte again. She would not even permit Sadie to hear her fingers stumble on the keys, but she continued. Because she had once loved it so, and because, with the help of Sadie's crochet hook, she felt her hands capable of more. One day she sat back content, on the piano stool. She would not hold a public concert anytime soon, but she had not missed a note of the simple air she had practised. And it was something to do now that she needed less sleep, and Lady Grant had begun to recommence the many social responsibilities of a fashionable lady.

Encouraged by Dulce and Sadie, she ventured into a long back garden behind the mansion. It was edged by trees and felt secluded and safe. Here she sat and read and, since the baroness asked her, drew up plans for a prettier garden layout, writing out lists of plants wanted to fill the beds. Gardening had once been a passion of hers, and since she had done much with Duvall Court, her old country home, this town garden was an easy task for her design skills. Sadie drew the straight lines for her, and measured, and swapped her pencil from one hand to the next, so that she was becoming ambidextrous. It seemed her injured hand gripped more firmly and her writing with it was nearly legible.

'Oh, Sadie,' Ursilla said once, 'Do you think, one day, that I might draw again?'

It was said with such shining eyes that Sadie's own eyes shone, and she nodded. 'Of course, miss. What you want, ses my Ma, is just a matter of hard work and added cow dung.'

Sadie was such a reassuring treasure, albeit, Ursilla giggled to herself, not a master of elegant speech.

Lady Aurora had tried to persuade Ursilla on three occasions to go to a milliner with her. 'One must *try on* hats my dear, shapes make such a difference on each lady.' But Ursilla could not yet go. But one day,

Lady Aurora brought in the biggest gun in her arsenal. Mrs Genevieve Fenton was to come too.

Somehow, Genevieve's presence was enough. All the other ladies, Lady Aurora, Lady Grant, and Dulce, Countess of Drakemire were prone to take mild offence at this. Why should the mannish Mrs Fenton possess the calming presence sufficient to get the petrified Ursilla from the house?

Ursilla herself was not clear why. But even with the promised accompaniment of Sadie, the huge George-coachman, the devoted footman William, plus the baroness, countess and Lady Aurora, it was *Genevieve's* presence that reassured her. Genevieve would permit nothing to harm her. Genevieve, unlike the other kind ladies, would see it before it occurred. Also, Genevieve inspired her to reach for bravery, for she was so brave herself. She wished not just to *please* Genevieve (as she did everyone else in the world) but to *impress* her.

But there was another presence at the lady's trip to Oxford Street. It was Lord Edmond Grant. He had considered accompanying the party, but this had seemed, when Dulce had suggested it carelessly to Grant, to have an inherent problem. The outing's purpose, as well as the purchase of bonnets and slippers, and sundry other items, was getting Ursilla to go into the streets of London once more, with confidence. For Grant to go, might suggest he too worried about the danger. It might underline it to her, and he did not wish to do so. His ambition now was that Ursilla Duvall should live a safe and contented life, that beyond her physical recovery there should be a recovery of innocence and high spirits. This was better achieved among such a set of excellent women as his mother, sister, and the two Mrs Fentons. But Grant, uneasy, dressed in a plain manner and followed at a distance, looking at each passing carriage and gentleman in the street, with all the attention he had honed when at war.

He saw, too, that Ursilla looked (when not observed by the others) over her shoulder, or to her side, in case Cole should show his face.

William and Sadie walked behind, as well as his mother's lady's maid Cross (which that motherly maid seldom was) and Lady Aurora's maid, he presumed. This last, a total Frenchwoman, rivalling many *ladies* in style, could hardly be Mrs Genevieve Fenton's maid, for Genevieve would have snipped off her many ribbons, Grant felt, as being annoying.

Ursilla looked fine in amongst them. She wore a pelisse of his sister's, and a bonnet of Dulce's also. He had seen the girl in the hall before they left, and he thought that the bonnet did not particularly become her. Ursilla had chosen it from an offered selection because the poke jutted out around her face and was close fitting, he believed. Grant had been glad of her choice merely because it did not allow much view of her strawberry blonde hair. One had to look at her full on before any hair was visible. As he followed on, he saw that Ursilla was at the centre of the ladies. But sometimes Lady Aurora stopped at a window display, or there was some chatter between the others, and suddenly she might be at *the edge* of the group, and Grant found that urgency rose in him, and he held his breath. He noted that Genevieve Fenton never left her side, and was calmed by it.

He laughed as he saw that there was also frequent conversation between Lady Aurora and Sadie. At one window that her ladyship was taken with, Sadie looked over her shoulder impertinently, but Lady Aurora only turned to her and pointed, and the two shared animated conversation. His mother had told him something of the ladies' first visit, so he was not surprised. Lady and maid were two enthusiasts of design. The French maid took umbrage, and did not reply to Sadie for two blocks, but when Grant's eye moved to them again, he wasn't surprised that the chatty maid seemed to have won her over somewhat, and the French woman seemed to be dispensing advice, too, by pointing at trimmings in a window.

There was a touch on his shoulder and Grant, in warrior mode, had grasped it and turned it up Wilbert Fenton's back before he knew who the hand belonged to. When a lady and a maid looked on, Fenton drawled, 'Yes, that's the trick, baron, but not in Oxford Street, I pray you!'

Grant had let go immediately. 'How did you find me?'

Fenton sighed, bored, and Grant gave a brief nod in acceptance of the elder's omnipotence. 'I saw Cole senior last night.' Fenton said briskly.

'Ah.'

'I am fairly sure he knew nothing of the events in his house. He doesn't live there, you know.'

'So says the *on dit*.'

'But he gets information from his butler of his son's whereabouts, so as to avoid him, I think. He detests the man. The long of it is, I think I have identified the missing women.'

'Sufficient for Bow Street? The sooner we can get him off the streets the sooner I can visit the races.'

Fenton regarded him, not believing his insouciance. 'Is that the young lady? Her walk is as normal now, I think. She looks much as others in the street, and yet she has suffered so much,' he mused. 'Let us go for coffee, my wife has made arrangements at the milliner's. They will be some time there. I have much to tell you.'

In the milliner's Miss Duvall was made to change into a great many more hats than she thought necessary, hats that showed her face more than she wished. Lady Aurora had taken charge and was assuring the fashionably dressed milliner that she would send pelisse colours as soon as they were decided on, for matching trims.

When Ursilla tried to opt for *disguise bonnets*, Lady Aurora would not hear of it, but it was Genevieve's wry aside to her that stopped all her protests. 'You may as well give up, Ursilla. I have long assigned all responsibility for my wardrobe to Aurora. Genius *cannot* be resisted.'

There were other patrons in the shop, but the two lady's maids and the footman essentially blocked all sight of Miss Duvall, as they had been charged to do by Genevieve Fenton. This was not quite the day for new acquaintances yet.

Ursilla was at first shaken to be outside, but to be surrounded by the dear baroness and countess and her new friends meant that she almost felt, even on the street (after the first five terrifying minutes), that she was back in the Grant's drawing room, safe and sound. The shop assistants had all been respectful to the noble party, and she had felt a reanimation in herself for the pretty things she had seen today. It had reminded her of the preparation for her first Season, that because of the death of her father, she had never attended. When first she had lived with the Coles, she had still been a viscount's sister, if not daughter, and if not welcomed, she was tolerated. Even then Susan Cole had requested that she lay aside her prettiest gowns so as not *'vaunt her superior position in her benefactor's home'* and so she had worn her simplest gowns, not her new town finery. Anyway, it suited her mourning for her Papa. It was only after the death of John that her position became one disdained by the whole family, and when her dress had been so radically altered, even her simpler muslin gowns taken away. But by then she had welcomed it, as a way of fading into the background and limiting the attention that Hubert Cole's coldly burning eye gave to her.

Now she said suddenly, 'I think the warmer pink becomes me better,' there had been a stunned silence from the ladies. Then Lady Grant, with tears in her eyes, was hugging her, 'Oh you are so *right*, my dearest girl.'

The milliner looked on, confused as to why so slight an opinion should cause such a reaction.

Ursilla gazed up at a ring of ladies with similar tears in their eyes, and felt moved by their concern. 'Well, but if it makes you all cry, I shall not say another word,' she said brightly.

When they all laughed, she had her reward. Lady Aurora said, 'And now...' and led the whole party behind a curtain. Here there was a woman with a mob-cap, with hair combs and scissors placed at a dresser, and curling irons on a stand over a small lit fire.

Ursilla's eyes moved to Genevieve who shrugged, 'Give in!' she recommended, and so she seated herself on a chair best placed to expedite their business here.

Lady Aurora was talking to the woman in the mob cap. 'I want the newest asymmetric curls style for the front cut.'

'Oh, how clever!' said Lady Grant, enthused. 'So that it will disguise the left side!'

'No, the curls will be on the right,' said Lady Aurora with lifted brows.

Ursilla looked up in horror at the smiling certainty of Lady Aurora. But her hair had been let down from her pins already, and her ladyship pulled a section forward over her right eye and to the side, the angle of her finger suggesting a long sloping cut from brow to jawline.

'Isn't she pretty?' She released one finger to touch the crescent scar, about an inch and a half long, that curled over Ursilla's high left cheekbone. 'It occurred to me that this might be just the position where our mothers', dressing for a ball, might have placed a crescent patch on their cheeks to draw attention to their lovely eyes. Let us draw attention to Ursilla's beauty, not mask it.' Ursilla was stunned as the faces behind regarded her in the mirror.

It was Genevieve that spoke, 'An honest solution. Or else one would be forever in hiding. But it requires courage. Are you ready, Ursilla?'

It was a large question. Ursilla looked into the glass. She had hidden, even from herself. But now, wearing Sadie's handmade gown in a lively colour of pink, and with a ribbon at her neck, she was not in hiding any more. These clothes were *inviting* regard, and this frightened her so much that she could bolt right now. But those kind, serious faces around her, and the challenge in Genevieve's eye, made her smile at Lady Aurora, 'So be it!' She was rewarded with a swift squeeze on her shoulder, and the scissors commenced their work.

When finished, her hair was pinned up again at the back and she saw a new female before her. This young girl had curls that angled from her middle forehead to one side of her jaw and skirted her long lashes, drawing attention to her large, pretty eyes. On the other side was undoubtedly a scar, but the crescent seemed to frame her eye too, making her ... it seemed too good to be true ... very nearly pretty.

Dulce, sighing, touched her cheek from behind, drawing a finger over the crescent, so revealed. 'It is lovely...!'

Ursilla frowned, embarrassed that such a word should be used for her scarred face, but looked in Dulce's sincere eyes, and held her breath.

Then an uncultured interjection broke her. 'Oh miss, you is *gorgeous!*' sighed Sadie.

This broke everyone's tension, and made the French maid roll her eyes, but the ladies laughed.

'You are quite right, Sadie,' said Lady Grant, mopping her eyes, '*gorgeous!*'

Chapter 12

Sadie Intercedes

Fenton, sitting at an angle on his chair at the coffee house, legs crossed, sipping some coffee, 'You seem ridiculously on edge, baron.'

'A murderer wants to harm a young lady under the protection of my mother, and she now walks the streets in broad daylight, what *should* I seem, Fenton?'

Wilbert Fenton stretched out the fingers on the hand Grant had grasped and said, ironically, 'Tense.'

Grant laughed harshly. He sipped his coffee and looked out of the window. The coffee house was on an upper floor of the street where the milliner's shop was, and Fenton said, 'They will be some time. We will await them here.'

'They are to come *here*?'

'My wife will see to it. Benedict joins us, and the ladies will happen upon us. It is my wife's notion. We will be her first gentlemen, and the safest.'

Grant put up a brow, 'Safety is not a word the world associates with *you*, sir. Rather the reverse.'

'Ah, but the World is not in my inner circle. My friend Ianthe says I am a kitten beneath the sinister exterior.'

Grant lifted his brows in amazement, 'Perhaps she does not know you sir.'

'Oh, Ianthe, Lady Fox, I should call her now, knows me rather better than most. From a child, you know.'

'The ravishing Lady Fox who has come from nowhere and charmed all London?'

'That is she. But she came from France.'

Grant cocked another brow, for Britain had been at war with France for an age, the hostilities only ended by a year.

'It is a long story, which she may tell you sometime. For now, I should say what I know about our business. I sent to all of the ... ah ... *establishments* on Cole's butler's list. There were strawberry haired ladies in three of them, and for the rest we know that he asked after a red blonde harlot in another. The landlords indicate that there are three girls missing. But again, that is just what we know of.'

'It is a rare colour, is it not? I am surprised ...!'

'Apparently, some girls with lighter hair *dye it,* using onion skins and roses or camellias. They are copying the most celebrated of the opera dancers, Miss Fletcher. Hoping to get a rich protector like their heroine.'

'Milsom's latest mistress?'

'I hear she moved onto an Austrian official, now. Not an earl, but much richer.'

'So, this craze for hair dye gives him more targets...?'

'I should say so.'

'We need *more* for Bow Street to take up a baronet's heir for murder.'

'Indeed.'

'I have had a thought about the trunk. We need to speak to Mosely.' Grant half stood, but Fenton crooked a finger. He said something to a server, who left.

'You summoned him?'

'Yes, via my groom. He will come here but await us outside. No need to disturb the ladies.'

'It's *him!*' said Grant tersely, standing once more, looking down at the street.

Fenton looked at a figure that *might* and *might not* have been Hubert Cole walking on the other side of the road from the milliners. He grasped the baron's arm. 'She is protected. I think your footman would be *glad* to kill his former master. The gentleman is passing. There is no need to worry. It may not be him. The man they looked down on met some others on the street and went off, chatting. 'It is not he.' Fenton removed his grip, and Grant sat.

'You value the young lady greatly,' remarked Fenton significantly.

'It is not what you suppose. She is someone I am responsible for. And the threat to her person is not an empty one.'

'I understand. But it *may* be what I, as you say, *suppose*.' He laughed at Grant's evil eye. 'Gentlemen, once a female — and in this case, from what my wife says, a frightened, but kind and generous female

— initiates our need to protect, it stirs an old, old, instinct in the male. It may be difficult to end it.'

'I have the same instincts for my mother and sister.' As Fenton looked unimpressed, Grant added, goaded, 'And I hardly see her, so there is nothing to end.'

'Well,' said Fenton, consoling, 'as long as she does not take up *too* much thinking time in your day or appear in your dreams.'

Grant's own cynicism had returned, 'Well, she appears in my *nightmares*, certainly ... in a trunk.'

'Yes, as I said, my boy. She's even in your dreams.' A lounging foot moved playfully in a way that reprised Fenton's tone.

There was a movement from the milliner's that stopped Grant's quashing reply at his companion, and he saw the ladies leave the building. Lady Aurora, recognisable by the silken shawl over her pelisse, pointed in the direction of the coffee house, and the ladies crossed the street to enter. He saw Ursilla hesitate, then his mother put her hand through her bent arm and guide her.

When Dulce went to her mother's chambers when they returned from the shopping expedition, they glowed at each other. 'Did not that go so well?'

'Oh, it did! And Aurora's notion for her hair was wonderful. Why, she has emerged from hiding herself *entirely*, and I could see she recognised it herself!'

'But the cost of Lady Aurora's taste! For we are not simply adding to poor Ursilla's wardrobe but creating an entirely new one!'

'Oh, the cost is nothing. Edmond will bear it, and says we need not scrimp. I told him that Ursilla's pin money had arrived, and that she had given it to me for safe keeping. She thinks, poor girl, that it is a great sum, but the milliner's bill *alone* might finish it, if we did not keep it from her.'

'Oh splendid! I do not think I could bear that she is even *more* grateful to us. I admit I prefer the *naughty* Ursilla that we begin to know.' Dulce giggled.

'But I think, you know, that it was Sadie who had the best time.'

'She and Lady Aurora share an enthusiasm.'

'But afterwards, I thought Ursilla did well in conversation with the gentlemen. I have always found Mr Wilbert Fenton charming but distant, but when he wishes he can be warmth itself. He made her laugh more than once.' Dulce said.

'And the warmth of Mr *Benedict* Fenton is entirely natural, I think. I am ashamed to say that I wondered if he married his wife in an arrangement, since they are so different. But it is easy to see that the handsome young god simply *dotes* on Genevieve Fenton,' said Lady Grant.

'As does Ursilla,' said Dulce and added, musing, 'I wonder what was said that day to make them such bosom friends?'

'I do not know, but she seems to inspire Ursilla with bravery as well as adoration.'

'We must be glad. I thought Edmond might be the one to do so, for he always bucked up my spirits when I was younger, but he still avoids her.'

But Dulce's mother narrowed her eyes. 'I am not so sure Edmond is as uninterested as he would like us to believe. I saw him look at her today when her head was turned. His eyes were smiling.'

'Why must men be so awkward about everything? What with Drakemire having no tact, and Edmond being stubborn, I'm glad the Fenton men, with their superior address, were the newest gentlemen she has met with.'

***

As Grant sat on the edge of Ursilla's bed that night, he saw that she did not wear a cap. He was gazing down at her and wondering what he was doing here once more and remembering Wilbert Fenton's ironic words. She lay to one side but rolled over onto her back and her fists clenched once more, her knees knocking against his side when she tried to pull them up in protection, balling herself into the smallest circle possible.

It had been, his mother told him, a triumphant day. Ursilla had been able to meet Wilbert Fenton, himself and Benedict Fenton too, when he had arrived five minutes later, ostensibly to join his uncle. It transpired that Lady Cynthia Fenton, Benedict's mother (a dark haired beauty who resembled him greatly), was also there with friends, and coming over to the table, they spoke briefly and pleasantly. It was altogether like the easiest of social occasions. Ursilla had still been wearing the close-fitting bonnet, and hid somewhat, but sat up at more attention when with the friendliest smile from Benedict's mama, they had gone.

The young girl spoke to the gentlemen shyly at first, and Grant had seen a new side of the urbane elder Fenton. There was a kind warmth in his eye that the gentlemen at his club would have been shocked to witness. But then he had teased Ursilla about her new coiffure, declaring her to be *utterly fashionable, and making the ladies at the neighbouring tables look cast into the shade.* Ursilla had laughed at his nonsense, and all had gone well thereafter.

But now Edmond Grant saw her terror again, and now began, as he had before, to tap on her closed fists.

'You did splendidly today, and now you are perfectly safe. You are at your home, where nothing can hurt you. Her fists unfurled, and suddenly she grasped his hand.

'John!' she said, still in her sleep.

'I am not John, but his friend. He has sent me to you so that you may be safe, Ursilla.'

As he used her name, she let out a long sigh and drew his captured hand to her cheek, resting the back of his fist on her face. 'I've missed you so...!' she said. She fell into a deeper sleep then, and though the hand that held his against her face slackened, he did not yet move his away.

When he had first sighted Ursilla in the coffee house, looking towards him, he had caught his breath, and Wilbert Fenton's laugh had made him look to his side, meeting his wicked eye. He had been shocked. Ursilla, whom he avoided seeing as much as possible, looked much different. The curls over one eye bespoke a sharply fashionable young lady, as did her pelisse, gown and accessories. Later he noted the worn boots but knew his mother would have that in hand. But the thing was that Ursilla, shy but smiling at a sally of Dulce's, was lovely. He wondered if he would have thought so if he had not seen the transformation from agonised, weak and starved, to a healthy, happy young lady. He wondered if he would have thought of her as in any way notable. But it had been a heady delight when she laughed or smiled or had opinions on the topics of the day: bonnet trims and dyed kid boots.

He looked at her now, his hand still at her face, wondering. *Was* she pretty? Her long lashes curled on her cheek, near her scar which, from the moment it had been accentuated by the blonde curls on the other side, seemed not a disfigurement at all. Her face was tinged with natural colour, her lips plump and rose tinted, her bones delicate. She was, he thought objectively, a lovely girl. When her eyes were sparkling, she was … but he could not even say it to himself. He had been sitting thus too long, he must move his hand at least before the impudent maid came in again. But it felt warm against her cheek, and it tingled in a way that was new to him. He vowed, as he looked at her, that no one would hurt her more. But as he shook his head to quash the sentimentalist, he pulled away gently. But she grasped the hand again and moved her head, trapping both hands, hers and his, between pillow and cheek.

The maid came in silently and was suddenly at his side, looking down at the scene.

'She thinks I'm her brother,' he explained. To a *maid*, he thought in disgust.

But Sadie only said, 'Yes my lord,' and bent over the bed, gently rolling her mistress's head so that he could move his hand.

He stood and wished to say more in explanation, but he curbed it and lifted his chin, then left.

A quarter hour earlier Sadie had been sitting at the top of the grand staircase, looking down at her clasped hands.

'What are you doing there?' hissed the butler, who was crossing the large square hall below.

'Thinking,' Sadie said, taking his words, as usual, as an enquiry rather than an admonishment.

'Well, *do not*! Return to your lady at once!'

'It's alright, Mr Baker, sir, the baron's wif her.' She said breezily, the looked distracted. 'I just have to think!'

Baker was stunned, 'The *baron*...!'

'Yes sir! He visits most nights, but only goes in sometimes.'

'The *baron*....!' Baker said again. He watched as she shifted her feet and dropped her chin again. The feet made a v-shape, toes joined, he noted, for no particular reason. But she looked worried, so, having been shocked out of his imperturbability already, he merely said, 'What is worrying you, girl?'

'Well, sir I'm worrying if I did aright. About the baron, sir.'

'If you are now seeing that you should accompany your young lady when there is a gentleman in the room, I am sure you should have known so.'

'Well, but she's *sleeping*, sir. It don't matter if she's *sleeping*. And he has a way of making her calm in her sleep when I cannot.'

Baker was about to inform her of the dangers of men in the rooms of sleeping females, but he forbore. He knew the baron was not a risk to the young woman, and besides, the other revelations he had just heard were more interesting. 'When did the baron begin ...!'

'From the first Mr Baker, just checking on the poor lady, only he don't visit in the day, just when she's asleep.'

'Don't want her to know he's concerned, I suppose,' said Baker to himself.

'I thinks so, Mr Baker. I reckon the baron is nicer than he pretends.'

'It is not your place to make judgements on your betters, my girl.'

'No sir, but it's hard not to, ain't it?'

Baker found her honesty irritating. 'So, what worries you about *tonight's* visit?' he asked, because he was concerned.

'Well, sir, I'd best keep that to meself.' She stood up, while the butler's jaw dropped. 'I'll just go and have a chat wif the baroness.'

She walked past, and he stood wondering why he had not cracked her head, when she was near enough, and ordered her to ... do something or other. The trouble was, he had not had the training of her, even though she had lived here for months now, since she was always with her lady. But he was glad he had not lowered himself to violence as he heard the baroness say, 'Oh Sadie, come in. Is she recovered from the day, do you think?' before she closed the door. Even his mistress treated that little one differently.

As Sadie remounted the stairs ten minutes later, having discussed today's expedition with the baroness, she thought of what she had done. It had been caused by some incidents she had noted today. The first was that she had witnessed the baron's sighting of their party, before Sadie sat on a bench in the corridor with the other servants. He was shocked, that was to be expected, but she was sure his dark complexion had darkened further, starting from his neck and moving up. Then, as the baron joined the smaller party of just Miss, his mother and sister (with William and her behind) she had witnessed the looks that both had given the other when the ladies were not looking. Their gazes had not met, but Sadie knew the significance of the stolen glances, because she herself was doing so towards William. They were interested in each other and could not *keep* from looking.

As Sadie brushed her young lady's hair, she now marvelled at the colour and the sheen. When Miss Duvall reached for her nightcap, Sadie had said, 'Not tonight, miss, it might disturb the curl.' This did not make sense, the maid thought afterwards, since the curl was principally at the front, but her mistress smiled sleepily and went to bed. She had enjoyed herself, Sadie knew, but it had been a great strain, nevertheless. She had fallen asleep quickly and Sadie waited for the hesitating step outside the door, for the occasional crack opening it for a moment, while her master ensured all was well. But Sadie heard the step and opened the door precipitately, going out into the corridor and saying, 'It's a hot milk night for sure, m'lord,' and she whisked herself away. As she looked over her shoulder, he had entered, and she sighed.

In the past the maid had thought that it was as bad for her miss to be interested in the baron, as it was for Sadie to be interested in William. No good could come of it. But that was before. Now, well it seemed to her that her miss was as good as *any* young lady. She looked so lovely ... there had to be a chance. And he ... well, he would not mind the scar, and he cared for her, and today it had seemed that there was more to it than kindness. But she could not be sure. And if her encouragement of attachment caused either of them pain, she had done very wrong. She knew from discussions of the baroness and her daughter while they were together in the drawing room with Miss Ursilla, that the baron's mother was daily awaiting his attentions to this young lady or that to come to some understanding. It seemed mostly, Sadie understood, to depend on dances at Almacks (them assembly room where balls were held for nobs outside the private houses) or at private balls. Had he danced *twice* with a certain lady, or just once? This question was significant to the baroness and the countess, and Sadie had asked Miss Ursilla about that. 'Why only one or two dances?' she'd said.

'Well...,' said Miss, '... *one* dance might be mere politeness, but *two* dances...' (her mistress's eyes had sparkled naughtily) 'are a mark of interest.'

'And three?'

'No one dances *three*, if unmarried. The lady would be considered *fast*, my aunt told me, and the gentleman would be considered no better than a *lecher*.'

'There's worse ways of being a lecher. There was a man who grabbed me after church onct ... anyway, I soon saw him off.'

'How?' asked Miss, interested.

'With the contents of me basket, all over his head.' Sadie said, swinging her hand in a mime, 'Potatoes miss. Big 'uns!'

'I am making a jest, Sadie, it is not so serious as *that*, it is only that three dances invite speculation, so my aunt told me never to do so.'

'And *did* you, Miss?' asked Sadie.

'I never had a Season, in the end,' said Ursilla, smiling a little sadly.

But when thinking about the baron, Sadie remembered the drawing room conversations. Though the baron did dance twice on occasion, giving his mother and sister hope, there did not seem to be the follow-up attentions they hoped for: of a drive out, or such continued gestures of interest — though the baron professed, said his mother, to be willing to marry. So, because of this, Sadie had acted. Her mistress was safe, she felt. She did not know of the visits, so they could not add to hope, like a smile from William did with her. And the baron's heart was not her affair.

No, she had acted aright. Tapping her lady's hand might give Baron Grant — that curmudgeonly, kind man — a clue to his own feelings. She thought the baroness agreed. 'Is the baron with her now?' she'd asked, ever so casually, and Sadie had nodded. The baroness had looked down at her book in dismissal, but Sadie knew she hid a smile.

Chapter 13
A Knowledge of Evil

Grant was a logical man. This logic had kept him from offering marriage on a number of occasions, and now it made him consider what he was about. He would never have thought of himself as someone who was seeking a damsel to rescue. In the hallway of Almacks Assembly Rooms, he had once watched a woman fall to the ground before him and had merely bowed, nodding a footman to help her up. It had been, he had arrogantly supposed, some method of gaining his attention. But Ursilla had not sought attention, she had borne her suffering alone.

He had guilt about this, guilt that he had not come home at once, or visited as soon as he did. She had suffered because of it. But as Southey said, he had not known. But he had seen, from afar, how she bore with it all, her bodily pain and social terror, her nightmares. She had done well not to go mad. But guilt was not a basis for marriage, nor was the need to protect her an admission of love.

Yet he was aware, from the first it seemed, that he should keep well away from her. He had assumed this was for her protection, in case she grew attracted to him (as many young women seemed to do) and suffered more pain as a result, but now he knew that was not all. There had been, even when he had looked at her outside Beltane Buildings, an awareness of her that he had never had with a woman who was not a lover. An attention to her he could not explain. She was the beloved sister of his friend, he'd thought, that was all. It set her apart in his attention. But looking into her eyes on every occasion of their meeting was a trial for him. They sucked him in, those large grey eyes, and it was months now, but he still remembered the feel of her light form when she had fallen into his arms. To desire a girl so broken had made him hate himself anew. But so it was — the stirrings of attraction, more tender than he had ever felt, had overtaken him.

Seeing her today was worse. She had been most of the way towards the bubbly child he had met for three minutes all those years ago. But now she was a woman, and her sparkling eyes had a deeper attraction, her smile more enticing. Her hair, cut to reveal the scar, not hide it, was a stroke of genius. The curls and the crescent both accentuated those lovely eyes, and he had been deprived of breath. He had felt a strong desire to converse with her, to make her smile directly at him, to display his wit and charm, to woo her. But beneath that smile was a fragile creature, broken and battered, and until he knew for sure what he was about, he must not inveigle her into his orbit. So, he had sat and watched, and had been aware of Fenton's knowing eyes on him.

Was she even intelligent? Sometimes she could be amusing, and that took wits, so he suspected so. Could they share interests? He knew from Genevieve Fenton that she could drive and ride. Books, literature? Opera? His mother read to her from appalling novels, but he had not asked Sadie yet about Ursilla's own taste. They could not share dance, surely, though she could walk once more. He walked for miles in the country; she probably could not. But as he thought these things he wondered if he had ever made such a list for his other women. Had he wanted them to match him in all things? No. So, why must she? Because she, he concluded, his logic carrying him places he had never wished to go, would be forever, or not at all. This was her haven; he could not taint it for her by the sadness of a failed romance.

Her face swum before him, and his hand was still warm where she had held it.

Jenks the butler at the Cole house was afraid. He had kept the baronet appraised of the young master's nightly doings, by asking his groom where he had been on the nights he took a carriage, or having him followed if Cole went out alone. But he had not told the baronet all the things that went on in this house.

The staff were at the board for their dinner, heartier this evening because the young master had failed to return to dine at home. Since the fish pie would not keep, said Cook, they had best finish it up. At a rap on the back door, the scullion had opened it and came back inside.

'It's someone for you, Mr Jenks.' Jenks thought it a trader come for payment or some such thing, and testily left the fish in rich cream sauce to go see him off. But in front of him was a man he did not know. A foot shorter than he, with a smile that made him shiver. Bow Street, he was sure. His early life had made him sniff a Runner from half a mile.

'I want a word with you, me old necker,' the man said, with that insinuating smile. And just like that he jerked the butler's jacket front and pulled him from the house. 'Been thinkin' about the list you gave to me friend. Your young master didn't take a groom *every* time, did he?'

Jenks, now up against the wall and too close to the soil buckets, did not pretend to misunderstand. Though he looked down on this man, gazing into his sharp, smiling face, he was completely sure the smaller man could do him serious harm if he tried. 'Sent Briggs to follow him.'

'Whozat?'

'Groom.'

'Where is he?'

'Stables. Master's at home now. Came in after dinner.'

'I know that. It's why I'm at me leisure to have this l'il chat wif you, old chap. Ain't it nice?' He let go of the butler's front. 'I'll see Briggs first.' The little man pressed his face up to Jenk's. 'But I know you knew what your young master did to that sweet young Miss Duvall, and never lifted a finger to help her, not even telling your *proper* master.' A sharp hand threw him back against the wall, but the little man was still smiling, 'He pay you?' He scoffed. '*"course* he did!'

He left with a last look, and went to the stables calling, 'Briggs! Friend o' yours here!'

It turned out that the groom hadn't returned at once on some nights when he followed the young master to his destination. If drink was served at an establishment, Briggs would have a quick one to keep the cold out. It didn't take much for Mosely to find out the rest.

After making a few more calls in the area, talking to informants of his own surrounding the Cole house, Mosely knocked on the back door of the Grant's house several streets away from Brook Street. Normally he was a front door man, but he was not proud. It might scare the females, or set them to speculating, if he came in that way. So, he was shown up to Grant's study discreetly, and he said, 'Hello there, me lord. Thought I'd tell you more. First about a blue striped cape.'

'The trunk!'

'Yup. Her that was in the trunk. We got a witness that saw a man of Cole's description wif her.'

'Fenton and I had a chat.' Grant said. 'He's organising the Runners to search certain parts of the river.'

Moseley whistled. 'It's a big river, and a mucky one.'

'But there are watermen that can search it. And we have some positions now. The river would move bodies, but some may be caught in reeds, or washed up nearby.'

'Nearest the inns that the butler told us of?' guessed Mosely. 'Well, Mr Fenton was always a quick one. I never thought of that.'

Grant did not bother to tell him that it was his own notion, following the impulsive move that Benedict Fenton had interrupted. Cole had asked that girl to walk to the river, Florrie the waitress had told Grant when he had spoken to her recently, and he thought he knew the reason why. It was a usual excuse for gentlemen not wishing to be seen entering a room in a low tavern, perhaps. There were bushes and trees by the river that gave shelter to men's desires on a warm night. If she'd gone with Cole, the girl would have have ended in the river, with a rock tied on her foot, perhaps. Like the rocks in the trunk that Bow Street found when they had taken out the terrible mess inside.

'If Fenton's men find anything, I think we have him!'

'We got 'im now, I'd say. He was wif the gel in the trunk, poor soul, he attacked the tavern maid, there's girls missing from places he's been, all wif the same-coloured hair. Baronet's heir or no, they'll take him in.'

'Fenton recommended to Sir Neil Cole not to try to save the cuckoo in his nest – though the baronet doesn't know from *what* as yet.'

'It will destroy the family name, I suppose.'

'Many of 'em deserve it. The women of that family did not even fetch an apothecary to Miss Duvall after the carriage accident, never mind a physician, and they must have seen some of her later injuries.'

'Don't expect that of gently reared ladies.'

'No.'

'I'm off to see the magistrate. He'll likely be at his supper at this hour, but I won't sleep until Pig-swill is locked up. He's mad, pure and simple. He'd break in here, even. Kill you and yours to get to her.' The little man pointed to the side table where a cut glass decanter sat with some glasses. He cocked and eyebrow at Grant, who shrugged. Mosely served himself a stiffener.

Viscount Gascoigne and the Fenton men were announced, and the viscount said quickly, 'Thanks for the report you had sent, Mosely. There may now be a way to get Cole faster.'

'Yes?' asked the baron.

'Yes,' said Gascoigne, 'It's all due to Benedict putting the pieces together. He got more out of the Briggs chap tonight than *you*, Mr Mosely!'

'Well, he was always a strong lad,' Mosely remarked calmly, 'I hope you allowed Briggs an apothecary.'

Benedict only grinned at this sally, while his uncle took snuff.

'Not needed,' smiled Gascoigne, putting a hand on Fenton's shoulder as he accepted a glass from the obliging Mr Mosely — who gifted him this boon as though the superior brandy were his own. 'Benedict used his other attribute, *devilish friendliness*. After talking to Briggs for an hour in a gin palace tonight, he has discovered something.'

Grant looked to the young man. Benedict commenced, 'Cole makes a diversion on his travels each night. To this house ....' Grant paled at Benedict's information, '...and to the tavern that I first saw the attack.'

'He still wants the girl he could not kill.' Grant said coldly, gazing off.

'Yes,' said Gascoigne. 'And if he were to see her *again*, we might catch him in the act.'

'It was my first thought,' admitted the elder Fenton, brushing snuff from a sleeve with delicacy. 'But on reflection, we cannot ask that girl to face him again.'

'Yes,' added Benedict, 'That would be too cruel.'

'But I had a different notion,' said the viscount, '*Another* figure in a plaid apron. When the news came and I told Delphine, our friend Phoebe Beaumont, who resides with us, wished to don the apron in the alley, since she is *also* slight, thus lure him in.'

'We could not ask it of her,' said Grant. 'The man is mad.'

'Yes, but she is anxious to help. The trouble is, she does *not* have strawberry blonde hair.'

'But I do,' a voice called out from the doorway, '*I* could don the apron.'

CHAPTER 14
Ursilla's Stand

'You!' said Grant. Seeing her standing in her nightrail and a peignoir of sturdy cotton, her plaited hair over one shoulder, he felt furious. Her maid stood behind, like a shadow, and in the gloom Ursilla's large eyes gleamed with a cast of tears. 'Sadie,' ordered the baron brusquely, 'take her to bed!'

Mr Mosley touched his head in salute. 'Seems I should be off!' he said, leaving with a smile in the middle of the charged atmosphere.

'You did not tell me he had hurt others *because of me,*' Ursilla said to Grant accusingly. She turned to Mr Wilbert Fenton, desperate. 'I wish to help, sir. Please make him let me.'

Fenton's hooded eyes looked down at her gravely. 'It is a great risk, my dear.'

Ursilla turned around to Benedict, 'Mr Fenton, sir! *Genevieve* would understand.'

Grant came forward but Ursilla turned to the tall, handsome man whom she did not know, 'You sir, *you* see, do you not, that it must be me?'

Gascoigne frowned, but before he could answer, the baron had come to grasp her shoulders and spin her to him, 'Ursilla! I will never permit it.'

She held his lapels and looked up and into his eyes, saying, 'Even if I *need to*, Edmond? Even if I *must!*'

He was shaken by her plea, her use of his name, by her nearness and by her looking so directly into his eyes. But he answered at once, *'No!'*

She pulled away from him, as though tossing him aside in disgust. 'Oh, *where* is Genevieve?' she exclaimed, looking around the male faces. '*She* could make you understand!'

'What do you speak of?' asked Grant, confused.

'*You* know!' she said passionately, turning to Benedict.

Benedict looked down at her kindly and held her eyes across the room. 'My wife believes,' he said quietly, 'that women should learn to save themselves.'

'Yes!'

'*No* miss!' said Sadie. 'The baron is quite right! There is *no need* to see that monster more. Why, the very thought of him still gives you nightmares. These gentlemen are more than capable of dealing with him.'

'But he may harm *Edmond!*' said Ursilla turning to her. 'I could not *bear* it!

Her tone as she said this held Sadie, and instilled silence in the room. All eyes shifted to the baron, who was looking at her astounded.

She turned towards them all and said, 'Gentlemen, I know that you all seek justice for me. But none of you but Edmond and Sadie know how that man ... no, I shall name him — Hubert Cole — how that man *still* invades my dreams. And now I know that he has harmed *others*...! I knew, even though everyone told me I was safe, that he would not easily give me up. I knew by the way his attention was always on me ... it was of an order beyond the normal. But I could not *explain* this fear, for it seems not to be rational. I am in the home of a man of rank, a powerful man in himself, more powerful even than Cole, I know it well,' Grant coloured at this, and the passion with which she said it, '... but he *cannot* understand the man's ...' she shuddered, '... and now you have confirmed it for me. That he plays out his madness on others, only because they have my hair colour. That he may *kill* my *saviour*. How *can* I stay still?'

'But you will,' said Grant dangerously and definitely.

'Hear, hear!' said Sadie.

'I would not let the tavern wench confront him again,' said Benedict gently, 'and *your* sufferings at his hands were so much worse, Miss Duvall.'

'You do not *understand*! To face him, to show him I am not his to oppress ... it might *free* me!'

'No!' said Grant again.

'You will all be there!' she pleaded, 'And...,' she added, smiling to herself, '...Benedict can gift me a pistol.'

'Go to bed, Ursilla!' Grant ordered in his most threatening voice.

Wilbert Fenton, who had been regarding this little scene with narrowed eyes came forward. 'I think it might work.'

'No!' exploded Grant.

'My dear baron, only consider! There are at least three crack shots here this evening ... I do not know *your* record, Grant, but I suspect I may add you to the list. Any *one* of us may put a bullet in any place we chose on the body of Hubert Cole, if he should get too close to Miss Duvall.'

'And if *he* has a pistol?'

'He does not want to shoot her,' Fenton said, calmly. 'Shooting would be too simple. His madness has demonstrated so. He wishes to *torture and hurt...*!'

'And so you would have this young girl face him?' said Grant viciously.

'Yes! And face him well. With a pistol near her, and a knife on her person, and all of us hidden in sight of her, ready to intercede. Don't you think this would be safe?'

'Safe? Perhaps!' said Grant furiously. 'But no one who has seen her in her sleep, as I have countless times, when she is drowned in nightmares of the man, can be anything but *terrified* of what confronting him might do to her.'

His third sentence had stunned the others, excepting Sadie.

'Oh Edmond,' you have visited me in the night? It is *your* calming voice in my dreams?' she said to him, eyes shining.

Grant flushed. 'That is beside the point! You will not go.'

'I must!' she said, full in his face.

'I agree!' said Benedict Fenton who had been mulling over his own clumsy attempts at saving his maiden once, and Genevieve's own efficient way of dealing with her husband afterwards. But only, she had said then, because Benedict's actions had shown her that she *could*. 'It is because you and your family have helped her gain the courage to do so.'

'*Yes!*' exclaimed Ursilla with delight, 'No wonder Genevieve loves you so, Mr Fenton,' Benedict flushed and was amazed that his taciturn wife should have expressed this to her friend. She turned back to Grant. 'You must trust in me, Edmond, I will not let him hurt you, or me, or anyone else ever again.'

Grant sighed. He looked at Sadie, who seemed as concerned as he. 'I don't like it, me lord, but me ma says, face your fears or be a scaredy-bogle till you die.'

He gave in. 'Very well!'

'I'll tell Mosely,' said Gascoigne, going.

'Tell him no Runners as yet. *We* shall escort Mr Cole to Bow Street. Miss Duvall's name must not be mentioned in their enquiries.'

'I expect we could bribe Florrie the tavern girl to say *she* was the one confronted again if the Runners want to talk to her,' said Benedict. 'We can let her know the details if we manage to lure him.'

'Very well, let us begin with a plan.'

***

It was to be the next evening. And perhaps, warned Edmond to Ursilla, for some evenings to come, for Cole might not yet appear.

But Benedict Fenton did not suppose so. 'The diversion to this house and to the tavern are nightly, according to Briggs. The only exceptions are when he has his own social functions to attend.'

'According to the weasel butler Jenks, whom Mosely just visited for a friendly chat,' smiled Benedict, 'he hasn't got anything else on tomorrow night, and besides which, he's twitchy!'

Ursilla shivered at the thought that her enemy had been *in this street* and held Sadie's hand. But she tilted her chin towards Edmond, who was looking at her suspiciously. She wrinkled her nose at him and smiled reassuringly, and he stiffened in shock and looked away.

That night, in her chamber, the waves of dread went more quickly than ever before. She would confront him at last, that monster who still inhabited her dreams. But something else inhabited them too, a cool, calm, deep voice infused her with courage there, and now she understood that this voice belonged to Edmond. Edmond had seen her at sleep *countless times* ... he had said so! However afraid she was at the plan they had made, this knowledge out-trumped it all.

Finally Sadie, too, admitted it, as put on Ursilla's nightcap before she went to sleep.

'The first night I needed to go to the kitchen for something, since I weren't allowed to *ring* then, Miss, and I just told the baron to look after you, and to talk rubbish to you to calm you if you was dreaming them nightmares again.' Ursilla laughed and imagined Grant's shock at being ordered by a maid. 'And then he came every night, in passing like, just to have a quick look and check you was alright, I reckon!'

Edmond had cared for her. He had always, though he had hidden it, cared more than just to supply her with a roof. It was like him. She felt she had known him somewhat by the words of his mother and sister, both of whose complaints about him scarcely could hide their love and admiration for their frustrating relative. They adored, and were adored, by him. Ursilla had divined it, but her understanding of him was much more. The goodness she had intuited, the honesty and reserve that hid his own hurts. His strength of purpose, his overwhelming masculinity. Even in the presence of the handsome male gods Benedict Fenton and Titus Gascoigne, one felt it. Perhaps only the elder Fenton, the charming and dangerous Wilbert, could rival the sheer power of his will.

But Grant was the man, her saviour, who had visited her in the night and talked to her.

'He were good wif you, Miss. His voice seemed to calm you, so when I needed to leave sometimes, I'd bring him in to make you tranquil for a minute or too.'

Ursilla could imagine the ruthlessness of Sadie's methods. 'But why did you not tell me of it, then Sadie?'

Sadie looked unusually reluctant to voice her thoughts. 'Well ... the baron did not wish me too...'

That would not have stopped the maid, Ursilla was sure. She raised her brows, but Sadie said no more.

'You did not wish me to get *ideas*...' mused Ursilla nodding to herself.

'Well, yes miss. The baron is kinder than he looks miss, and would probably rescue...'

'Injured animals, I know.'

The thought was lowering. But there was something, something of joy in her. Edmond had cared for *this* injured animal from the first, had sat by its bedside at night, while ignoring it in the day. Even if this meant no more than a proof of his goodness, it brought her a warmth that she could not explain, and an excitement she would work hard to quell in herself. If he knew that it had made her heart flutter when she had grasped at him tonight, they could not continue contentedly in this happy house.

She would not let him see. One day they might share the kind of intimacy he shared with Dulce, perhaps, but that could all be broken if she showed herself to have a *tendre* for him. She would calm herself and learn be his friend.

But tonight, only for tonight, she would hug her new knowledge of the baron to banish the fear of the battle she faced ahead. Tonight, she would let herself dream of him, to keep away the nightmare of a monster.

***

In the alley that evening, the grim group arrived and waited for the call. Mosely was following Cole closely and would send word if he approached.

A groom ran forward from Mosely to tell them that the man was on his way. The gentlemen — the handsome viscount, the dangerous Mr Fenton and his nephew, and Baron Grant — disposed themselves around. Titus Gascoigne's large figure blocked the tavern door, hidden on the threshold, for they wished for no interference from drunkards once their man appeared. Grant was in a shallow gap between tavern and the ramshackle house beside it, the gap only just accommodating him sideways (and a family of rats, he noted grimly, but he stamped and drove them off), Fenton senior was behind the corner of the tavern at the other side, with Sadie (who had insisted on coming) close by him. Benedict was flattened on top of a drayer's cart at the opposite end of the alley mouth, his black coat and hair making him indistinguishable from its covering in the gloom.

URSILLA AND THE BARON'S REVENGE

And so it was that Ursilla, dressed in a plain gown with a low bodice and a loud plaid apron, stood washing tankards in the alleyway. Her back was to the direction Cole would come, and to Grant and Benedict, and her heart was beating fast. But when she looked up, she could see the muzzle of Wilbert Fenton's pistol, its silver chasing glinting in the moonlight, and felt relief. After three turns of the tankards in the trough water (a disgusting practise, thought Sadie, watching from behind the elder Mr Fenton's back), she heard the signal. Fenton was the only one of them with a view of the direction that Cole was coming (all other eyes were on Ursilla's back), and he had tossed a small stone, the sign that Cole was in the alley. Her heart almost stopped, she had an urge to turn behind her and run to Grant, but she stayed swilling tankards, humming to herself an old song.

She heard the footsteps echo in the unnaturally quiet alley, William and James, two footmen from the Grant house, were blocking the patron's entrance from the opposite end beyond Fenton, she knew, and the tavern babble, which had seemed shockingly loud and noisy to her at first, seemed muted now, far away. There was only hurt, and the footsteps.

The world turned red. Her breath held and an old, old dread shook her inside organs. The footsteps stopped. She forbore looking over her shoulder, and his voice, that priggish upright voice full of derision and some other thing, that voice she feared above all others, said, in a insinuating sneer 'So you are out of bed, I see, my dear.'

She pulled herself up, back straight in the manner of her friend Genevieve, and turned slowly, 'Yes, Hubert, I am, as you see,' she said smoothly, her voice displaying no trembling. She was proud of that. The red was dispelling now, seeping into the torchlit gloom. She found herself breathing again, the constriction in her chest lighter as she found her voice. She looked him full in his masked face and smiled sardonically, 'And quite well!'

'*You* ... how?' he thundered.

He looked at her apron, confused, but then she saw his wave of elation rise as he took a step towards her and reached to grasp her, his eyes too drunk with the vision to wonder why it should be her, and why she was dressed so.

'Now, I'll have you!' he breathed, stepping two steps, but Grant's body and Wilbert Fenton's bullet reached him at the same time, the baron stepping between Cole and Ursilla.

'You shall not touch her!'

But Cole was on one knee now, blood pouring from his wound, and Ursilla stepped from behind Grant's body and looked down at him. He groaned, cursing.

'It is as Genevieve said,' uttered Ursilla, surprised, 'you are *pathetic*. You whine at the least pain, as you jeered at me for doing.'

'Pathetic? You say so now that I am at your feet, you harlot.'

Grant grasped his neckcloth and was stopped by Ursilla's hand, which amazingly, held a knife.

'Edmond!' she warned him and pleaded both. Then she said to Cole. 'No, I have *always* found you pathetic. But a murderer, too...!' she said in disgust.

'Your fault! Your fault...!' the madman cried, trying to reach for her.

Grant kicked away his supporting leg and he screamed as he landed face down on the street.

'An admission of murder, you all heard it gents?' said Mosely coming in energetically as usual. 'That'll speed things up. I'll take him in, sir,' said the happy voice of Mr Mosely to Grant, who stood looming over the fallen man, 'I brought some friends 'n' all. Runners. Brewster and Chattel is the names.'

Two figures, one short the other burly, came into the alley.

'*Mosely!*' said Grant, furious.

Mosely merely winked at the baron who frowned, putting a protective arm behind him to prevent a view of Ursilla Duvall, then turned to the two Runners by his side. 'The gel standing behind this gent here is Miss Florrie Plunkett, who works in that there tavern. He threaten you, wench?' he called to Ursilla, then looked back to the burly Runner. 'Poor gel, she's that afeared.' In Ursilla's direction he said, 'Just you stay behind them broad shoulders, me darlin'. Ain't nobody goin' to hurt you now.' Mosely nodded to Sadie, who now stood beside the viscount.

Benedict Fenton, distracting one Runner from peering behind Grant's back, said, 'He tried to kill Florrie once, I saw him, but I stopped him. She had broken bones, poor girl. I hoped he would be lured out again when Florrie came out of her bed.'

'We been following up on some missing girls with Florrie's hair colour,' said the big Runner.

'You have your man here, Brewster,' said Grant, taking charge. 'We are friends of Mr Benedict Fenton, who saw the past attack on Florrie, and then later recognised the man in town as her attacker. When he pointed him out to Viscount Gascoigne, Lord Gascoigne informed Fenton that the man was named Hubert Cole, an heir to Sir Neil Cole. Given Cole's position, and Fenton's determination to bring him to justice for the savage attack he had halted, we thought the magistrates might better believe in this man's wickedness if *we*, Mr

Fenton's friends and uncle, were witnesses. I am Baron Grant, this is Viscount Gascoigne and Mr Wilbert Fenton, the Prince Regent's close friend, you know.'

Titus Gascoigne raised an eyebrow at the baron at his unusual puffing off of their consequence.

'I am afraid,' said Wilbert Fenton, drawling lazily, 'that I put a bullet in the man's leg.'

'You did right sir, by the sounds of it,' said Brewster.

'Gels like that is probably used to bein' approached by gents. Makes money from it,' sniffed Chattel.

Mr Mosely slapped the back of his head. 'Don't get paid to have her arm broke and her ribs cracked and put in the river after, like he's likely done afore.'

'You ain't a Runner no more...!' said Chattel resentfully, holding the back of his head.

Brewster slapped him too, 'That ain't what ye said last monf when the boss gave you the whereabouts o' them highway robbers, now was it, you nodcock?'

Sadie had joined the skulking Ursilla, whose back was now to the Runners, and now said in a vulgar fashion, most unlike her soft country voice 'Come on, Florrie me old mate, let's get you to my place, you'se been through the mill tonight.' She put a hand on her hip and looked at the men standing to one side of Grant. 'Runners, eh? Well, you poltroons can come back and talk to her tomorrow. She'll be out like a light after me ma's remedy.'

'Let's go. gel!' said Ursilla's voice in a similar tone, to Grant's amusement. For some time now the sole of Grant's boot, which he sincerely hoped was covered in all the worst detritus of the foul alley, had been over Cole's mouth, to stop his voice upsetting Ursilla. Sadie and she walked off and the man squirmed beneath his boot, still trying to get to her like a rabid dog. Grant leant forward, making Cole squeal.

The Runners had only seen Ursilla's hair and got a glimpse of the loud plaid apron before Sadie put a woollen cape over her. They were moving to William's end of the alley, and Grant's carriage was only a street away.

'I do not suppose we need a crowd at Bow Street,' remarked the elder Fenton, in his urbane voice of command. 'My nephew and I will go with the officers, and you two gentlemen may go home. Thank you, Grant, Gascoigne. I will see you both tomorrow at the club, no doubt.'

Grant moved off, but he found Sadie holding up the swooning form of Ursilla Duvall on a corner of the alley mouth. He scooped Ursilla up and into his arms, feeling a scratch on his knuckle as he did so. She was still clutching the knife, with the same ferocity as she had once held his finger.

'Take it from her, Sadie,' said the baron quietly.

Sadie tried. 'Easier said than done, me lord.'

'Never mind, we must get her home.'

Ursilla stirred and opened her eyes, jerked a little by his fast pace.

'Oh, Edmond! Did I do well?'

'You did splendidly, my Valkyrie.'

'I'm sorry I fainted. But at least he did not see me. He must think me a little brave at least.'

'You *are* brave,' he said, sitting her in the closed carriage, then joining her. Sadie, hesitating, finally got on the box, leaving them alone within, and they drove off.

Ursilla was swooning again, and her head lolled on his shoulder.

'Try to let go of the knife,' Grant said, after he had tried to prise off her fingers from it without hurting her.

'I cannot seem to...!' she said, beginning to shake. 'Horrid thing! Edmond, take it from me.'

He looked at her ruefully, then raised the grasping fingers to his lips and kissed her knuckles, which dropped the knife immediately.

'Edmond!' she protested faintly.

He just caught the knife with his other hand before it impaled his leg.

'You were very, very brave, Ursilla'

'No, I had you,' she said, sleepily.

'And the Fentons, and Gascoigne.'

She laughed. 'What an honour guard,' she murmured. 'I am blessed.'

'Yes, now sleep if you wish.'

'On your shoulder?'

'We have no cushion,' he said, somewhat distantly.

She giggled, still half asleep. 'So afraid to be kind. But it was only *you* who made me feel safe...' he stiffened a little at this. '...and the cook's knife...' She added to herself, smiling, finally spent and asleep.

He also smiled to himself. He pulled her cape around the low bodice and plaid apron, for it disturbed him. Making sure she was really asleep, he moved her forward and inserted his arm behind her, pulling her to him. He was trembling too. Any mistake tonight and Cole might have managed to *touch* her. The thought had revolted him, but he had promised Mosely to delay his appearance until Cole was surprised by Ursilla, since it might loosen his tongue. It had.

In the alley, Grant had held his breath until he could stand between them. He had wished to pummel the madman to the ground, but Fenton's bullet had made it unnecessary, which was, Grant reflected, probably its purpose. He'd known that her presence would rob him of the satisfaction of turning the face of Hubert Cole to tenderised beef, of breaking every bone the monster had broken on Ursilla. He felt denied, but her warm head on his chest, her soft curves in his arms made him better. She was safe, and exactly where he wanted her. When the carriage stopped, he would take her to her room and leave her. Then, just as *she* must, lay down his obsession for revenge and protection.

After which, his life could continue, just as it had before she came.

Chapter 15

Retribution

Lady Cole was with her daughter Susan at breakfast when she received a missive from her husband. She looked at his slanted hand derisively, and set it beside a plate.

'Who writes at this hour, Mama?'

'Your Papa,' said her ladyship pulling sharply on the poke of her muslin cap, 'I shall ignore it.'

But she had not quite finished her morning chocolate when she looked at the letter again, resentfully. Her spouse did not correspond with her, so why he had sent her this, and at this hour, had intrigued her, annoyingly. She picked it up, making her mouth prim against him before she began to read, hardening herself against the rebukes or unpleasant words she expected to find there, but it was not long before she cried out, dropping the letter and almost fainted away in her chair.

'Mama!' said Susan, leaping up to go to her, 'Whatever...!'

'It is *Hubert...!*'

'Hubert? Is he not abed?'

Her mother held out a shaking hand and Susan read:

Edwina,

Your blasted by-blow has ruined us all. He is at Bow Street now, or perhaps Newgate Prison, had up for assault and murder. He is the hell-born fruit of your loins whom you held up as a pillar of rectitude, and I hope you know your own folly now. You were aware, so I have been informed, of how he treated Miss Duvall under your roof, so you too are at fault here, you cruel and despicable woman.

Better you and Susan go to Arthur Park to reside before the world knows of it. I'll not see you starve, for Susan's sake, at least. Don't look for me, for I'm leaving the country.

Cole

'Mama ... *murder?*' squealed Susan. 'Oh, the shame!' She clutched the letter to her and looked aghast, 'Does that mean I cannot go to the Gascoigne's ball?'

Her mother threw a roll at her. 'You stupid, stupid girl! We shall never visit town again. All is *over!*' she turned to the footman, ignoring Susan's wails. 'George, have all our trunks packed and the carriage called for a half hour hence.'

'A half hour, my lady?' said the footman, hardly able to imagine it.

'If you need the kitchen staff to help you, I do not care. No longer than a half hour.'

'Mama!' wailed Susan. 'What about Hubert? Should you not visit him?'

'*At Bow Street?* Are you *mad?*' she grasped her daughter's elbow and moved her forward, both wailing as they went.

Chapter 16

The Submission

There was a slight deviation from Grant's plan of a return to his old life.

On the night of the arrest, he had left Ursilla's chamber, shaken, and tried to persuade himself that her gratitude, when she had kissed his hand as she stirred, was that of a sister and no more.

But next morning he was in his room, and the door knocked. Since his man was with him and Baker never knocked, he was perplexed, but he put a loose robe over his shirt and buckskins while Trump, his valet, opened the door.

'Your mama,' called a bright voice from the doorway, 'bids you come down for breakfast, my lord.' Ursilla sounded far too lively for one who had faced down her demon last night, and he wondered if she were showing him she was quite well after her ordeal.

'I breakfast in my room, Miss Duvall,' he answered in a cold tone.

'Ursilla!' exclaimed the bright voice, 'We are *family* are we not? *Please* come down, Edmond! Your mother said that you frequently did so before my arrival, and I feel guilty that she is spared your company on my account.'

He was sure his mother would have volunteered no such thing.

'Very well,' he said, to be rid of her.

He came down, treasuring the words of distance she had offered. *We are family are we not?* Yes, she was telling him her actions of last night had been the gratitude of a sister.

But when he came down to the table, his mother and she smiled up at him. Ursilla was wearing a primrose dress with a fawn stripe, and had a heart charm on a ribbon tied at her wrist. Her hair framed the face again, though it was only dressed in a simple coil at the back, but the spread of her smile as he crossed the threshold held him back. He tried to look bored.

'You requested me, Mama, and here I am!'

'Ursilla has just told me the news! How *did* you manage it, Edmond? You *must* tell us!'

'*I* did not manage it; I was simply *told* of it. I just asked a friend why Cole was blackballed from our club, and I was told that young Mr Benedict Fenton had witnessed an assault on a tavern wench and the club stewards were somehow informed of it. The Fentons, Wilbert Fenton and his nephew Benedict that is, took it over from there. They thought an ex-Runner friend of theirs might be interested, and so it proved.' The baron's tone was off hand, but the ladies looked at him with admiration, nevertheless.

'*And?*' his mother prompted. Grant looked at her significantly.

'Oh, do not ask him, Lady Grant, he had *nothing* to do with it whatsoever!' It was Ursilla's voice, but light and laughing, and she looked naughtily at him. 'He will not be thanked, I know!'

'But now that Ursilla's fears are relieved you will begin to dine with us again, Edmond,' said his mother, 'It has been so *boring* without you, my dear.'

'My lady!' said Ursilla, in a teasing tone of shock.

'You know what I mean to say, dear girl. Edmond tells me gentlemen's gossip, you know, which I would never hear about else.'

'Gentlemen do not gossip,' said Ursilla in a grave tone that Grant suspected was a mimic of his own.

His mother evidently thought so too, for she giggled. 'But you will come, Edmond?' she said.

'If I am not engaged,' he conceded.

And so, breakfast and dinner together became his norm once more, and then Ursilla asked him to show her how to drive a team, because Genevieve was from Town, and so they tooled around the park together. People began to ask about his pretty little relative, and hardly anyone mentioned the scar. Lady Aurora's magic held. The hair said *here it is*, but also said, *and aren't I stylish?* at the same time.

He was glad of the beginning of her social ease, but was uncomfortable to be always by her, since he thought that she had been more relaxed on their drives than he. Those people who remarked on her to him included, he noted, some eligible friends of his. He did not know why, but he found their interest insinuating. For many were less interested in *why* Grant was driving her, than in where they might meet Miss Duvall again. Townsend, in particular, who had also been a close friend in the regiment, was delighted to think of meeting John

Duvall's sister, and such a charming young thing. On hearing that she resided with Grant's mother, he said he intended to call on her. Grant explained that this was not quite convenient at the moment for his mother, but that he would give his old friend the nod when it was.

Townsend had raised a suspicious eyebrow.

The night before her brave summoning of Edmond to breakfast, Ursilla, who had awoken suddenly, and had asked Sadie to tell her *everything* about the baron's night-time visits. Sadie had tried to turn the tables to discuss what might happen to Hubert Cole, but her mistress was strangely less interested in Cole's incarceration than Edmond's visits. The maid was a little reluctant, and issued many vague phrases, but finally told her all.

Ursilla had hunched her knees up and thought, once Sadie lay down to sleep. Grant had visited her. The reason he did not want her to know, she guessed. It was, she saw, too easy for a young girl to become attached to her hero, and she was not the sort of sophisticated lady that he seemed to be attracted to again and again.

As for her, she knew she had been attracted to him from the first. His avoidance of her had led her to sneak looks at him. She had noted his walk, always a stride, full of power and purpose, she had listened in on his conversations with the servants when in the hall, patrician, but never rude or bullying, like her father or Hubert Cole. He exchanged an occasional dry jest with the butler, and once asked after a footman's mother.

In the past she had been distracted from her lady friends whenever she heard his arrival in the hall. And there had been, in words and looks between his mother and sister, some recognition of her interest, and some smiling encouragement.

She could never have him, perhaps, but she could attempt to restore him to his family by making it less awkward for him to be in her company at home.

Lady Aurora had said something quietly to her in the coffee house on that day when they had all met up. 'Lord Grant has been energetic in his work to protect you, my dear.'

'He has offered me a home and I am amazingly grateful.'

'Of course you are!'

'But I feel I make it awkward for him at home. He does not wish to talk to me, I do not interest him. It must be a trial to have another lady reside with him.'

'If you do not interest him, why does he constantly steal glances at you?'

'Oh, he does not!'

'Oh yes he does, as you do to him.'

'It is only that I seldom see him and I ...'

'Of course. You know, Ursilla, very often gentlemen are not aware of what they feel at all.'

Mr Wilbert Fenton, overhearing, lent forward to say, in a voice not discernible to the others, 'I myself mistook my emotions for my adorable one for *years* until she showed me the way.'

Ursilla giggled.

'And while I was not aware of my own emotions, I am known for noting the state of others.' He had looked at the blushing girl. 'Grant has done a great deal for you that he will never tell you, my dear. Indeed, since you arrived in his house his attention, whatever he would have you believe, has been on little else. But while these are the acts of a protector and a gentleman, he is too *emotional* about this business. He is normally a cool head, like me, but no longer.' Mr Fenton had raised his brows, smiling sardonically, 'I wonder why?'

And so, Ursilla thought, hugging her knees, *he has done so much for me. I must do something for him.* Sadie, looking over from her bed, thought that Miss looked a little naughty sometimes these days.

And the next morning she had started by inviting him to breakfast, using the low trick of guilt.

In the next days, trembling at her own daring, she played many low tricks. She had noticed that when, over breakfast, she made a request that the baron coldly denied, she only had to look at him with puppy-dog sadness for him to reconsider, in an incensed voice.

She began to think that she was *more* than annoying to him, as when a gentleman, whom they had met in the park when he was giving her driving lessons, had called upon her. Grant had fumed all the way through his visit, though this was Mr Townsend, a friend of her brother John, and of Grant himself. She was rather afraid to think what this behaviour might imply.

When his mother invited Grant to comment on Ursilla's new gown, or her attempts on the pianoforte, he sometimes blushed, even though his words were dismissive. On one of their rides, Ursilla had grasped his hands, insisting on taking the reins, and she had laughed at his jerked reaction. 'I shall not bite you!' she had said.

Was she flirting? He evidently thought so, for he said admonishingly. 'Really? I find you bite these days a great deal.' They had exchanged a look, and it was some acknowledgement of the game she had begun, and she hung her head in shame. 'Head up!' he'd said, 'the patrons of the park will think I am being cruel to a young lady.'

She had looked up and held his eye in challenge, 'Sometimes you *are* cruel.'

'Is that so?'

'Do not try so hard, my lord,' she had smiled a wise smile, 'I will try my best *not* to like you *very* much.'

'Another bite!' he said, below his breath.

Ursilla attended the play and the Opera. In the opera box, she had sat at the front with the two Mrs Fentons and his mother. He saw the wisdom of his mother's positioning, for as neighbours looked towards his box, they saw a happy young woman, laughing with her friends before the performance commenced. His mother had then asked Ursilla to cede her position to Dulce, and he had found himself seated beside the girl, and so aware of her that he wished to move. But then her shoulder had brushed his, and he looked at her, and realised she was venturing again, embarrassed and naughty both. Well, he had always admired confident women, and she was recovering her lost confidence. But he found that the bravery it required for her to press him, and the shyness she exuded in doing so, moved him a great deal. She left him room, always, to escape.

It was only his fear of their strange beginning that made him pull away.

Ursilla slowly embraced the Town's best offerings. She went to musical evenings, and visited collections of art, had tea at Gunther's, walked and drove in the park with her new family or friends, and ended by agreeing to go to a ball, if no one would require her to dance.

But Dulce, who was present at this conversation, would not hear of it and set footmen to move chairs around the room, and insisted that Edmund, who had just ventured into the room, practise with Ursilla to prove that she still remembered her steps, and could now perform them. As Ursilla was left, blushingly abandoned in the middle of the countess's makeshift ballroom, and his mother sat to play, it seemed that he would be churlish and unbrotherly to avoid it.

They performed the minuet together, and if her steps were not all grace, it was because she was rusty, and confoundedly embarrassed at his touch, not because of a discernible injury.

Southey was announced at this time for a less frequent visit to his patient, and remarked to the countess as he watched Ursilla dance, 'It is a miracle!'

'*You* managed it, dear sir, how often Ursilla praises you as her saviour.'

'The miracle belongs to all of you. She had landed with the kindest of families.'

The countess smiled warmly. 'But she truly is a darling!' She said behind her hand, 'You know him, Dr Southey, do you think Edmond realises it?'

Looking at Edmond's stern face, and his chiding words to the lady, he said, 'I think Edmond is trying very hard not to know it.'

'Mother has that in hand!' Dulce confided to him with a mischievous smile.

As though by magic, Lady Grant cried at this moment, 'Now the waltz, Edmond!' Southey grinned at the countess.

Edmond looked desperately around, spotting his friend, 'Southey waltzes better than I,' he protested. 'Ursilla is better off with him.'

Reading the messages in the baroness and countess's eyes, Southey said, 'I'd be charmed, but I sprained an ankle yesterday, and I cannot.'

Grant gave him a dark look and turned to Ursilla.

She bent forward and whispered to him, blushing, 'If you'd rather not, I'll plead fatigue.'

'It makes no odds to me!' he said casually, and turned to take her hand for the start of the dance. But this dance did not go well for either of them. His male closeness made her stumble and that made him hold her waist longer than the dance required. She shook but pulled herself together and away. The music continued, they danced again, she casting down her eyes. Then when they must, as in the minuet, raise their hands and look into each other's eyes, Ursilla trembled, and began to pull away, her eyes filling with tears suddenly.

But by this time Grant, too, was trembling, and he pulled her to him violently, '*Oh Ursilla!*' he said, 'Oh, my *darling* girl, don't cry!'

His sister and Southey gasped; his mother stopped playing; footmen left the room. None of it did Edmond Grant see. He only saw her lovely eyes swimming in the tears she had tried to hold back.

'Edmond!' she said looking back at him finally.

'Don't pretend you did not know! *You* knew before I did, and you have played me like a lute with your smiles and your breakfasts and your looking prettier every day. It was not fair on me.'

'Not fair at all,' she agreed, but laughing a little.

And then he kissed her. The kiss was such that it caused his mother to tidy her music noisily and his sister to take a rapt interest in Dr Southey's blue superfine coat. When Edmond backed his little prisoner towards a sofa, Southey thought his friend in the grip of insanity, and he coughed once, twice, thrice.

'Southey,' said Grant straightening up and pulling Ursilla to stand by him. 'You here?' the baron said, though he had previously addressed him. But Grant was obviously not himself.

'Yes, my lord. And I am glad you have *rejoined* the company,' he added with an ironic eye.

Grant coughed. 'Mama, Dulce, Southey, I have to announce my engagement to Miss Ursilla Duvall.'

'Oh!' said Ursilla.

He looked down at her, 'That is alright my love?' he asked, then his eyes snagged onto her lips once more.

'Oh, I should th-think so,' obviously no more sensible than he.

He looked down again at this. And those dancing eyes that he had seen years ago in her family home, looked back at him.

'Should you not approach the viscount, as head of her family?' asked Lady Grant, in a bid to have things settled.

'I shall *inform* his lordship, no more,' said Grant haughtily.

Dulce raised her head, looking every inch a countess suddenly. 'If he even deserves *that* courtesy.'

Then the ladies rushed forward and claimed Grant's prize. Just as well, thought Southey, noting his friend's drugged gaze as he looked at his love.

'Oh, my dearest Ursilla!' 'My own daughter now!' were the most heard of many words.

Grant, ousted, strolled over to Southey.

'I thought it might end this way,' the physician said.

'Because knights rescue maidens?'

'No. Because she is such a brave, funny and thoroughly nice girl.' His friend replied.

'I was avoiding knowing so, and only spied on her at night.'

'Sadie told me.'

'She *would*!'

Sadie burst in, carrying sewing she had been completing in the other room. 'Oh miss, I just heard from William!'

'Sadie!' said Ursilla, throwing open her arms into which the maid ran full tilt, thrusting the sewing onto Grant as she passed.

Grant looked down at the fabric he was now holding, pierced with a needle, 'What *can* I do with her?'

'She wants to marry William.' Southey said.

'There are no married servants *here*.'

'It would keep her out of your hair for a few hours at a time.'

'I'll think about it,' sighed Grant.

'Oh,' his betrothed was saying, 'I must tell Genevieve, and Lady Aurora, and the two Mr Fentons, too!'

'Might we at least go for a walk in the park before you do so?' interjected her betrothed, moving towards her.

'No!' protested his mother. 'You will give your status away by the way you are looking at each other, before we have even informed our closest friends.'

Ursilla, who had come to take his hand again, said, 'Oh, that is quite true! We must go *today*.'

Grant looked rebellious, like a child.

'Put in your bottom lip, Edmond. Walk around the garden, if you must have her to yourself.' But his mother's chiding was full of joy.

'I will!' he said and pulled Ursilla to the garden doors.

'Can we go to Genevieve's later?' asked Ursilla, once they had moved to the garden, Sadie having run for her cashmere shawl and delivered it with a grin.

Edmond took his love's face in his hands. 'I want to keep this just to the *family* today, my love. I am surprised at myself. I have done such a good job of pretending, even to myself, that I do not love you ... or only as a sister ... that I am adjusting to my happiness now.'

'Are you *sure* Edmond?' she said, anxiously looking at him. 'Have I thrust myself at you too much?

'Was I right in my suspicions? Did you *mean* to do it?'

'I did. I gave you room to back away, but I was so happy after that night you came to my room, and then, I had felt your heart beating so hard when I lay on your chest in the carriage...!'

'That is normal when a male is near a female.'

'Oh, I thought it was like me ...,' she said, disappointed, 'that it might be ... love. And so, I wanted you to know me ...*awake,* you know ... because I hoped you might like me.' She looked up at him hesitantly. 'And then, after you were gone, I started to remember the voice in my dreams, the calm, loving voice, and I knew it was *you*, and that you must have come so many times.'

'Well, I did. I was worried, but I did not then wish to befriend you.'

'I can guess why. In case I became attached to you. But you became such a figure of interest to me precisely because I did *not* see you.'

'And I could only see *you* at night.'

'You had an unfair advantage on me. And yet, you still put distance between us.'

'I was afraid that you might become attached in a way that might hurt you. I know myself, and you are not at all the sort of woman I normally spend time with.'

'Dulce and your mama have told me so, and even pointed your chosen ones out to me. They are all taller and more beautiful than I. And all look very confident, sophisticated and intelligent.'

'Yes. Rather like Mama and Dulce, in fact. But though I liked them, and felt easy in their company, somehow, I could go no further.' He touched her cheek. 'But you are more beautiful than them *all,* you know.

'You do not have to say so,' her hand going to her scar.

'I do not. But I do, because it is true. Do you know how many fellows who have seen you in the Opera box or in the park who ask after you? I can guarantee that your first ball would have been replete with partners. But now *I* may dance with you all night long.'

'If I could just be sure that it is not pity ...!'

'It is not pity, Ursilla. It is true, I know that it must be *me* who saves you from all suffering from this day on, but I could have done *that* as your brother. But since we sit together at the opera and tremble to be near each other, and since my hand is scorched when you take it to dismount the carriage...!'

She blushed. 'I realised you seldom let it go at once.' She smiled that naughty smile that showed him her return from the darkness.

'I *never* want to let it go,' he said kissing it. 'I avoided you, but I would hear you laugh, even from my study, and it would bring me such joy.'

'Even when your face is grim, your eyes *burned* at me, and it gave me hope.'

'The grim face was trying to contain the emotions that had to be *certain* that I would be good enough to you. You, of all people deserve full devotion. You have suffered enough.'

'You have *always* been good to me.'

'I ignored and avoided you.'

'So that a poor girl would not fall in love with her knight. I understood that.' She laughed. 'But *you* gave me Sadie.'

'And have lived to regret it,' he said, sounding more like his sardonic self.

'You like her. And that is good. For maid or not, she will always be my dearest friend.'

'I see why. She has been totally devoted.' He gave a half smile. 'But *did* you? Fall in love with your knight, I mean?'

'I did. But it took dedication, for you gave me no encouragement.'

'Clever girl. But I think I longed for you very early on.'

'Not with a limp and a scar and a mouth that could not speak!' she said dismissively,

'I think so,' he admitted.

'Goodness!'

'Yes, *goodness*, you had it in great quantities. You were as brave as John when you rescued Cole, you were kind to street traders and beggars, you smiled amidst your pain. I began to think John *bequeathed* you to me. Or it was fate. I have no words to describe what you have come to mean to me. All those nights, when I could look at you without disguise, when I touched your hand to comfort you, *I* was the one comforted. You became my obsession, as you were Hubert Cole's.

'Obsession?'

Grant gave her an edited version of Southey's theory of Cole's obsession.

Ursilla nodded. 'It makes sense. He is very proud. Had I met him at a ball as John's sister, perhaps he might have pursued me openly, as being worthy of him. I always felt his attention was … you know.' Her gaze faltered when she said so, and Edmond held her hand. 'But I had fallen in life, and he could not have borne to admire such a person any longer. He was obsessed with status, yet he could not bring himself to marry the earl's daughter whom he danced with twice. She is not, according to Susan at least, well-favoured. And, *'Lady Maude would not have you in her house,'* he told me once, for he must have mentioned his poor relation to her. It was as though he planned to take me *even to his marital home*. I wanted him to marry her, that woman who would not have me, and live elsewhere. Or I would have, if I had been in my right mind. As it was, I tried *not* to think in those days, for it never did me any good.'

'There was nothing you could do.' But he paused, 'Did you write to your aunt?'

'I did.'

'I suspect your mail to have been intercepted.'

'Perhaps. He controlled everything else.'

'It is all over now, my love,' he said, pulling her even nearer.

She pulled away to look at him honestly. 'I have played with your feelings these last days, Edmond. But I thought, perhaps, that you wanted me.'

'I did. It is only that the feelings I have for *you* are unprecedented for me. I hope I was never *cruel* to women, but they existed for the pleasure I could *receive*, not what I might *give*. And so, when I felt very differently for you, so protective and possessive, I thought it might be pity indeed.'

'But it is not?'

He held her close. 'I do not pity your naughtiness, or your prettiness, or your kindness or your enthusiasms. They are all part of you, and those I love. But there was something there from the start that knitted me to you, even as I watched you in the street as you visited your lawyer ... and that belongs to God, not to me.'

'Yes, I know! Even when we did not speak, or I hardly saw you, I felt it. A connection.'

'You are *for* me ... and very different from what I *thought* I wanted. Someone to love, not just be loved by.'

'But I do love you, so very, very much. I *felt* your goodness, even when you tried to hide all you did for me. I was afraid of men, but very soon, not of you.'

'Shall we visit John's grave together and tell him?'

'Oh yes! My darling, let us do so.'

'We will!' he smiled at her, but then his dry voice returned, 'You bring out the sentimentalist in me.'

'I shall show you what John wrote about you, if I can get my letters from their hiding place at the Cole house. John knew you had the deepest heart of them all behind your stone exterior.'

But Grant was looking at her lips and hardly listening. 'You are mine now,' he informed her.

'You sound quite fierce!'

'Well, there are other fellows who have seen you now, and it worries me.'

'You, too, are mine, Edmond. Do not think of tall, sophisticated young ladies anymore.'

He laughed and hugged her, and his mother and Dulce, overlooking from a window, exchanged a contented look.

'Do you think,' said Lady Grant guiltily, 'that the untold damage that man did her ... might she not be able to have children?'

Dulce said, looking at her happy brother, 'I do not think it matters in the least.'

'Not matter?' said Lady Grant, appalled.

'Mama, Edmond would *never* have married any of those sophisticated beauties he professed to admire.'

'No,' her mama agreed, thinking of it. 'But *why not?*'

'Because they were not Ursilla,' said Dulce, sagely.

Her son, in the garden with the baroness's dear girl, picked her up and twirled her around. 'No. You are right, Dulce dear. They were not our dearest Ursilla!'

Chapter 17

Dinner with Friends

The next day Ursilla went early to the Fenton home, Sumner House. She found Genevieve trying to catch a little boy whose preserve-stained fingers was destroying upholstery as he went. Genevieve backed him into a trap and a nursemaid caught him and lifted him aloft. 'Now My Lord, enough of that!' said the maid.

Benedict entered and swung the boy out of the nurse's arms and on to his shoulders.

'Papa, papa!' he cried. 'Run, run!'

Benedict did so and Genevieve sighed. 'He has smeared strawberry preserve all *over* your hair. Burke will be furious,' she said, referring to her husband's valet.

'It will not hurt!' laughed Benedict.

'If you do not obey next time, Oswald, I shall not let you ride your pony for a week,' said the stern mama.

The child began to cry.

'Don't worry old chap, you may ride Papa instead.'

'Giddy-up!' said the little fellow, kicking his legs.

Father and son left together.

'Ursilla, you visit alone?'

'You had to be the first to know, Genevieve!' said Ursilla, bubbling with excitement. 'You will *never* guess.'

Genevieve Fenton looked at the shining face and pretended ignorance. 'Be seated and tell me all!' she said.

That evening the two Fenton families changed their plans and had dinner at the Grant house.

'To think,' murmured Wilbert Fenton to Lady Aurora, 'that once she could not speak.'

'She will make up for her betrothed's taciturnity, certainly!' laughed her ladyship in return. 'But only see how proud he looks behind it all.'

'Can you afford her a team, Grant?' inquired Genevieve Fenton briskly. 'I saw a comfortably matched foursome the other day that I think Ursilla could learn on before she attempts your bays!'

'You shouldn't speak of money, Jenny,' laughed her husband, teasing. 'You might make the baron blush!'

'Pshaw!' said Genevieve.

'I daresay I could manage it,' said Grant. 'But do you really want to Ursilla?'

'If Genevieve says I should.'

'You are small, and four horses require...'

'Good hands! Do not scare her, Grant. Ursilla will do well!'

'My brother is cowed!' said the countess, laughing.

'Well,' said the bluff Drakemire heartily, 'she knows, ye know!'

'I have lived a retired life,' confessed Ursilla, quietly, looking around the table at her family and friends. 'And so I must learn and take advice. In the matter of elegance of dress I shall consult the females of my family and dear Lady Aurora, on all matters of manners and fashionable decorum I shall consult Mr Fenton, on skills of friendliness, I shall look to Benedict, and for all things horse related, I shall listen to none other but my dear Genevieve.'

Grant uttered a protest at this, but Ursilla continued, 'on all emotional matters I shall consult ....' Grant gave her an open, loving look at this, '....Sadie.' Grant's face fell.

'Is there *anything* my son is worthy of giving you hints upon?' laughed the baroness, looking at Grant's face.

Ursilla wrinkled her nose. 'I cannot *think* of anything at present...!' she replied, sneaking a look at her betrothed.

Grant, grave-faced, leant towards her and whispered something in her ear. '*Edmond!*' she squealed, pulling back, blushing.

'A toast!' said the Earl of Drakemire standing his solid bulk upright and raising his glass. 'To the tiniest bear, who was able to capture the most arrogant,' his wife nudged him, 'but *best* man in all of England!' They drank, with some shouts of 'here here!' 'When I think,' said the earl, mopping tears from his eyes, 'what that little lady had put up with...'

'Drakemire!' admonished Dulce, faintly, but her husband went on.

'... I only hope that however little you smile at one Edmond, you make the kindest husband to her, for she deserves it!'

'I know it!' said Grant, moved. 'You few all know something of what my darling has been through. But now that the villain is behind bars, we have resolved to lay it to rest. Drakemire is a sentimental old fool, but what he says is essentially correct. I want to thank you all for helping me pay back Cole and also for helping Ursilla. But I, who do not usually wish to talk of myself, feel that I should disclose something. I did not betroth myself to help a broken angel. As well as brave and lovely, my lady is also a naughty minx who needs schooled by a character as strong as mine....'

'Edmond!' protested Ursilla looking at him with puppy dog eyes.

He looked down, 'Do not...!' he protested.

'Sit down, Edmond,' said Wilbert Fenton cynically, 'for you are a defeated man.'

'Yes, my son. Just a look from Ursilla and you are conquered.'

'As it *should* be!' said Lady Aurora.

'Nonsense,' said the baron, to right himself. 'I am known to be a stern individual.'

Sadie, who had arrived with a shawl for Ursilla, said derisively, 'Stern? *You*, my lord? When your eyes went all mushy as you looked at her suffering them nightmares.'

'*Did* they, Sadie?' said Lady Aurora, Sadie's friend.

'Oh, yes, me lady. He used to come into her bedchamber—'

'*I say*!' said Benedict disapprovingly, enjoying himself.

'...and tap her fist and talk rubbish to her for ages at a time, my lady, wif a tear in his eyes sometimes.'

Ursilla touched her maid's hand on her shoulder and giggled.

'Yes, yes, you dratted girl! Get off with you!' said Grant.

'Yes, me lord. I weren't a teasin' you, me lord. It's only because you is a kind gentleman, says I. The roughest skinned turnip's got the sweetest pulp, says me ma.' She bobbed a curtsy and went off, but no one was surprised as she piped up again. 'Lady Aurora, I got trouble with these sleeves...'

'I am busy in the morning, Sadie. Perhaps I might come and look at them in the afternoon.'

'Well, if'n it was the morning, I could get them finished for tomorrow night, your ladyship...!' said Sadie hopefully.

The butler pushed her from the room forcibly.

'We truly must deal with that girl!' sighed the baroness.

Ursilla giggled. 'I have just had a thought. Once we marry, Edmond, Sadie will outrank all those servants who disapprove of her, saving Baker.'

'*Must* you have her?' sighed Grant.

'I must!' replied Ursilla, firmly. 'Always.'

'Oh well, my future baroness!' sighed Grant, kissing her cheek. 'I suppose.'

'*I* shall be a *dowager!*' shrieked the baroness, suddenly seeing it when her son had named his betrothed in jest.

'Oh Mama, but a *splendid* one!' said Dulce, appeasing.

'Oh, yes,' said Lady Aurora, 'and you can save the poor young girls at Almacks who are bullied by those dowagers of carping habits.'

'By disparaging those dowagers myself! Yes! I have scores to settle.'

'But tonight, I think, we need a simple toast to happiness,' said Mr Wilbert Fenton.

They raised their glasses, all, and regarded the happy smiles of the betrothed couple, Ursilla beaming with delight, and a warm fire in Grant's eyes as he looked at her.

'To happiness!' they cried, looking at its embodiment before them, in the glowing lovers aura.

Later, when the baron walked Ursilla to the foot of the stairs, he said to her, taking both hands in his. 'Let us marry with all possible haste, my darling girl!'

'You are so anxious to wed, Edmond?' she said laughing up at him.

'I confess that since the first time I held you in my arms, they feel empty when you are not in them. I can barely sleep at night.'

'You are lonely for me?'

That was not precisely how he would describe it, but Grant nodded, his harsh face full of something that pulled her towards him and into his arms again. 'Then *soon*, sweetheart.'

Sadie watching this from above, and seeing how the comforting embrace turned into a crushing kiss, the baron's hungry mouth almost consuming his weak-kneed betrothed, moved to the top of the stairs and placed her hands on her hips.

'Here! Miss!' she called, and the butler, who had being trying to remain invisible in the hall, blanched at this rudeness. 'Best come upstairs now, Miss, I just warmed the bed.' The baron looked up at her threateningly. Sadie's gaze in response was just as threatening as his.

Sadie's evident thoughts corresponded so much to Baker's opinions on the matter that he temporarily forgave the little maid's impudence. Lord Grant had never been in love before, the butler reckoned, and he was having a hard time behavin' himself. Best get the young Miss married as soon as possible. The baron, Baker knew, was like honey for all those females out there. It was a strong power to have, but his master hadn't taken much notice of it, just went about his day, unless he took a mild fancy to a woman for a while. But it was as if he now knew its purpose, that honey-power he possessed. The man sent looks to Miss at the dinner table that would make any legs go weak, he touched her hand with a light gesture that made the poor little Miss's face fire up. Playing tricks by word and deed. Thank God for Sadie. But he would alert all the household of the necessity of interruption. Lord Grant was not, at present, rational. It was their job to keep him respectful at least. But no one who had seen that first kiss, backing an innocent maiden towards a sofa, could have any doubt that the man lost control near that sweet young girl. Baker and the staff would ensure the proprieties. In the house at least. In the open air, Sadie must do her best alone.

'Yes, Sadie, dear!' Miss Duvall was answering the maid.

The incendiary look the master gave Miss Duvall's back, confirmed the butler's worst fears. If the baroness sought to delay the ceremony for her love of pomp, Baker would drop a word off in her ear. His master had long ceased to view Miss Duvall only as one to be protected. Now she had become his prey.

Grant's prey skipped upstairs to Sadie happily, infused with her own mind-shattering response to his arms. She would joyfully await being caught again tomorrow.

She thought suddenly of the broken body and spirit that had first mounted this staircase to the bedchamber, and that girl seemed very far from her, a thing of the past. She could hardly believe the difference. She was loved and cared for by everyone within these walls, she felt. Maybe that special care was a gift of the pity they had felt for the broken Ursilla Duvall, but it continued even more now. She was loved, and turning her head, she looked down at the man whose dark eyes almost consumed her, even from this distance. Oh yes, she was loved, and she loved so, so, deeply in return. She gave him a teasing smile and took Sadie's hand, so happy she could hardly bear it.

A gentleman growled like an animal.

Hearing this, the Butler wondered if a Special License was out of the question.

CHAPTER 18

Epilogue

'Lady Cole!' called a voice in the park, hailing a carriage.

Ursilla, Baroness Grant, dropped the ball she had been about to throw at Freddy, her youngest son, a stout two year old. Her husband, with little Marjorie held aloft in his arms, came to her, setting down the child gently and nodding the nursemaid to her duties. 'Darling!' he said, concerned.

They both looked over at the landau, which held two adults on the box, and three children in the rear, the gentleman driving himself, apparently. Grant took the shocked Ursilla's hand through his arm and walked forward. The lady who had hailed the carriage was moving off, having finished her chatter, and the stoutish gentleman at the reins prepared to go on, when the baron cried, 'Cole!'

Ursilla could hardly move the steps toward them, but Grant pulled her along.

'Sir Neil, I should present my wife, for I do not think you have met her, Miss Duvall she was, now Baroness Grant.'

Ursilla was in a dream as the watery eyes looked down at her sympathetically. 'Honoured, Your Ladyship!'

She held up her hand and bobbed a curtsy, in a more childish manner than was usual for her, her fear retreating somewhat at the sight of the big open face so unlike his son's. But of course, that man was not really the baronet's son, as Edmond had explained to her.

'My wife was rather startled to hear the name called out, I am afraid.'

'Oh, thought it was the old harpy, eh?' said Cole. 'No, no, she's dead these many years. Died six months after she left London for the country that year.' He looked to his side, 'this is now my Lady Cole, my dear wife.'

A pleasant woman in her late thirties smiled down at Ursilla in a sensitive fashion, seeming to see and understand her confusion. 'You do not care for the Cole name, I imagine, my dear, so much as you have suffered.'

Ursilla could not even manage an answer.

'Well, well,' said the baronet in a bluff but slightly apologetic manner, 'do not fear to see us too much in Town, Your Ladyship, for we are not much received. But we come to London anyhow, for we have still have some good friends here and we see the play and such, ye know.'

Ursilla nodded, still dumb. As Lady Cole expressed in a sincere tone how nice it was to have met her, and as Sir Neil picked up the reins to go, Ursilla managed to say, 'And Miss Cole?'

'Susan you mean?' said the baronet in his open fashion, 'ah, she lives in our Dower House these days. I thought I should take her in with us after the old witch died, but she is dashed unpleasant to my wife and children. She is not much liked in the area, I'm afraid, not received even as my wife is. But then my Jenny lady, who knows how to get on with people. There seems no saving Susan. She is arrogant and bitter still.'

'She too, was cruel to you?' asked Lady Cole, anxiously.

'She was, my lady.' Ursilla said, surprised to hear herself admit it. She looked to the back seats of the landau, to the happy children chattering among themselves. 'Do not leave your innocent children alone with her. Her voice does great violence.'

'Oh, I know it, Lady Grant!'

The baronet looked to Grant. 'That's my eldest boy there. Silly thing is, I had to adopt him. In case my lady should fall with another boy, ye know.'

'Ah, the legitimate younger would be your heir, of course.'

'It is better that we do it properly, says the lawyer.'

'Mmm!'

'I think that you have a better heir this time, sir. And you are the nicest Lady Cole I have ever met,' Ursilla smiled at the baronet's wife.

'I am so pleased to have met you, Lady Grant,' that lady replied.

'I too, dear lady,' said the baronet.

With final goodbyes, Sir Neil drove off.

'That was rather a deeper conversation than is usual after hailing a carriage in the park.' remarked Grant. 'Darling, you are still shaking. Should I not have approached them?'

'No, I always wondered how the females of that family fared. It seemed they had escaped their misdeeds, but apparently not,' she held his arm tighter and smiled up at him.. 'It is another nail in the coffin of my fear.'

'Yes, I thought so. You are always so brave.'

'Look out!' screamed Sadie's voice. But after a look, neither of the Grants were worried. Sadie, who favoured their children greatly, was apt to be critical of their nursemaid, a female who wished to establish her authority as their carer. But the children and Sadie disagreed. It was Sadie who had the final word. She grabbed at brave four-year-old Marjorie's feet to stop her attempt at tree climbing, and took her in her arms. She walked towards the Grants with child in hand.

'Bring Miss Marjorie back,' called the nurse.

Sadie shrugged, sniffing as she grinned at the baroness. 'She's nothing more than the children's laundry maid, my lady, what's she shouting at me for?'

'But Sadie,' said Grant, with his habitual sigh when talking to the impish maid, 'we have employed her as more than that. And you should not hoist the babe in your own delicate condition.'

'Well, but Miss Marjorie does naught but cry if that bunch o bones tries to lift her, and Master Freddy cannot stand her.'

'Well, we do have you, Sadie. But you cannot do everything. Nurse is help for you.'

'The children is no trouble, My Lady. I must tell the Dowager Baroness my latest idea to improve the household, such as telling Lady Muck over there what her duties are confined to.'

The nursemaid looked after Sadie resentfully. She had only been employed with the Grants a few months ago, had never been in such a household. All was run regularly by Mr Baker, the butler, but that there was a married lady's maid and footman in the house, and that the maid, moreover, seemed to be shut up with Lady Grant and Lady Aurora Fenton each week to draw designs for a lady's dressmakers that

Mary, an upstairs chambermaid said was *owned by Sadie* shocked the nurse. And she was not cast off when in the pudding club, like what a normal maid would be. Mary said that you had to think of Sadie as, well, a *friend* to the young ladyship, and not offend her no how. 'A friend?' had scoffed the nursemaid, but it seemed so. Once the baron and baroness had *visited Sadie's home in the country*, and even had dinner there, Mary said, though they stayed at an inn in the village, while Sadie and William (the footman husband) slept at the farm. Sadie and Lady Grant both had taken all the care of Miss Marjorie and Master Frederick before Nurse's arrival, and Mary said that the nursemaid had just been employed because Sadie was to have a baby, and Lady Grant was worried that her maid had too much to do.

'So then, she just does as she pleases, that Sadie?'

'Well, no,' giggled Mary, 'Sadie don't give herself airs and is always respectful to Mr Baker and *appears* to do as she is bid ... but she has always been a cheeky one, and never properly schooled in service before she got the job as maid to Miss Duvall when she was poorly. And when Miss Duvall became the baroness, she stayed on, like.'

Despite all this, the nursemaid tried for dominance of the children so as to keep her place, but Mary had shaken her head at her, sadly. Sadie was Sadie. There was no explaining it if you hadn't lived through it like Mary had, and Nurse would be stupid to challenge her.

Now, since Sadie had joined the baron and baroness and spoken of the dowager, Grant and Ursilla exchanged grins. 'My mother will be *happy* to hear your plan, I'm sure, Sadie,' said Grant with all the sarcasm that still failed to register with his wife's maid.

Grant became aware that Ursilla was still trembling somewhat, and pulled her closer. 'Darling! All is well now.'

'Oh, I know! ' She smiled up at him and then gazed off at her children being marshalled by Sadie and the nursemaid. 'How did I become so happy? You know, sweetheart, sometimes I am even grateful to *him*, that murderous monster.'

Grant exclaimed.

'Because without him I should never have come to your house. I should not have been given the happiest life a woman could ever have!'

'Darling, my darling,' he breathed.

But Ursilla knew that look. Her husband was a dangerous scoundrel again. Even in public, he could still be overborne by his feelings, her cold-faced baron. She laughed and ran from him, going back to the closed carriage where it was safer.

'Sadie, see to the children,' she cried. 'The baron is called home urgently.'

Sadie laughed. Her William was often urgent hisself, she was glad to say. There went the best master and mistress in the world, she reckoned. Miss Marjorie kissed her, and Sadie tickled her and ran for Master Freddy.

Chapter 19

First Chapter of Honoria and the Family Obligation, The Fentons #1

Blue Slippers

'He has arrived!' said Serena, kneeling on the window seat of their bedchamber. She made a pretty picture there with her sprigged muslin dress foaming around her and one silk-stockinged foot still on the floor, but her sister Honoria was too frozen with fear to notice.

'Oh, no,' said Honoria, moving forward in a dull fashion to join her. Her elder brother Benedict had been sitting with one leg draped negligently over the arm of the only comfortable chair in the room and now rose languidly to join his younger sisters. After the season in London, Dickie had begun to ape the manners of Beau Brummel and his cronies, polite, but slightly bored with the world. At one and twenty, it seemed a trifle contrived, even allowing that his long limbs and handsome face put many a town beau to shame.

Serena's dark eyes danced wickedly, 'Here comes the conquest of your triumphant season, your soon-to-be-fiancé.'

Dickie grinned, rather more like their childhood companion, 'Your knight in shining armour. If *only* you could remember him.'

'It isn't funny.'

Serena laughed and turned back to the window as she heard the door of the carriage open and the steps let down by Timothy, the one and only footman that Fenton Manor could boast.

'Oh, how did it happen?' Honoria said for the fifteenth time that morning.

Someone in the crowd had said, 'Mr Allison is approaching. But he never dances!' In confusion, she had looked around, and saw the throng around her grow still and part as her hostess approached with a tall gentleman. With all eyes turned to her she stiffened in every sinew. She remembered the voice of Lady Carlisle introducing Mr Allison as a desirable partner, she remembered her mother thrusting her forward as she was frozen with timidity. She remembered his hand lead her to her first waltz of the season. She had turned to her mother for protection as his hand snaked around her waist and had seen that matron grip her hands together and glow with pride. This was Lady Fenton's shining moment, if not her daughter's. Word had it that Mr Allison had danced only thrice this season, each time with his married friends. Lost in the whirl of the dance, she had answered his remarks with single syllables, looking no higher than his chin. A dimpled chin, strong, she remembered vaguely. And though she had previously seen Mr. Allison at a distance, the very rich and therefore very interesting Mr Allison, with an estate grander than many a nobleman, she could not remember more than that he was held to be handsome. (As she told Serena this later, her sister remarked that rich men were very often held to be handsome, strangely related to the size of their purse.)

There was the waltz; there had been a visit to her father in the London house; her mother had informed her of Mr Allison's wishes and that she was to receive his addresses the next afternoon. He certainly visited the next afternoon, and Honoria had been suffered to serve him his tea and her hand had shaken so much that she had kept her eyes on the cup for the rest of the time. He had not proposed, which her mother thought of as a pity, but here she had been saved by Papa, who had thought that Mr Allison should visit them in the country where his daughter and he might be more at their leisure to know each other. 'For she is a little shy with new company and I should wish her perfectly comfortable before she receives your addresses,' Sir Ranalph had told him, as Honoria's mama had explained.

Serena, when told, had thought it a wonderful joke. To be practically engaged to someone you could not remember! She laughed because she trusted to good-natured Papa to save Honoria from the match if it should prove unwanted; her sister had only to say "no".

'Why on earth do you make such a tragedian of yourself, Orry,' had said Serena once Honoria had poured her story out, 'After poor Henrietta Madeley's sad marriage, Papa has always said that to marry with such parental compulsion is scandalously cruel.'

And Honoria had mopped up her tears and felt a good deal better, buoyed by Serena's strength of mind. To be sure, there was the embarrassment to be endured of giving disappointment, but she resolved to do it if Mr Allison's aura of grandeur continued to terrify her.

'And then,' her sister had continued merrily, 'the rich Mr Allison may just turn out to be as handsome as his purse and as good natured as Papa — and you will fall head over heels with him after all.'

The morning after, Honoria had gone for a walk before breakfast, in much better spirits. As she came up the steps to re-enter by the breakfast room, she carelessly caught her new French muslin (fifteen and sixpence the yard, Mama had told her) on the roses that grew on a column. If she took her time and did not pull, she may be able to rescue herself without damage to the dress. She could hear Mama and Papa chatting and gave it no mind until Mama's voice became serious.

'My dear Ranalph, will you not tell me?'

'Shall there be muffins this morning, my dear?' said Papa cheerfully.

'You did not finish your mutton last night and you are falsely cheerful this morning. Tell me, my love.'

'You should apply for a position at Bow Street, my dear. Nothing escapes you.' She heard the sound of an embrace.

'Diversionary tactics, sir, are futile.'

Honoria knew she should not be privy to this, but she was still detaching her dress, thorn by thorn. It was incumbent on her to make a noise, so that they might know she was there, but as she decided to do so, she was frozen by Papa's next words.

'Mr Allison's visit will resolve all, I'm sure.'

Honoria closed her mouth, automatically continuing to silently pluck her dress from the rose bush, anxious to be away.

'Resolve what, dearest?' Honoria could picture her mama on Papa's knee.

'Well, there have been extra expenses – from the Brighton property.' Honoria knew that this was where her uncle Wilbert lived, her father's younger brother. (Dickie had explained that he was a friend of the Prince Regent, which sounded so well to the girls, but Dickie had shaken his head loftily. 'You girls know nothing. Unless you are as rich as a Maharajah, it's ruinous to be part of that set.')

Her father continued, 'Now, now. All is well. If things do not take with Mr Allison, we shall just have to cut our cloth a little, Madame.' He breathed. 'But, Cynthia, I'm afraid another London Season is not to be thought of.'

Honoria felt instant guilt. Her own season had been at a rather later age than that of her more prosperous friends, and she had not been able to understand why Serena and she could not have had it together, for they borrowed each other's clothes all the time. Serena's intrepid spirit would have buoyed hers too and made her laugh, and would have surely helped with her crippling timidity. But when she had seen how many dresses had been required — one day alone she had changed from morning gown to carriage dress to luncheon half dress, then riding habit and finally evening dress. And with so many of the same people at balls, one could not make do - Mama had insisted on twenty evening gowns as the bare minimum. However doughty with a needle the sisters might be, this was beyond their scope, and London dressmakers did not come cheap. Two such wardrobes were not to be paid for by the estate's income in one year. Honoria had accidentally seen the milliner's bill for her season and shuddered to think of it — her bonnets alone had been ruinously expensive. She had looked forward to her second season, where *her wardrobe could be adapted at very little cost to give it a new look and Serena would also have her fill of new walking dresses and riding habits, bonnets and stockings. If she were in London with her sister, she might actually enjoy it.*

'Poor Serena. What are her chances of a suitable match in this restricted neighbourhood?' Mama continued, 'And indeed, Honoria, if she does not like this match. Though how she could fail to like a charming, handsome man like Mr Allison is beyond me,' she finished.

'Do not forget rich,' teased her husband.

'When I think of the girls who tried to catch him all season! And then he came to us – specifically asked to be presented to her as a partner for the waltz, as dear Lady Carlisle informed me later — but she showed no triumph at all. And now, she will not give an opinion. She is strangely reticent about the subject.'

'Well, well, it is no doubt her shyness. She will be more relaxed when she sees Allison among the family.'

'So much rests upon it.' There was a pause. 'Dickie's commission?'

He laughed, but it sounded sour from her always cheerful Papa. 'Wilbert has promised to buy it from his next win at Faro.'

'Hah!' said Mama bitterly.

Honoria was free. She went towards the breakfast room rather noisily. 'Are there muffins?' she asked gaily.

'How on earth do you come to be engaged to *him*?'

Honoria was jolted back to the present by Serena's outcry. She gazed in dread over her sister's dark curls and saw a sober figure in a black coat and dull breaches, with a wide-brimmed, antediluvian hat walking towards the house. She gave an involuntary giggle.

'Oh, that is only Mr Scribster, his friend.'

'*He* you remember!' laughed Serena. 'Is he as dull as his hat?' Honoria spotted another man exiting the chaise, this one in biscuit coloured breaches above shiny white-topped Hessian boots. His travelling coat almost swept the ground, and Serena said, 'Well, he's more the thing at any rate. Pity we cannot see his face. You should be prepared. However, he *walks* like a handsome man.' She giggled, 'Or at all events, a rich one.'

The door behind them had opened. 'Serena, you will guard your tongue,' said their mama. Lady Fenton, also known as Lady Cynthia (as she was the daughter of a peer) was the pattern card from which her beautiful daughters were formed. A dark-haired, plump, but stylish matron who looked as good as one could, she said of herself, when one had borne seven bouncing babies. Now she smiled, though, and Honoria felt another bar in her cage. How could she dash her mother's hopes? 'Straighten your dresses, girls, and come downstairs.'

Benedict winked and walked off with his parent.

There were no looking glasses in their bedroom, so as not to foster vanity. But as they straightened the ribbons of the new dresses Mama had thought appropriate to the occasion, they acted as each other's glass and pulled at hair ribbons and curls as need be. The Misses Fenton looked as close to twins as sisters separated by two years could, dark curls and dark slanted eyes and lips that curled at the corners to give them the appearance of a smile even in repose. Their brother Benedict said they resembled a couple of cats, but then he would say that. Serena had told him to watch his tongue or they might scratch.

The children, Norman, Edward, Cedric and Angelica, were not to be admitted to the drawing room — but they bowled out of the nursery to watch the sisters descend the stairs in state. As Serena tripped on a cricket ball, she looked back and stuck her tongue out at the grinning eight-year-old Cedric. Edward, ten, cuffed his younger brother and threw him into the nursery by the scruff of his neck. The eldest, Norman, twelve, a beefy chap, lifted little three-year-old Angelica who showed a disposition to follow her sisters. On the matter of unruly behaviour today, Mama had them all warned.

As the stairs turned on the landing, the sisters realised there was no one in the large square hall to see their dignified descent, so Serena tripped down excitedly, whilst her sister made the slow march of a hearse follower. As Serena gestured her down, Honoria knew that her sister's excitement came from a lack of society in their neighbourhood. She herself had enjoyed a London season, whilst Serena had never been further than Harrogate. She was down at last and they walked to the door of the salon, where she shot her hand out to delay Serena. She took a breath and squared her shoulders. Oh well, this time she should at least see what he looked like.

Two gentlemen stood by the fire with their backs to the door, conversing with Papa and Dickie. As the door opened, they turned and Honoria was focused on the square-shouldered gentleman, whose height rivalled Benedict's and quite dwarfed her sturdy papa. His face was nearly in view, Sir Ranalph was saying, 'These are my precious jewels!' The face was visible for only a moment before Serena gave a yelp of surprise and moved forward a pace. Honoria turned to her.

'But it's you!' Serena cried.

Everyone looked confused and a little shocked, not least Serena who grasped her hands in front of her and regarded the carpet. There seemed to be no doubt that she had addressed Mr Allison.

Honoria could see him now, the dimpled chin and strong jaw she remembered, and topped by a classical nose, deep set hazel eyes and the hairstyle of a Roman Emperor. Admirable, she supposed, but with a smile dying on his lips, he had turned from relaxed guest to stuffed animal, with only his eyes moving between one sister and another. His gaze fell, and he said the most peculiar thing.

'Blue slippers.'

To read on:
getbook.at/Honoria

Chapter 20

First Chapter of Georgette and the Unrequited Love, Sisters of Castle Fortune #1

Prologue

If you were to see all the Fortune sisters together in a line, you would be living in a fairy tale, for the girls, first because their mama was a trifle frail, and later because she was no longer with them, were too unruly ever to have been held in line for more than a second without some of them escaping to another room in the cavernous

URSILLA AND THE BARON'S REVENGE

Castle Fortune, or into the rivers and wilderness beyond.

For the benefit of this presentation, we will imagine them all kept in place to shake your hand. We shall capture them all in this day of 1813, and make it a sunny day. First will be Miss Fortune as was, the lovely and gentle Violetta, twenty-three, who must now disappear into the mist of Scotland to be with her husband. Loud and vibrant Cassie, twenty-two, is next, but her equally loud swain, Mr Hudson, has swept them off to Somerset, where the whole neighbourhood may hear their business from a mile away. Next there is Georgette, twenty-one, who is the principal subject of this tale. She has particularly large eyes, and has now become Miss Fortune in her turn, being the eldest unwed sister. Mary, twenty, her romantic and wilful sister, ran off with a Mr Fredericks, a music master, and they made their poor home in Bath. If Mr Fredericks hoped that marriage to the daughter of a Castle might increase his wealth, he was disabused of this notion after he met his father-in-law, Baron Fortune. Susan, eighteen, the plainest of the girls (which is to say not plain at all), married sober Mr Steeplethorpe, and seemed quietly content at her bargain.

So, our reception line now has only the unmarried Fortune ladies. Georgette now lives with the shame (her neighbours said) of having two younger siblings marry before her. Next is the sprite Jocasta, at seventeen not too like a fairy of the tales in behaviour, but who nevertheless entranced London this season with her wispy gaiety. The final four girls are not out yet and have seen little beyond the castle grounds and their few friends in the district. Red-haired Katerina, at sixteen, still thinks boys are boorish and stupid, an opinion no doubt suggested by her closest male acquaintance, her brother George (at twenty-five the only male sibling and proud heir to his father's dignities and debt). Portia, at 15, was rather more romantic, with hair a shade between the blond of Jocasta's and the brunette of Georgette's. She is taller than her sisters. The little twins, at 14, were probably the prettiest of the bunch (which is to say very pretty indeed), with still-white blond curls and big blue eyes. They would arrest the eye together in a ballroom in another three or four years.

Georgette, the median age of all her married sisters, was now on the shelf, doomed to haunt the shades of Fortune Castle till her death, unless her brother George were to eject her on the day of his inheritance. If George remembered the days of her childhood when Georgette had still seen the point of poking a bully in the eyes, perhaps he would do so, and swiftly, too. But most probably, he would let her stay to keep up the numbers of people he could ignore, insult and command.

Chapter 1

She was invisible, Georgette discovered. Quite invisible. She had suspected as much in the glazed-over glances the other guests to this house party had cast over her during the introductions, but this longed-for but entirely unexpected meeting with the Marquis of Onslow had completely underscored the matter. He had even reached past her to shake her father's hand and had touched her arm in passing, raising her heartbeat until it seemed the organ would leave her chest, without any seeming awareness of having done so.

One *could* blame Papa perhaps, but with ten daughters and one son (heaven be praised) to provide for, and no wife living to aid Lord Fortune with understanding the subtleties of female feelings, she did not really think that she could. She had quite understood that she, the third daughter of the impoverished baron, had to surrender her place in the London season to allow her younger sisters their turn at society. Their eldest sister, twenty-three-year-old Violetta (named for their dead mother) was already wed to her Scottish gentleman before Georgette had come out. Georgette had enjoyed two seasons already, one with elder sister Cassie, who had married the eligible, if very loud, Mr Hudson. This slight defect that Georgette had discerned in his otherwise excellent, convivial character was shared by Cassie herself, who talked as though addressing a congregation even at breakfast, and who had been used to clattering downstairs in satin slippers as though the blacksmith had shod her. After Cassie's baby was born last year, Georgette had visited her home in distant Somerset and had informed her father afterwards that the child's lungs seemed to have double the capacity of each parent, making him audible ten miles hence. Her father had remarked that he would write to his daughter, kindly understanding that such a journey as the three days it would take to reach Castle Fortune should on no account be undertaken with an infant, and that they could henceforth meet during the London season for his beloved daughter's convenience. How thoughtful.

Georgette's second season had been with her younger sister Mary, who married (much to her father's wrath) a mere Mr Fredericks, who had been employed to teach them the pianoforte. Both sisters could play, but not exceptionally, and their father had conceived the notion that it was young ladies of musical talent who snared the richest, that is the most eligible, of gentlemen — an opinion he came to rue. Mrs Fredericks now lived in genteel poverty with her swain in Bath and seemed happy enough, thought Georgette, but where they might dispose of future children in two rooms was beyond her. Perhaps they might be suspended in tiny hammocks on the ceiling, she'd considered as she'd regarded the linen slung on the washing pulley in their tiny kitchen, but what to do with them on laundry day exceeded her imagination.

Susan, 18, had wed a quiet country gentleman much in her own style. This had occurred in the previous season, when Georgette remained at home to make way for Jocasta Fortune, her pretty blond seventeen-year-old sister, who had already shown herself popular in town, so she had heard.

With three of her sisters wed already after Georgette's second season, her father's looks toward her had suggested that she had rather let him down. The cost of each season was a prodigious run on the estate every year, and some decent settlements from an eligible *parti* might have eased a situation which, with six daughters still to provide for, seemed never-ending. After her last season, two years ago now, when they had returned to the crumbling Castle Fortune, he had looked at her from beneath his bushy eyebrows. 'You are not bad looking,' he barked, as though contemplating inwardly, 'even if your bosom suggests you might run to fat at a later date.' Georgette had swallowed with difficulty. 'But young men don't think of that. You don't have much conversation of course, but your birth is good and you have a small portion from your mama, which makes you at least respectable. All those gowns and bonnets,' he lamented, 'and *no one* could be persuaded to take you!' He shook his head and tutted.

When Susan got married the next year, he could not look at Georgette for a week without audibly betraying his great disappointment. 'Still here, miss? Eating my meat when even your younger sisters—' he shook his giant head with the shaggy mane of hair and muttered into his soup, 'Females! What use are females at all — especially unwed females? A leech for life, I suppose.'

There had been two people prepared to take her, who had indeed offered for her, had her papa but known, and others whose interest Georgette had, with difficulty, discouraged. The first offer was from a deliciously conceited, round-bodied clergyman, bound for a bishopric, he told her confidentially during only the first dance. It was in the family, it transpired, that all the second sons became bishops (though his grand-uncle had disappointed his family by rising no further than Dean). Georgette had accepted his offers to dance as was polite, but Cassie had been unable to understand why she allowed the fusty cleric to walk her to the supper room, or take her apart to sit and talk a dance away. The sad truth was that Georgette, though listening with a grave air to the Reverend Mr Fullerton's conversation, had been inwardly bursting with delight. He was so utterly ridiculous that she found herself fuelling his climb to the precipice of bumptious absurdity. The dreadful propensity of hers to judge the ridiculous was understood by none in her family since the death of her mother. They looked upon Georgette's placid exterior as her substance, never guessing the bubbling cauldron of devilry beneath. 'I hold,' said the reverend gentleman, 'that the exercise of dancing may become injurious to the health *and*, to the *morals* of the nation.' Georgette was sipping a negus cup in the throng around the supper table, and she answered, as his bulging eyes looked at her expectantly, 'Indeed sir, you think dancing *dangerous* to the body?'

'I see you are surprised, my dear Miss Fortune! I do not wonder at it. It is so *common* to think of dancing these days as *beneficial*. Indeed, parents employ dancing popinjays to teach their daughters.

Then those same young ladies are encouraged to dance every dance and quite wear their feet away.'

'It is the feet, then, which you seek to protect?' said Georgette, still sipping the negus.

'Worse than the feet, I fear, are the temperate humours that keep the passions in check. These are vital to our health, yet let a man (or worse, a lady, I suggest) caper about a room for even an half-hour, and these have been so agitated that the very rules of civilisation may be ignored because such excitations have been allowed. Why, the English temperament becomes ever closer to the *Latin*.' Georgette's eyes widened in faux shock over her cup. 'We know how *they* conduct themselves. It is, in my idea, the product of the heat and being ill-bred.'

'I expect you warn your parishioners of the dangers,' remarked Georgette, enjoying herself shamefully, still sipping at her cup.

'I do. It may be that the upper classes might just possess the discipline of spirit to control themselves in a ballroom, but all country dances for the working man are to be discouraged. A young gentleman, but ten years ago, was taken ill after much dancing and when the surgeons opened him up there was seen to be *putrefaction* of the organs. Ah! I have shocked you, I fear. I might have spared your delicate ears such sad truths. But a warning I must give to those I regard.' Georgette gave a jolt to be included in this company, but stilled as he continued. 'I myself have felt the ill effects. It is not *natural* for a man to jump and shake his innards so! It was not thus decreed by the Almighty. You have observed that persons beyond the age of thirty restrict such posturing. With age comes wisdom, perhaps.'

Or exhaustion, thought Georgette. 'But I have met you at three balls already this season, Reverend Fullerton, and I do not believe *you* would seek to injure yourself.'

'You are very wise, my dear Miss Fortune, very wise. *I* dance, it is true. But here is the secret, my dear.' He bent forward, as though imparting one, but his voice was still booming. 'I do not dance to excess, *never* to excess.'

'It is true, Mr Fullerton,' said Georgette as though much struck. 'You danced perhaps three dances all evening, I have observed. When you did me the honour to dance with me this evening you did so with the most economy of movement. I remarked upon it. It was almost as though you were not dancing at all ...'

Then came the moment that changed her life. For over the shoulder of the vicar, and over the shoulder of a gentleman with his back to him, Georgette met the humorous eye of a tall, blond gentleman who seemed to have been listening for some time, perhaps. In that look, which caused the lines around sky-blue eyes to deepen, she saw his shared joy of the absurdity, and his knowledge of her own role in encouraging the display. The six feet between them seemed to retract as the look held, and she felt as though his whole being was closer to her than any gentleman had ever been, excepting her father and brother. But it was a simple illusion, neither of them had moved. She dimpled and blushed — then his attention was taken once more by his male companion. It was the work of but two seconds.

The Reverend Mr Fullerton continued to praise her for her observation and she hardly heard him. She had turned her face towards him once more and saw the fleshly lips move and bulging eyes search her face, but was only vaguely aware.

Someone had seen her, really seen her — and she was shaken to the core.

She was so aware of the tall gentleman that her peripheral vision grew larger. He moved away with his friend in the direction of the ballroom and she was able to notice a thatch of blond hair whose curls disobeyed pomade, whose tall frame was elegantly covered in a black coat and buff knee breeches, and whose large form carried away with it her heart.

This was the Lord Onslow that now, two years later, had not even recognised her.

to read on:

getbook.at/Georgette

About the Author

Alicia Cameron lives between her homes in rural Scotland and rural France. She reads avidly, laughs a lot, and is newly addicted, unfortunately, to Korean Dramas ... for which she refuses treatment.

Here is a link to get **Angelique and the Pursuit of Destiny** for FREE! https://BookHip.com/XSNQVM   It puts you on the list to receive Alicia Cameron's book news and offers, occasionally.

All Alicia books are available on Amazon and as audiobooks on Audible. Some are available in several languages, German and Spanish especially.

You can find out more here :

The website   https://aliciacameron.co.uk(books, audiobooks, translations, free book, occasional Regency Blog)

Amazon Author's Page: https://www.amazon.co.uk/stores/Alicia-Cameron/author/B01A3JY8L4

Facebook   https://www.facebook.com/aliciacameron.100

Twitter   https://twitter.com/aliciaclarissa2

Bookbub   https://www.bookbub.com/authors/alicia-cameron

Also By

Regency Romance

Angelique and Other Stories: Romantic Regency Tales: mybook.to/Angelstories

Angelique was named by her French grandmother, but now lives as Ann, ignored by her aristocratic relations. Can she find the courage to pursue her Destiny, reluctantly aided by her suave cousin Ferdinand?

Beth and the Mistaken Identity: getbook.at/Beth

Beth has been cast off as lady's maid to the pert young Sophy Ludgate, but is mistaken as a lady herself by a handsome marquis and his princess

Desperate to save the coach fare to London, she goes along with them, but they do not let her escape so easily.

Clarissa and the Poor Relations: getbook.at/Clarissa
Clarissa Thorne and her three friends have to leave their cosy School for Young Ladies after the death of Clarissa's mama. all must be sent off as poor relations to their families. However, Clarissa suddenly inherits Ashcroft Manor, and persuades the ladies to make a bid for freedom. But can she escape their unpleasant families? The Earl of Grandiston might help.

Delphine and the Dangerous Arrangement: getbook.at/Delphine
Delphine Delacroix was brought up by her mother alone, a cold and unloving childhood. With her mother dead, she has become the richest young lady in England, and is taken under the wing of her three aunts, Not quite trusting them, Delphine enters a dangerous arrangement with the handsome Viscount Gascoigne - but will this lead to her downfall?

The Fentons Series (Regency)

Honoria and the Family Obligation, The Fentons 1 https://getbook.at/Honoria

Honoria Fenton has been informed that the famous Mr Allison is to come to her home. His purpose? To woo her. She cannot recall what he looks like, since he made her nervous when they met in Town. Her sister Serena is amused, but when Allison arrives, it seems that a mistake might cost all three there happiness.

Felicity and the Damaged Reputation, The Fentons 2 https://getbook.at/Felicity

On her way to London to take a post as governess, Felicity Oldfield is intercepted by Viscount Durant, who asks her to impersonate his cousin for an hour. When, in an unexpected turn of events, Felicity is able to enjoy a London Season, this encounter damages her reputation.

Euphemia and the Unexpected Enchantment, The Fentons 3 https://getbook.at/Euphemia

Euphemia, plain and near forty, is on her way to live with her dear friend Felicity and her husband when she is diverted to the home of Baron Balfour, a bear of a man as huge and loud as Euphemia is small and quiet. Everything in her timid life begins to change.

Ianthe and the Fighting Foxes: The Fentons 4 https://getbook.at/Ianthe

The Fighting Foxes, Lord Edward, his half-brother Curtis and Lady Fox, his stepmother, are awaiting the arrival from France of a poor relation, Miss Ianthe Eames. But when Ianthe turns up, nothing could be further from their idea of a supplicant. Richly dressed and in high good humour, Ianthe takes the Foxes by storm.

ALICIA CAMERON

The Sisters of Castle Fortune Series (Regency)

Georgette and the Unrequited Love: Sisters of Castle Fortune 1
https://getbook.at/Georgette

Georgette Fortune, one of ten sisters, lives as a spinster in Castle Fortune. She refused all offers during her London Seasons, since she fell in love, at first glance with the dashing Lord Onslow. He hardly knew she existed, however, but now he has arrived at the castle for a house party, and Georgette is fearful of exposing her feelings. She tries to avoid him, but Onslow treats her as a friend, making Georgette's pain worse, even as he makes her laugh.

Jocasta and the Cruelty of Kindness: Sisters of Castle Fortune 2
https://getbook.at/Jocasta

At a house party in Castle Fortune, Jocasta's beau had fallen for her sister, Portia. Now Jocasta is back in London and has to suffer the pity of the friends and family that care for her. Only Sir Damon Regis treats her without pity, and she is strangely drawn to him because of it.

Katerina and the Reclusive Earl: Sisters of Castle Fortune 3
https://getbook.at/Katerina

Katerina Fortune has only one desire, to avoid going on her London Season altogether. On the journey, she hears of a recluse, who dislikes people as much as she. Katerina escapes her father and drives to offer a convenient marriage to the earl, who refuses. But an accident necessitates her stay at his home, and they discover they have more in common than either could have believed.

Leonora and the Lion's Venture: Sisters of Castle Fortune 4
https://getbook.at/Leonora

The pretty Fortune twins come to Town, and Leonora has only one object in view: The Honourable Linton Carswell. But Foggy Carswell is too craven to be caught – he is not a marrying man. While trying to save her twin Marguerite from the results of her own romantic naivety, Leonora has her work set for her. But a number of family alliances begin to aid the unlikely pairing.

Marguerite and the Duke in Disguise: Sisters of Castle Fortune 5 https://mybook.to/Marguerite

Marguerite Fortune, bereft of her newly married twin Leonora, is heading back to her Castle Fortune home with only her two unsympathetic male relatives for company. At an inn she meets another Leo, this time a man mountain, who saves her from harm. When her father diverts their journey and abandons Marguerite to make a match at Dysart manor, Leo arrives too. They are soon embroiled in awful plots, kidnap and even murder.

The Wild Marchmonts (Regency Series)
Naomi and the Purloined Journal #1

Edwardian Inspirational Romance

ALICIA CAMERON

(typewriters, bicycles, and leg-of-mutton sleeves!)

Francine and the Art of Transformation: getbook.at/FrancineT
Francine is fired as a lady's maid, but she is a woman who has planned for every eventuality. Meeting Miss Philpott, a timid, unemployed governess, Francine transforms her into the Fascinating Mathilde and offers her another, self directed life. Together, they help countless other women get control over their lives.

Francine and the Winter's Gift: getbook.at/FrancineW
Francine and Mathilde continue to save young girls from dreadful marriages, while seeing to their own romances. In Francine, Sir Hugo Portas, government minister, meets a woman he could never have imagined. Will society's rules stop their union, or can Francine even accept the shackles of being in a relationship?

Printed in Great Britain
by Amazon